DANIEL'S PRIZE

Second Edition

Jack Crawford

Copyright © Jack Crawford 2014
This book is sold subject to the condition that it shall not, by way of trade or otherwise, be lent, resold, hired out, or otherwise circulated without the publisher's prior consent in any form of binding or cover other than that in which it is published and without a similar condition including this condition being imposed on the subsequent publisher.
Published by Createspace 2014.
Published by J.M. Crawford Publishing 2016.
The moral right of Jack Crawford has been asserted.
ISBN-13: 978-0-9935704-0-7
ISBN eReader: 978-0-9935704-1-4

To my wife Joan whose belief in me has never wavered.

This is a work of fiction. Names, characters, businesses, organizations, places, events and incidents either are the product of the author's imagination or are used fictitiously.

Any resemblance to actual persons, living or dead, events, or locales is entirely coincidental..

CHAPTER 1

Outside the weather scoured the paint-faded, shabby house, weeds elbowed their way up through cracks in the broken and crumbling concrete that served as a pathway into the gloom, dust and disarray of the interior. Furnishings, such as they were, dated back to the distant origins of the farmhouse, but lacked any patina associated with civil use over time. Rather there was an air of passive vandalism where worn and broken items lay where they fell, patched and propped among the collection of detritus being an accumulated by-product of the existence of previous inhabitants. Neglect hung around like a poor man at a bordello. The same decaying path that led in, pointed like a crooked finger on its way out, to distant hills where low, curdled clouds lay heavy like worry on a brow. A raven, Dracula black, cloaked a lazy beat across the rain-drizzled, mist-mizzled, weary fields.

A man in his early twenties, short, stocky, with a ruddy, weather-scrubbed face and dark, wiry hair as wild and tangled as the gorse, wielded a spanner with careless ease in the guts of a tractor as ancient and battered as the hand-me-down grease and mud-decorated boiler suit and jacket that claimed a precarious hold on his being. Around him lay the rusting, skeletal remains of engines and wheels and metal carcasses in a bone yard of parts that had proved to be beyond even his healing skills. As the spanner gripped and turned, he gave himself a running commentary of his task.

"Just give that a couple more turns to fetch it up, then connect up the starter." The wrench seemed to dip and peck into the open belly of the time worn vehicle. His gaze was almost unblinking and he had an air of exaggerated seriousness that some adopt when they are competent at a craft, but have few other abilities.

"Haven't you finished with that yet?"

He straightened slowly, his one free hand slowly stroked and picked at the front of his jacket. He looked back at the object of his recent labours then back at the other man. He moved with a controlled stumble, barely lifting his clod shod feet.

"I keep telling you, Dad, it's bloody knackered, you can't keep on bodging it up. It needs new parts."

"New parts costs money and we ain't got no money."

"You got money alright," the younger man opined, waving his spanner towards a distant spot, he continued. "You've just sold that land from Grandfather's place. That fetched a tidy sum. I saw the price in the agent's brochure when you left it on the kitchen table."

The older man recoiled at the thought of his carelessness. "Listen, boy, I keep telling you we ain't got no money, this farm is ruining me, just one bill after another with nothing coming in; it's gonna take me to an early grave. Selling land," he snorted. "Them agents is like vultures, you just got to keep giving them money - and them bloody grasping lawyers, had to pay them thousands. Hardly had anything left and what was left went to the bank." He nodded his head in his son's direction as if to say, 'that's the money issue sorted.'

His son twisting the spanner in his hands with his head cocked to one side, gazed at a point over his father's shoulder, hesitantly retorted, "But you didn't pay them straight up, they threatened to put the law on you 'cause you couldn't put your hand in your pocket when you should have done. As usual." His head nodded vigorously as if to emphasise the fact and show that he had scored a telling point.

He shuffled closer to his father. "Why are you so bloody tight-fisted? You can't take it with you. Although you would have a sodding good try."

The stature and features demonstrated the clear blood link between to the two, but with the older man being bent and stooped with the weight of the years. His face, all deep reds and purples like a bruised sunset, had been shaped by the pushing and pulling of time's cruel fingers. The twist of his mouth, in which his teeth, the ones he had left, mimicked staggering tomb stones in a forgotten churchyard, the narrow eyes suggested that, as one who had rarely received a trusting hand, he was one who viewed the world at large as not deserving or entitled to even a small portion of largess. It would be a sign of weakness, something to be turned back on him. The two men faced each other, although only feet apart, there was a void between them that was beyond measuring. It was a space that they always adhered to, a no man's land not to be encroached upon. When they spoke to each other it was as if across a chasm. Intimacy between them was an alien concept, both incapable of reaching out to touch each other, either physically or emotionally. They were held in their own personal gravity that kept each of them in a fixed orbit that maintained a measured distance into which neither man was able to venture. The father seemingly had never been capable of, or desired any form of closeness that may have plumped out his grey, two-dimensional existence. The son, almost as a matter of osmosis, sucked up the sterile emotions of the man who had fathered him.

"What about my pay? I haven't seen anything from you for ages. I'm entitled to my money."

"Look, boy, I told you, I'm investing it for you, you would only go off wasting it in town, getting up to no good. I gave you some a while ago and what did you do with it? Drinking and chasing bits of skirt." The old man's voice guttered up in a slow burble from deep within his chest.

"Chasing skirt, chasing skirt?" The young man's voice rose in parallel with his incredulity. "You must be joking, what woman is going to look at me - what could I give her? I look like a tramp. I live in a pig sty. They laugh at me, say I'm simple. How could someone like me ever get a woman? The only time I went into town, after half an hour you come looking for me to fetch me back. They laugh at me."

"You don't want to go wasting your money on tarts and drink. It will ruin you." The retort showed that the older man chose not to hear the protestations of his son; it was a suggestion, advice to one who needed it.

"What money? You don't give me no money. I'm entitled and you know that. And how could I be ruined? I am ruined, I ain't got nothing that's mine. I do as much work here, no I do a lot more than you do, round the farm. We should be what they call 'partners', I should be like an owner. It's going to be mine when you pass on, so you should put my name down on the papers to say that I own some of it, like we was a proper business. Why can't you do that then?"

"Well you know it's hard for you with learning things, its proper that I look after you, take care of you. How could you deal with bills and paying for stuff? Things like that. You don't know about all these things, you don't understand it." The old man's standard, prickly rebuff was stumbled over like a bad actor rehearsing his lines. It was when issues surrounding his eventual demise and handing down the farm arose, that he couldn't quite hide the germ of an emotion, a feeling that he did not realise he had. Whether it was concern for the boy or for his own existence, it was so wrapped in the deep layers of his mind, that it didn't knowingly trouble him.

"The only thing you take care of is money, my money, I'm entitled. I could have done learning, but you always kept me back from school to work here. There's nobody better at fixing engines and things like harvesters than me. You know I fix for Mr.. Reece and Mr.. Tomlin, they always ask me, and I know they give you money for it, that should be my money."

"Don't go on about it, you will get all this when I pass on."

"You may well pass on, but I will never be shut of you." Now the spanner was being thrust in the direction of the target of his rising anger. "You'll come back and haunt me when you see me spending you're money, but I'm gonna spend just you wait."

"There ain't no money, you're just too daft to understand it all."

The older man flagged down his arm to signal the end of any further part he would take in the exchanges. He turned and walked away. It was a sign the younger man was all too familiar with.

"I'll have my bloody money, just you see, I'll bloody have it, it's mine anyway." The words now having no target other than the speaker's wrath, dispersed like smoke in the wind. The young man stared into the distance, it was the only way he could go beyond the confines of his narrow life. He was existing in a backwater, cut off from the eddies and currents of life that could swirl in changes and push him along into different paces and places. He didn't know this, he kept looking out into what he thought he wanted but was held by bindings that he couldn't see or feel, although they were as real as a tether on an animal. He could not reach out and touch and take that which would give him a character, an identity. There were no markers in his life that would enable him to use his past to plot something ahead or to look back on. He had no friends or enemies who may have added some form to his character. His swings of joy and disappointment were shallow curves that did little to enrich his being. He had no memories, his mother was a dark distant cold corner of his mind. She was never spoken of or acknowledged; there were no photographs or mementos. The pressures and hum drums of life were shouldered by his father. He had never dealt with a bill, or seen a final demand. He had never faced a buttoned up bank manager, never negotiated a purchase. His existence was a flat line of repetitive menial chores. Only the seasons changed, all this meant was that sometimes he took his coat off.

If he found any solace at all, it was his own small secret space. A narrow, brick-lined, cramped room created in the distant past when his forebears had added on to or had extended one of the outbuildings. The imperfect planning of the day had left a space, which abutted an interior supporting wall in what was once the coach house. The omissions of a succession of his ancestors had allowed it to settle into a silent, still placed where memories, if there were any, had soaked so far into the fabric of the structure that they remained locked in. The insidious weeds of time had carelessly and casually dressed walls and floors in a gritty black dust. The sills by windows had scatterings of the dried husks of a selection of winged insects that had seen the light but had fallen, like so many, in trying to reach it. At floor level in his room there was a small area of glazing, which was the top of a window from the floor below, allowing some light through the dust filtered glass. He had found the space one day a vague number of years ago when he was looking for a piece of timber. He went to the top of the old coach house, where yards of discarded furniture lay propped without thought of future use or rescue. In his days on the farm, he had rarely ventured into this part of his domain. It had always been there merely as walls and old odd spaces. His lack of curiosity meant that exploring even his own bailiwick was an exercise that had no point to it.

He had climbed the open wooden stairway and worked his way along the yards of carelessly and casually stacked distressed artefacts. His searching had taken him towards the end wall at the far reaches of the building. There, under a barricade of dust dry timber, he saw what might be of use. Propped tight against the wall was a small stout wooden door, as he pulled it away, he saw that it covered an opening into a small, narrow, brick-lined room that was at a slightly lower level that the main floor. He peered into it, then turned with a degree of alarm to confirm that he had not been observed whilst making the discovery. The old building, blindly silent, chose to maintain the secretive code it had abided by for the past many years. The stillness offered him assurance, he pushed the door to one side and, with his heart thumping loud enough to rouse the slumbering coach house bricks, he squeezed into the space that was to become his, and only his. This was to become his sanctuary.

When his father was in town on some sort of business or at the market, he would shift his way through the old furniture that guarded his room and just sit and watch and look. He found a loose floorboard that, if pulled away from underneath the wall, could be lifted up to reveal a space. Over the years he collected items, which were of little or no use or value, but they were his. This collection was his other secret. With time, his collection grew. Some coins, a brochure on farmyard equipment, a ticket from a visit to the cinema he made years ago and a train ticket from a journey he made for a hospital appointment. There were also four books, the type that children use when learning to read. Scraps of paper, in an awkward hand, contained passages copied from his nascent library. There were also some shotgun cartridges that he sneaked one at a time from his father's drawer. These few trinkets and this space described him, these were his. Nobody else knew about them. Here was escape from the rattle of his father's constant upbraiding, a relief from being directed as to how his time was to be allocated. By having grown into his sanctuary, he could, at times, be his own master and even look down on his day to day tormentor. On occasions he pretended he had to do tasks at the remote parts of the farm, which he had already done. In this stolen time he could look down into the yard through the cobweb-laced section of the window. Sometimes he could see his father scanning the lower fields with escalating impatience.

"Where is that boy, what's he up to now? Don't he know he's got jobs up here? Down in Small Acre field I 'spect. Boy, boy, where are you? Get up here."

Looking down on his father's futile efforts to locate the errant boy, he watched as the old man twisted and turned like a terrier in a barn. He sat on an old combine harvester seat, watching, holding his breath, statue still, unblinking until his father moved on. Often his father would challenge him.

"Where you been, boy? I've been looking for you. You got jobs to do."

"I was down at the bottom the big field, down at the stream."

"Well I never saw you, boy. I called and called. I was going to come and fetch you."

"I never heard, anyway you never go down there, you won't walk that far and you don't like taking the Land Rover down there."

As the boy grew and gradually developed an awareness of his situation, his feelings of being regarded as no more than a piece of equipment, an inanimate resource that was constantly called into use, hummed inside him. For some time the boy felt a resentful anger creeping through and around his being like ivy insinuating itself around a tree. Eventually ivy will kill a tree.

As the old man entered, the bell on the door of the shop jangled its gentle apologetic alarm, informing that the boundaries of the premises had been violated. Outside the narrow cobbled main street of the little town coped with the hum and bustle of the monthly market. The volume of collective conversations and street noise rose and fell like waves at sea. The store, a cathedral of quiet and gloom, smelled of oil and tar and hessian. Open sacks of various seeds and tubers slouched in a casual huddle beneath an arsenal of forks, spades and hoes. Behind the counter, small pigeon holes of drawers with worn scooped brass handles attended with their contents marked in pen. Screws of different virtues, nails in varying lengths and gauges. On the scrubbed wooden counter a set of scales with brass weights stood by waiting so as to supply this hardware by the pound. Shelves, which tram lined into the far reaches, were laden with tins and packets that would either prevent or delay deterioration in wood, metal or in plants. On the same shelves other packets claimed to fix the same ailments once the items had succumbed to time and nature. A large wooden clock watching from its own space in a shadow infused corner quietly ticktocked, chopping seconds off the minutes. The old man had slow, heavy steps as though walking through a ploughed field. As he passed over the scrubbed wooden floor, he stirred the air into small eddies and whirls. Sunlight through the windows showed the slowly revolving dust and then seemed to highlight the counter like an actor's mark. Before he spoke the old man gently rubbed his hands up and down the remnants of the jacket he was wearing. His lips moved silently as if rehearsing his lines.

"Davey, alright?" The words were delivered without emotion or movement. He softly cleared his throat. His expression suggested a form of approval for his opening.

"Sam, and you?"

The other speaker was a thin middle-aged man wearing a brown, neatly pressed buttoned overall. His black hair was greased and smoothed flat so that it looked almost like a piece of glistening porcelain, a small neatly trimmed moustache thatched a thin tight lipped mouth. He stood to attention, behind the long wooden counter as though to guard the integrity of the store. Neither man appeared to consider this exchange, despite its brevity and detachment, as anything other than normal and entirely acceptable.

"Yes, yes, not bad, been better." He shuffled up to the counter and leaned on it with one hand. The support was not just for his physical needs.

"Davey." He paused and sighed deeply. "Davey, I could do with some supplies for the farm." The statement was left to hang in the air for a moment. "Yes, a few supplies."

"I see." The other man leaned forward slightly and bounced gently on the balls of his feet. He coughed quietly and he too leant on the counter as if in a mirror image of his customer.

"Thing is, Sam, it's your account, you could do with clearing some of it off."

"My account, Davey?" The old man did a slight, if somewhat theatrical, stumble backwards. "My account? Davey, you know I've been coming to you, and your father before you, for nigh-on forty years. My account has always been sorted. Why me and your dad…"

"My dad nearly went broke because he never chased up his bills." The interruption was assertive. "I'm not saying it was just you, but I can't work like that, I've got to have the money coming in regular. It's what they call cash flow, the bank and the like." The last sentence being delivered with added gravitas.

"Cash flow, Davey, that's a new one." The old man took his cap off and scratched his head. "Well Davey, what you saying? I would pay if I could, but right now thing's is not good."

"Sam, we all know you just sold your father's place. That brought in a tidy sum. We know what it fetched. Tidy sum."

"Thing is, Davey, yes, I got something for it, but I had to pay off the lawyers and the bank as such. Then I got my son's wages."

A sudden expression showed that he thought this aspect of his explanation of dwindling finances could be developed to add weight, if not poignancy, to his submission. "Back wages in fact, quite a decent amount, Davey, I can tell you. Not a great deal left." At the end of the explanation, the old man nodded his head gently, slightly dipping it in the direction of the shopkeeper indicating that his plea had reached its conclusion, and now a response was anticipated. The shop keeper stood straight, tucking his chin in. He made no comment, not wishing to entertain any further development to the old man's plea. His stare posed the question.

"Well, Davey, what do you think, what could you be going on with?"

"Sam, at the moment it stands at over four hundred and fifty pounds."

"I could give you a hundred."

"Three hundred would be better."

"I could give you two."

"Two-fifty?"

The old man winced as if receiving a minor wound and turned away to ferret into a deep pocket of his shapeless coat. The shopkeeper heard a faint rustling. Occasionally the old man would glance back accusingly at his adversary. There was a heavy sigh, a hand thrust back down into his pocket. He slowly wheeled round and flourished a wad of notes almost in the manner of a magician who had just completed at trick.

"There you are, Davey, two hundred and fifty. Alright?"

"Yes, thank you Sam." The hint of sarcasm was missed.

"Now then Davey, here's a list of those supplies. I can pick them up when I leave town."

"Sam, when are you going to leave town? Thing is, occasionally you hang on a bit, sometimes until after we close. Do you aim to leave when the market finishes, or might it be later?"

"Well sometimes I stay a bit longer, catching up with the news, sort of thing. If there is not much doing, I'll be off by early afternoon. Davey, you couldn't, you know, if I leave my truck here?"

"All right, Sam. Leave your old Rover outside and I will load it up for you."

His exit from the shop was a deal sprightlier than his entrance.

Outside the old farmer merged with the town's inhabitants and its visitors. He took a long sniff of the air and ambled along the High Street, briefly acknowledging and returning the salutations directed towards him.

Occasionally he encountered other farmers with whom he had some form of acquaintance. The general opinions were that farming was still going through bad times; the weather contrived against successful growing of crops, milk prices were too low, vets bills were too high. He stopped off at Hunter's newsagents for two pouches of tobacco and his usual lottery ticket.

The Golden Fleece was a pub as old as his farm. It was in a row of buildings of similar vintage, all of differing height and girth and pressed together at the shoulders as though squeezing forward for a better look at the High Street. Inside it had benefitted, to some degree, from periodic but basic improvements, usually a coat of whitewash. The doorway was recessed into the thick stone walls and gave way to an interior that, in accordance with the demands and wishes of its patrons through time, had seen no basic changes. The closing of the door on entering muffled the business of the street. The snug, a slate floored room, with simple rough-hewn wooden tables, benches and chairs worn smooth with time's rasp, spoke to the generations of farming stock who had swapped stories across the tops of pots of beer. Generation after generation, grandfather, father, son, grandfather father, son, in a comfortable wheel of time had left their memories sucked into thick stone walls. The white paintwork had now matured to a hint of tobacco. The old man paused momentarily nodding to those who caught his eye. A general murmur of acknowledgement was directed towards him. One or two uttered an abrupt, "Sam," but there was no effort to develop any further relationship. Conversation was permitted, but persuasive custom and practice ruled that it should be conducted with low voices and spaced with frequent intervals. After pausing in the doorway and satisfied that convention of greetings had been completed, he trudged towards the bar. The middle-aged, trim woman behind the bar smiled briefly. In contrast to the suggestion of melancholy that seemed to infuse the premises, she was brightly and neatly dressed in blue jeans, white blouse and pink sweater. It appeared that the years of serving behind the bar had not wearied or eroded her cheerful demeanour.

"Hello, Sam love. How are you, usual, pint of bitter?"

He nodded first. "Yes, that's right, pint of bitter. Thank you Sarah." Only now did he remember to take his cap off, which he scrunched between his hands. His bald head, garlanded about by wisps of sweat matted grey hair, glistened even in the dim yellow glow given off by the bare bulbs.

"There you are Sam." She pushed the pint glass across the bar.

He stared at her, his mouth moving slightly, almost pouting like a fish. Any words he was looking for did not come. He nodded and raised his glass.

"Hear you did well when you sold your dad's place. Got a good price didn't you? I thought you would have had a nice new suit. Going to get a new car?"

"No, not really, I'll just keep what I've got. Does me alright." His reply was matter of fact. He then started to sip his beer, but before it reached his lips, a faint questioning look overtook his face. "Well, I might, you know I might, I'll have to see how it goes. You never know."

"Because you could well afford it now, Sam, rich man like you. I thought you might take me out to one of them posh expensive restaurants for a nice meal."

His perceived intimacy of the conversation caused him to avoid looking directly at the landlady. It was too overwhelming. The thought of taking a woman out, especially one who was clearly above his station, going to a restaurant and parting with money, caused him considerable concern. As he pondered the implications he muttered softly to himself and trudged off to find a seat. As he did so, he missed the mutual knowing smiles between Sarah and the regulars behind him. He settled into his usual seat and prepared himself for the first of his several mugs.

CHAPTER 2

"Mr.. Reece, Mr.. Reece." The panicked cries were made above the rattling engine of the old Land Rover before it came to a stop. "Mr. Reece, Mr. Reece, are you there? They've done Dad, he's not moving. Mr. Reece I'm frightened. Mr. Reece." The boy jumped from the vehicle without turning the engine off leaving the windscreen wipers on. His splashed and irregular path around the farm yard that reflected the agitated state he was displaying. Reece walk towards the Land Rover from his barn. He viewed the young man in front of him, whom, he noted, was pale and shaking. His blazing eyes searched for answers and help.

"What you saying, boy, Daniel, what are you saying?"

"Mr. Reece, you better come now, they've done him, he's not moving, I'm scared. I'm really scared."

"Daniel, what's happened, what you saying?"

"You better come now, Mr. Reece, come and see."

"Do you need the police, an ambulance? Did you call them?"

"We ain't got no 'phone, I don't know how. You better come Mr. Reece."

"Is he bad, Daniel, is he bad? Daniel you've got to tell what happened. Is he badly hurt, has he had an accident, is he moving?"

"He's not moving, least I didn't see him move. I tried to shake him, but he's just lying there. He's bleeding awful bad, awful bad, not saying anything, not moving, I didn't stay long mind, but there's a lot of blood."

"I think I better call the ambulance from here, Daniel. Then I'll drive over there you don't look in any state just now."

Reece and Daniel arrived at the farmhouse a few minutes before the ambulance arrived. As it slowed to a stop, Reece walked over and told the crew, "I think you had better call the police, he's dead, I think he's been shot. Don't know if he did it himself, can't see no gun. The lad's in a state, he found him, that's him over there." The ambulance staff, having satisfied themselves as to the correctness of Reece's findings, sheltered in their vehicle.

The two plainclothes police officers, clad in waterproof jackets that held some of the rain at bay, surveyed the scene with a practiced nonchalance. Dead bodies were part of their job, they had seen them before and they would see them again. There was a determination not to be anything other than casual. Casualness under circumstances such as lay before them, was a badge to be displayed to let others know that, whatever it is, we have seen it before and dealt with it. Real police work is what we do. It sets us apart from the pen pushers. Eagerness to deal with a crime scene was frowned upon. Any suggestion of enthusiasm was the reserve of new entrants and those college graduates who were employed to rise rapidly to senior officer level. The view that pertained was that enthusiasm and common sense were strange bedfellows. Old-fashioned police work and graft were what counted in forming an effective officer. The police headquarters was stuffed with bright eyed, cherub faced, posh speaking university types whose main aim in life was to be intensely interested in whatever function they were given and to demonstrate unstinting devotion to their commanders. Their uniforms pressed cardboard flat, buttons and pips gleaming, they moved with an earnest haste that was obviously the prerequisite to achieving a task of some moment. When they conversed with the 'men', there was a deep and thoughtful, but transient interest to the matter in hand. Questions answered in accordance with the current policy. The story used to demonstrate the rift between the two classes was that one old, time-served constable on yet another management course at headquarters was leaving the gents, and an inspector a third of his age, said, "I say, constable, when I went to boarding school we were taught to wash our hands after going to the toilet."

To which the reply, according to legend, was, "Son, when I was in the army we were taught not to piss on our fingers." Never walked the beat, never felt a collar, never been crossed-examined in court.

The detectives arrived at the farm equipped with paper cups containing coffee. Both men showed the effects of their chosen occupation. Months and years of no regular hours or routine, grabbing what fast food was nearest to hand, frequent lunch time pub meals washed down with the local beer and the habitual ending of the day of the day by stopping off for a quick one that never was just a quick one.

Inspector Malcolm Curran was a forty-five year old born in London and raised in and around a couple of council estates, part of a steady family content with its lot. His first position after leaving school with an unexpected clutch of 'O' levels was as a clerical assistant in a civil service office. The boredom of the menial tasks that made up his working life, together with a realisation that promotion was a mythical beast, caused him to cut his ties. He considered following his brother into the navy. Encouraged by a fellow member of the local football team, a young policeman, he joined the Metropolitan force. He seemed to sprint through the initial few years, gaining commendations and praise from those whom, he assumed, mattered. He brushed aside the world weary cynicism of his more established colleagues who found amusement in his desire to impress. Although aware enough not to believe he was changing the world for the better he enjoyed his job and the status amongst his community as one who had achieved an acceptable station in life. He was quickly promoted to inspector and then out of uniform into CID. Here his sprint slowed down under the weight of internal politics. Assurances as to his future always sounded promising, but he came to realise, his circle of colleagues was not the one that mattered. His enthusiasm for his job slowly withered.

In his words, "I thought they were whispering in my ear, but all they were doing was pissing down my leg." Gradually he accepted that his fate was to remain at his current level, he decided to move to a peaceful part of the country and find a pace more to his liking, somewhere where he could use auto cruise for the remainder of his service. Now being a bigger fish in a small pool, he did not expect to rise through the grades, but there was still hope. His second marriage seemed to be working. The flexible hours of his working life did not give rise to any questions in respect of irregular absences.

His constable, Barry Fenwick, was twenty-five years and, at six foot one a few inches taller than his opposite number. His mother, a single parent to her only child, had succeeded in life, rising by ability and commitment from secretary to personal assistant then to the sales director of a multinational company. She liked to treat her son, the two-seater soft top he drove was a gift from her. He had his own apartment in a more exclusive area of the town, obtained with considerable assistance from his mother. Off duty, he had an assured manner and his reasonable looks had not yet completely surrendered to the ravaging of his chosen profession, so he wasn't short of female partners. However, never seeming to find anything to get serious about, he never formed nor seemed to want, a more permanent attachment. Women tended to pass through life on an irregular basis. As plainclothes officers, their business was dealing with liars, cheats, thugs, thieves and members from a class of society that seemed to be reserved exclusively for the squalid end of the law. Social outcasts who would steal from their grandparents, parents, their children, the poor and the needy without any semblance of remorse or regret and, given the opportunity, would repeat the process. Even if caught *flagrante*, the usual litany of defences would be blindly thrust forward.

"I was going to take it back, I thought he said I could take it, I was looking after it for a friend, I didn't think he would mind. I was defending myself." The officers knew, beyond doubt, that there was no honour, no accused person ever said that they felt better for making a clean breast of it.

They were used to hearing innocence being professed: "On my mother's grave," or, "On my children's eyes," only for the same protesters to plead guilty when faced with a bag full of evidence against them.

When your job is not to trust anybody and never to be surprised at how spiteful and squalid a crime or an offender can be and not to expect anything much more than hostility and deceit from the objects of your work focussed attention, you need a shield. Complete and yawning indifference will do and, perhaps, a good helping of cynicism. The shabbiness of their lives was matched by the shabbiness of their clothes. Curran, now pudgy and grey with cropped black hair, was wearing his usual attire of cheap chain store sports jackets and slacks. His pastel coloured shirts would be complimented by startling ties that never embraced a top button, showed a determination that he was not interested in being a slave to fashion. Fenwick was slightly more upmarket, usually favouring a blue two piece suit. However, their practice of downing a few pints after work then finding somewhere to eat, meant that, more often than not, ties and shirts would be liberally dressed with sauces from a favourite Asian restaurant.

Two uniformed officers sheltered from the rain in their marked car, doors slightly open. They shouted across the yard towards their plainclothes colleagues who, dodging the puddles that now looked as if they were joining up, skipped over in an exaggerated form of hopscotch, to the marked car. The uniformed constable was the first to speak.

"Alright, Malcolm, Barry. Looks like we've turned up a nice little tickle for you blokes. Old Sam Hamblin's copped it. Thought he might have topped himself, but we don't see a gun."

The inspector from the car nodded his greetings. "You lucky buggers, Friday afternoon. Got it down in our notebooks, called out at four fifteen. The ambulance was here first, saw the state of him, suspected suspicious death and called us in, the crew saw he was a goner. We haven't been inside. I did cop witness statements from both crew, I'll get them typed up and sent over to you. We had a look at him but we haven't been inside."

"Not wishing to contaminate the crime scene?" ventured Fenwick.

"Crime scene, my arse. Health and Safety. Our beloved leader, he who never makes a decision, said that from our description, the farm buildings could represent a hazard."

The uniformed inspector moved closer to Fenwick, tilted his head and raised it so as to be able to direct his conversation directly into Fenwick's ear. His voice was low and soft, as he spoke his lips barely moved. "You know who that is, the chap standing by the ambulance?"

Fenwick, who had stooped in order to almost couple with the uniformed inspector's only working parts, now stood up and casually surveyed the area. "No, you mean the bloke who looks like a farmer?"

"Well he is the only other bloke here, and he looks like a farmer because he is a farmer. Yes that's him - Bill Reece, he's got the farm next to this one. He's the one that called the ambulance. Apparently when the lad found his father, he went and fetched Reece."

"Why didn't he call us?"

"He made the call from his farm, he didn't know what was really going on. When he got here, there's no phone, so he had to wait for the ambulance crew to tell us. I haven't taken a witness statement from him, it's a bit more involved than the ambulance crew, it would be better if you do that. But watch him, he's got a very short fuse, and, shall we say, he is not our biggest fan. Just thought I would let you know."

The two plainclothes officers stood in the doorway of the building, craning their necks into but without actually entering the premises. Curran took a sip of his coffee and stepped back. Fenwick stood on the threshold of the gloom and saw, feet from the doorway, the body lying beside an upturned chair. Blood spatters radiated out. Moving closer to the figure, he could see the unblinking eyes looking up to the top of the head and the lips that in life gave a defined outline, but now looked deflated and shapeless. Perhaps optimistically, he felt for a pulse. He stepped back.

"Well, Inspector Curran, what do we have here?"

"Well Constable Fenwick, I think we've got a dead bloke, old Sam Hamblin. Yeah, I would say he's pretty dead."

"Inspector Curran, I concur entirely that he's dead, but pretty, isn't that pushing it a bit?"

"Constable Fenwick, as always your observations are both succinct and germane to any investigation you embark upon. Whereas we will never know what caused him not to be pretty, what, do you deduce from your observations, caused him to be dead?"

"I deduce what caused him to be dead is a bleeding great hole in the middle of his chest, which, if I am not mistaken, was in turn caused by his failure to get out of the way of a shotgun."

"Excellent, Constable Fenwick, any further observations?"

"Inspector Curran, I would have to say that the absence of such a weapon as a shotgun in the surrounding environs means old Sam either flogged it in the nanosecond between being hit and passing on to that great farmyard in the sky - which, knowing old Sam, is not impossible - or somebody shot him and, in the vernacular of the trade, buggered off with said firearm."

"Again Constable Fenwick, excellent, excellent. So, applying your finely honed investigative skills, what sort of crime scene do you think we have here?"

"Well, having ruled out the illegal sale of a firearm, I think I would have to plump for murder."

"Exactly, Constable Fenwick, and this being a murder at a remote farm and this being a Friday afternoon, what does that suggest to you?"

Fenwick puffed out his cheeks and splayed his arms as if looking for an answer. "Shed loads of overtime, if I may be so bold."

"Exactly. Shall we call it in?"

"I think I should leave that to you, Inspector, privilege of rank."

"Why, thank you, Constable. OK, better tell the firearms mob. They've got to come over from Newcastle, so that will be an hour. "Still, they will no doubt circle the wagons. Mind you, you never know, there might be a crazed gunman out there. He must be crazy to think he would get anything out of old Sam."

Right, I'll tee up forensics, medical examiner, scenes of crimes. Where's the son?"

Curran indicated the ambulance and the huddled figure now inside.

Fenwick nodding towards the ambulance asked his inspector. "What about the lad? Is he likely to be in the frame?"

"I doubt it, apparently he's a bit daft, soft in the head. Always has been. The old boy takes care of him, looks after him. Always has done. Apparently all the lad has been saying since this happened is, 'Who is going to take care of me now?' Daft bastard."

Fenwick was slightly taken aback by his inspector's assessment, but chose not to say anything about it, but then said, "Shall we take him in? I mean at the moment he's all we've got."

Curran pondered the question momentarily. "Might as well. Get the overtime started. Yeah, we could rack up a few hours interviewing him. Stanley is bound to let us have it. He'll authorise it alright, he would love a nice murder on his patch. It's been a long time since we've had one. He will be out there in front of the TV and press telling the world that 'my men' will leave no stone unturned. Yeah, we can take him in, but I don't know if the lad has got the motive, the balls or the brains to do it. I mean if he had, there would be evidence all over the place. Yeah, might as well grab him. We'll shake him up a bit."

The rain was easing now. Fenwick puddle hopped over to the ambulance and addressed the figure wrapped in a blanket. "What's your name, mate?"

"Daniel, Daniel Hamblin. Am I going to be alright? Who will look out for me? Is somebody there to help me?"

"Can you tell me what happened, Daniel?"

"Well, all I know is that I was in the bottom field clearing the drainage, you got to do it a couple of times a year or the stream gets blocked up."

"Can you just tell me what happened?"

"Right, sorry, and I thought I would come up to the house for some tea. And I saw him, he didn't move. I shouted and shouted, 'Dad get up, get up.' But he didn't. I tried to shake him, but he didn't move. Then I went and fetched Mr. Reece. I don't know what to do. Is somebody coming to sort things out for me?"

"Look, Daniel, we need to talk to you about all this, about your dad. Obviously he has been shot and we need to find out what happened. We want to clear this up, we can't let some nutter with a gun go running around the countryside. We have got to find him. I know it is a real mess, but we have got to clear this up. We need to talk to you at the station, see what you can tell us. For the time being, we want you to stay here until scenes of crime arrive. Then you will have to give us the clothes you are wearing."

"Me clothes, what am I to do? I don't really have any others. I had a jacket and trousers once, when I went to the hospital, but they're gone now this long time since. Can't I stop here? I think I rather stop here."

Fenwick tried to interrupt the lad's verbal flow without success. "No, if it's aright I'll stop here. Mr. Reece will…"

The officer found it hard to hide his growing impatience and was aware that his colleagues looking on may be of the opinion that he was not controlling the situation. The tone of his voice was moving from that of authority to being demanding. "Look, lad, you have got to come with us. Scenes of crime, will give you some overalls to wear, paper ones with boots, right. We are going to talk to you about this and you better tell us everything you know or it might not look too good for you."

"Not good for me, what do you mean? What are you saying? Do you think I've done something bad? You're not saying I did this to me dad, you're not are you? Why are you saying this to me? Where have I got to go to, you're not putting me in prison, not locking me up? I don't want to go, I want to stay here. I'll stop here with Mr. Reece, he can look after me. I help him, with fixing his machinery, I'll stay with him."

"Listen, mate, don't bugger me about, you're coming in and that's it."

Across the yard, Reece, who had been conversing with the ambulance driver, caught the tail of the conversation. He straightened and started to walk towards Fenwick, who turned and walked away back to Curran. Reece stopped and stared at the officer.

Curran had just finished a 'phone conversation. "Right, got forensics sorted, they were at the nick anyway. Be here in about fifteen or twenty minutes. Tommy Lucas is the inspector, good bloke. Sound as a bell. What's up with the lad?"

Fenwick thrust his hands deep into his pockets. "Oh, he got the hump because I told him we wanted to talk to him in. Says he doesn't want to."

"I would play it a bit pear shaped if I were you. You want to watch that bastard Reece. I was watching him giving you the once over. He's only a farmer but, if he can, he will start trouble. Right twisted prat."

Fenwick drained his coffee cup. "Yeah, uniform just said he can be a bit awkward. What do you mean, what's he done?"

Curran, with his back to Reece explained. "A few years back, the drugs squad were doing observation from his land. The farm looks onto a couple of cottages that, according to Intel, was being used as a drugs distribution centre, allegedly cannabis coming in from the coast from Holland. Our blokes were using an old outhouse on the edge of his farm, it wasn't used for anything, just storing bales of hay. Anyway, Reece cottoned on to all this."

"Didn't they tell him what they were doing?"

"No, if they did he may have inadvertently tipped somebody off. If he mentioned it to some local from here, that would be it, be round the place in no time. It protected him. If he didn't know about it, nobody could accuse him of either supporting our boys in blue, except they were in camouflage gear, and nobody could say he gave a nod to the druggies. Well, one night he stumbled across a couple of our blokes, fully kitted up. He says he didn't know who they were, thought they might have been terrorists. Then he found out they were using his outhouse without telling him. He went ape, saying that we had made a mess of his straw, used it as a toilet. They did leave a few chip papers lying around and some empty pop cans, but nothing serious. I mean it's only bloody grass, there's a lot of it about. He said it was for his winter feed. Said he was going to speak to the chief constable and his MP. It hit the fan. Said he could do us for trespass and criminal damage, a right bloody carry-on. In the end our blokes had to get out of the outhouse and go back to using the obs vans. Our wonderful management agreed to pay him damages for his grass. The inspector on the obs team got a bollocking for not clearing it with him. Reece swore blind if the police ever came near him again, he would write to the press about intimidation, complain to his MP, all that old malarkey. What a dickhead."

Fenwick digested the foregoing for a few seconds then asked, "Did they get the druggies after all that?"

"Bit of a problem, our blokes got the wrong village. The cottage they were eyeballing was being lived in by a middle-aged spinster music teacher. By the time they twigged it, the druggies, in the next village, had it on their toes. Never saw them again. Well in fact they never saw them at all come to think of it. So be a bit careful of matey there."

"I thought he was giving me a bit of the evil eye a minute ago when I was having a word with the son."

As the story ended a car pulled into the farm. Curran walked over to the driver. "Well hello, Inspector Lucas. How is the world of forensics these days, still keeping you out of trouble?"

Curran had been a friend of Lucas since he arrived in the area over fifteen years ago. Lucas had steered him through the vagaries of internal politics and the ebbs and flows of the canteen gang culture. Lucas, due to retire within the year, had a reputation as a reliable and methodical officer who played it by the rules. His thick grey hair was swept back, recently it had been allowed to grow longer than it had ever been. Not much above medium height, he had a strong heavy boned clean shaven face, the angles of which had not been masked by the addition of the pudginess that was a feature of most of his colleagues. He smiled easily and his large brown eyes, which had a direct gaze, were capable of showing both humour and compassion.

"And how is Mrs. Lucas looking forward to having you under her feet?"

"Thrilled just isn't the word. She says she is dreading me being there all day, but she has sorted enough jobs out for me to keep me there for the next half a dozen years. Still I won't be sorry to leave this lot behind. Well, what have you got for us this time?"

"Old Sam Hamlin, the owner of the farm, well now ex-owner. Deceased, obviously a shotgun. Looks like homicide as there is no gun around, whoever did it had made off with it. Old Sam had been in town today, which, as you know, is market day. Rumour has it from some of the locals, according to uniform, he had been flashing a big roll of notes all over the place, mainly twenties from what they say. He had just sold some of his father's land and was a bit flush. We reckon that some punter had clocked him in town and either knew where he lived, or followed him out here to get his hands on the cash."

"So we may have tyre tracks, mind you, this rain won't have helped. Nor have we, charging up here like the fifth cavalry and there may be a wallet, that, if it has been taken, is likely to be dumped somewhere. Well, have a scout round for that. Who is the young man in the ambulance? Looks like he belongs here."

"That's the son. Haven't really spoken to him, but he says he saw nothing."

Lucas, as he wriggled into a white boiler suit, asked, "Do you think he might have done it? You know, most murders, relatives and all that?"

"I doubt it, he's a bit simple, not quite the full deck. I don't think he has got the ability, or the reason. His old man looked after him, apparently did everything for him, kept him, fed him. All the lad had to do was a few jobs around the yard. All he keeps saying now is 'Who is going to look after me?' Anyway I reckon it was a shot gun from not more than a few feet away. Whoever pulled the trigger would be splattered with blood. I had a look at the lad's clothes, we've told him that you will need them for examination, but there's hardly any blood on them. A bit on the sleeves around the cuffs and the bottom of his trousers, if you can call them that. He did say that when he found the body, he shook it, I think he thought he could wake his dad up." Lucas then indicated to one of his team to obtain the young man's clothing and supply him with a white paper coverall. "Bag the clothes up and make sure the exhibit labels and your note book correspond. I don't want any more cock ups." He turned to Curran.

"Well done, Inspector Curran, I think you can have my job in a couple of months. I suppose you notified Firearms?"

"Yeah, I spoke to them. They're on their way from Newcastle, should be here within an hour or so."

Lucas gave a furtive look around, then, in a conspiratorial whisper said, "Do you know who the inspector is now?"

"No, no idea. Haven't used them for years."

"Well I can tell you it is Simon 'Storming' Norman."

"You are pulling my plonker. Storming bleeding Norman, a sharpshooter? They've given him a gun? That man couldn't hit a cow on the arse with a banjo."

"Exactly," sighed Lucas. "Let me know when he is close so I can take cover. John Wayne doesn't come into it."

Curran reached for his phone. "I'll call him, tell him there is no gun, no gunman near here and suggests he makes a sweep of the country side looking for a farming type with a shotgun. That'll keep him and his band of merry men out of harm's way for a while. Right, I'll let you get on."

A Mercedes saloon swept up the drive, Lucas ran towards it waving his arms, signaling it to stop. The car continued past him and stopped in the farm yard. A large sleek man wearing a dark blue pinstripe suit emerged from the vehicle. "Hello, Tommy. I take it you were waving at me because you were excited to see me."

"Not exactly Doc, I was trying to keep the number of tyre impressions down. Maybe our killer used a vehicle to get here."

"Oh, right. So what have we got here?"

"Sam Hamblin, the owner of this farm. His lad found him, about an hour ago, maybe a bit more. He's in the house, if you can call it that. Complete tip."

"OK, anyone move the body?"

"No, the inspector and constable, you know Malcolm and Barry." The doctor's nodded acknowledgement to the two officers was returned.

"Well they just checked that the area was secure, no trace of anyone running around with a gun, the usual stuff, but they would not have moved the body. Hamblin's son apparently, when he found his father, shook him."

"Shook him?"

"Yes, he's got learning difficulties or something, thought he might wake his dad up."

"Oh, I see. Well let's have a look at him."

The doctor and the forensics officer walked towards the farmhouse.

"I hear you are up for retirement, Tommy. Can't be bad. How long to go now?"

"About seven months or so."

"A tip from me, if you haven't done so already, take up golf. It will get you out of the house for the day. You don't want to end up under the wife's feet all the time. I can get you an introduction to my club if you like. Nice bunch of chaps."

"Golf? Thanks. Can I let you know?" As the doctor moved away to attend to his duties, Lucas, in a stage whisper addressed Curran. "Bloody golf, I tried it; had some lessons; no good."

"Why not?" Curran returned the whisper from the side of his mouth.

"Well, it's a bit like sex or having a pee, I can't do it if anybody is looking at me."

The doctor bent over the body, shone a torch into its eyes and felt its fingers. "Well he's dead and it's a shotgun. Not much more than two or three hours ago. I'll let you know after I've done the autopsy."

With the doctor standing beside him, Lucas turned and addressed Curran and Fenwick, in a louder than necessary voice announced, "Doc says he's dead."

Fenwick shouted back, "Bugger me, how does he do it? And here's us thinking he cut himself shaving. What must it be like to have a brilliant mind?"

"Says it was a shotgun."

It was Curran's turn. "There you are you see, all the benefits of a higher education." The doctor, impervious to the remarks walked back towards his car, shouting over his shoulder, "He's all yours. Get him back to the morgue when you have finished. Let me know about the golf club."

Curran spoke to Daniel now enclosed in a white coverall. Look, lad, I know it's been hard for you, but we have got to speak to you at the police station. You won't be able to stop here for a few days. We need to investigate, search for clues. Look for things."

Daniel looked up, his eyes darting. "That other man said I've got to go to the police station. I don't want to. Why do I have to go? Will you keep me there? How do I get there, where will I stay. I've never stayed anywhere except here. What will I do?"

Fenwick waited for a minute or so, exchanging glances with Curran. Fenwick, looking up and apparently taking a general interest in the sky eventually said, "You can get a taxi into town then can't you, sort out a nice hotel for yourself to stay in when we have let you go. Somewhere posh perhaps? I would book a suite if I were you."

Reece, standing a few feet away, strode over his face as dark as the inner storms that had just erupted within him. "Oi, I know you're coppers, above the bloody law, but don't take the piss. You know what the lad is like. Think that is bloody clever do you, well you sort it for him and sort it now."

Curran closed in what was already a short distance between him and Reece, raising a finger into Reece's face, the distance between the two men shortened.

"I don't want you telling me what to do or how to run an investigation. You should back off."

Reece erupted. "Or what?" Then in a slower, more controlled tone but still with the command he had just demonstrated, "Or bloody what?" Each word was given its own space. "Run me in, check my car for road tax and insurance. Listen you two useless gobshites, you two who are the joke of the town who couldn't investigate a hole in a bucket. Find a killer, you couldn't find your mouth with a meat pie. You want to do something? Put me on a charge, no problem, no problem at all. We all know where you do your afterhours drinking, putting the arm on the landlords so they keep open for you. Have you ever thought about paying for your drinks, eh? Well, have you ever? Or is it still a 'gift' from grateful landlords? Do you still drive home pissed as rats? Do you still get your meals at a 'special rate' from the local restaurants? What does you're missus think you are doing when you are on night time investigations, eh. That's about the only time you find anything. We know, we all know about you, we let it go for a simple life, but by Christ if you bugger this lad about, it will all stop and your feet won't touch the ground. You think we are all thick farmers with mud on our boots and straw in our hair. Some of us have got kids that have done well, been to university, got jobs as lawyers. Well, are you hard enough when a man stands up to you? Now sort that lad out, do it now. If I find you've been messing him around, so help me I'll see that you two are the next behind bars. You two are not from round here, now think on that."

Curran pursed his lips and stared at the ground. Fenwick moved in towards Reece glaring at him, his anger welling up, filling the space in his chest, unable to believe that his authority had been challenged. Curran grabbed Fenwick's arm and pulled him back.

"You too, sonny, you too, now then, what are you going to do?" Reece was now back in erupting mode. Curran tugged Fenwick away from the scene, saying, "Come on leave it. Just leave it, alright."

Reece, putting his arm on Daniel's shoulder announced to him, "Don't worry, Daniel, these policemen are going to look after you nicely. I think they will take you to a little hotel or guest house where you will get everything you want. And you know what, Daniel? These policemen are going to pay for everything, everything, so you don't have to concern yourself. Isn't that right officers? Look, Daniel, if it's not all right, you got any worries or complaints, you tell me all about it. I don't think you will be needed at the police station tonight. They can leave that 'till tomorrow."

Curran, his head bowed and nodding slightly, looked up at Reece. "Look, Reece, we have got to speak to that lad tonight. We just cannot let go without speaking to him. There's been a bloody murder for Christ's sake. The lad will not be spoken to until we get him a responsible person to look after him. We will get one of the agents from a local solicitor. All right.

He is not a suspect. Not at this time. All right? He is needed to help us to find his dad's killer. All right? We will sort out accommodation with him and speak to Social Services. All right?"

Reece inhaled deeply. He did not rush to reply. "Daniel, go with these men. They are going to look after you. There is no need to worry, because if anybody does upset you, I will sort it out, good and proper." The commotion had caught the attention of those present. Lucas did not try to hide his disapproval, he looked somewhat uncomfortable. Curran and Fenwick knew they had lost this one, and had lost it in a public way. For a few moments they stood, trying to find something to look at, something to divert their attention, but there was nothing. Curran gave a slight shrug of his shoulders and tucked the matter away as an experience. It was just one of those things. It was not to be forgotten. He would chose his time and place.

Without speaking Curran indicated to Daniel to get in the police car, holding the rear door open for him. From outside the car he dialled a number on his phone. He said to Fenwick, "I'll see if Claire Knowles can put him up. Social services will pick up the tab. I sure she's got room." As the 'phone rang, he turned and walked a few paces away from Fenwick.

CHAPTER 3

"Hi Claire, Malcolm, that's right, you all right? No I'm working. Good, listen have you got a room? It'll be down to social services. It's for a lad whose father has just been killed. Well I say lad, he must be in his early twenties. No, it's quite alright, he's not suspected, he just needs looking after. He's in a bit of a state, in more ways than one. Do you know him? Old Sam Hamblin's boy, the farmer about four or five miles outside town. It's Sam that's copped it, looks like he was shot and his wallet taken. Robbery gone wrong. This lad, Daniel, he's going to need clothes, at the moment he hasn't got any, no I'm not joking. Could you talk to your friend from social services and see if she can do something for him? He's about five eight, five nine, well built." As he spoke he circled the car. After a few minutes he snapped the 'phone shut. The four or five miles into town took about fifteen minutes and were undertaken in complete silence.

Daniel wondered if he should speak to the two policemen who just stared tight lipped and with an unflinching gaze in the direction of travel. He couldn't remember if he had ever been in a proper car before. It was smooth and warm and lacked the smell of diesel and the ever present farmyard odours that had seeped into the fabric of his father's old Land Rover. His father's vehicle, on the occasions he travelled in it, used to bounce, rattle and sway through the lanes with gears crunching. In winter the windscreen would steam up, a window opened to clear the condensation let the icy wind in to prod around and finger its way down into him where the fit between body and clothes was generous. In this car he couldn't see over the hedges, couldn't see how the crops were coming on in the neighbouring farms. In the winter he would have been able to see those brown, fecund fields, ploughed to a corduroy stripe. He knew that now they are green and plump, but they were masked off by the tall hedgerows. He missed not being able to see the broad run of the landscape with its shallow billowing curves that played down into the hazy distance, to places he always imagined as holding some fascination for him. He didn't realise that he would want to see and judge these everyday issues that were part of his life.

In the police station, Daniel, still in the white coverall, was left alone in a square and dimly lit windowless interview room. Curran had told him that he would be back soon to talk to him. With the exception of the table and chairs, which he discovered were bolted to the floor, it was completely empty. He constantly surveyed the area, his head panning and tilting as though searching for something that could cause him harm, or to convince himself that there was nothing of that nature present. He found being alone, as he had been for some time now, with no information as to what was wanted of him, or what was about to happen, made him increasingly anxious. His initial fear grew being fed by the solitude, quietness and the not knowing. Occasionally voices and footsteps would pass by. At first he was glad when they kept moving past. Then he wished that somebody would come and tell him he could go home.

The police station was stark and functional. Metal desks were littered with forms and some time to be finished reports, grey filing cabinets were topped with unwashed coffee mugs. Notice boards that nobody ever noticed. In the large open office, most of the seats were empty. One or two of the occupants were engaged in telephone calls. One officer splayed over his chair, another hunched over in earnest and dark conversation. A small group congregated at the work station of a colleague, conversed animatedly, with occasional intervals of subdued laughter.

The two officers who had in the past hour returned from Hamblin's farm were sitting in front of Superintendent Stanley. Better dressed than his two subordinates but showing to greater effect the benefits of a more prolonged life of irregular hours and dining habits.

"Right you two, so old Sam Hamblin's copped it. He was a miserable old bugger, still won't do the figures any harm. We haven't had a murder for quite a while now, who was the last one? Wasn't it that Miss Taylor the school teacher who was having it off with that young barman, what was his name now?"

Curran leaned forward in his seat. "That was Charley Blakemore, Boss, a few tears ago now. Ted Blakemore's lad, you know Ted, he's been done for all sorts of petty stuff, nicking mainly. Apparently she, who was nearly twice his age, she was giving him the elbow because she'd found another lad who was even younger than Blakemore. He got potted for manslaughter, no doubt he'll be out soon, if he's not out already."

"Aye, Blakemore." There was a slight reflective pause. "But this one sounds like straightforward murder, shotgun through the chest. No sign of the weapon, ruling out suicide. What did you find?"

Curran leaned back in his chair with his hands clasped behind his head. "The lad, that is old Sam's son, reported it, well he went to the next farm to fetch help, that's Reece's place. Apparently the lad was absolutely bricking it. Old Sam was lying face up beside an upturned chair complete with said shotgun hole. The place is an absolute tip, you wouldn't think ordinarily that anybody would target it for a bit of thieving. But, apparently the old boy has recently sold his father's land, which, according to uniform, every local knew about. He was in town today, it was market day, flashing a wad that could choke a donkey. He paid off a large bill in Jones's supplies, he was seen in a few shops and then he was in the Golden Fleece trying to impress the barmaid with it. The money that is."

Stanley sat up and pushed himself back from his desk. "Isn't that that Sarah Blanchard? Tommy Blanchard, who used to be the vet, isn't she his daughter? Bloody hell, no wonder he was trying to impress her. I wouldn't mind flashing my wad at her myself. Wasn't she doing a line with that bloke who run the garage over at Haltwhistle?"

"That was ages ago, Boss." Curran unclasped his hands and put them in the pockets of his jacket. "Don't know who she's with now."

Stanley, after pondering momentarily and pursing his lips, continued his debriefing. "So, what do we know?"

Curran leant forward slowly rubbing the palms of his hand together. "Well, the wallet was gone. So was Old Sam's shotgun. Could have been some punter who saw Sam flashing his cash; thought he would help himself. Maybe Sam, being confronted, was going for his gun. But it looks like he was shot while he was sitting in his chair. Uniform have checked for a licence, he didn't have one. Apparently he just left it lying around. Maybe matey panicked, got there first and shot him. From what we can find out, it was a pretty knackered old blunderbuss, maybe a light trigger, just went off. We've brought the son in for a chat, just as a witness. He's not quite right, a bit simple. We're waiting for somebody to hold his hand when we speak to him. It isn't beyond the bounds that he did it, but it doesn't look like it."

Stanley sniffed loudly and suddenly. "We don't want any of that, accidental shooting stuff, we don't want another manslaughter. We will have murder. The crime scene shows robbery, Sam shot at close range and the punter was sharp enough to make off with the gun. No, this is a murder enquiry. Alright?"

"Right Boss."

"Right, Boss."

"Anything else?"

Curran and Fenwick looked at each other, then Fenwick took the lead.

"We found tyre tracks in the yard that would fit a Land Rover, we know that every bugger for miles around has got a Land Rover, but this one had mixed tyres on it, one was badly worn and one had quite a large split on it, so quite a distinctive marking. We got Scenes of Crime down there doing casts and photos. It's a bit iffy as the rain has washed away most of the tracks. We contacted all local stations and asked that the local bobbies check as many Land Rovers as they can."

"Good work, well done. I can contact other senior officers in the area and make sure their lads are on the ball. I presume you checked the tyres against Sam's vehicle?"

Fenwick continued. "Yes we did, Boss, completely knackered tyres but completely different. We checked the neighbour's, Reece, as well. Nothing there."

"What about the lad?"

"As we said, lad's half daft, Boss."

Now it was Curran. "We tried to speak to him, but he was shaking and crying. Kept asking who was going to look after him now. His dad, Old Sam, looked after him because he's thick in the head, he relied on the old boy for… well for everything. The lad said he'd been working in one of the lower fields. That would be about six seven hundred yards away, well away from the house and out of sight of the drive up to it. He was doing ploughing or something, so with the noise of the tractor he wouldn't have heard anything or even seen anybody coming up the drive. We've put him in an interview room, by the time somebody gets here from a solicitor's office, he might have calmed down a bit."

Stanley hunched forward over the desk, waving a ballpoint for added emphasis. "Look, let's get this lad rowed out of this, I mean out. I don't want any smart arsed newspaper bloke coming up here and pointing fingers were they shouldn't be. Let's be absolutely clear on this. If the lad is ruled out, then that leaves the way clear for us to conduct a proper murder enquiry and find the toe rag that did this. Am I clear, well am I?"

Fenwick looked down at his feet nodding slightly, then looked up. "Clear, Boss, absolutely clear."

Curran added, "Absolutely, Boss."

Stanley leaned back in his chair and threw the pen onto his desk. "Right, you two, what's to be done?"

Curran looked at Fenwick and indicated that he should proceed.

"Well, Boss, we will talk to the lad, check his timings. Confirm his story like." Stanley nodded sharply. "By the way the doctor reckons that old Sam had only been dead for not more than two to three hours. That puts the shooting at about two to three this afternoon. Just about the time when the market is emptying out. There will be the usual report. Do a search of the premises, that could take a while, there's loads of outbuildings and sheds and stuff. Check the main house where he was found, look for prints, dropped fag ends and the like. Check the area outside for footprints. See if we can firm up on vehicle type from the tyre spacing. Find out if there is any CCTV in the area that might identify a vehicle."

Curran, sensing that his partner was flagging slightly took over. "We would need to speak to them in town old Sam came into contact with. See if they can identify any scallywags from outside. Have a word with the shops he had been in, and the pub."

Stanley held his hands up in mock defeat. "I can see you lads have got it well boxed off. How many bodies will you need? I'm presuming some uniforms for the farm search. What about feet on the ground with enquiries?"

Curran. "I think the thing is, is to try and trace this vehicle, that really means covering farms in a radius of say fifty miles. If we could get uniformed from the surrounding areas checking, then reporting back to us, that would be a big help."

Stanley looked at his watch. "I don't want to hurry you lads, but I'm meant to be meeting a mate of mine for a pint soon. Look, I'll get the uniforms organised, I'll make sure they report back to this nick. I don't want some bloody superintendent from across the way trying to stroke us on this one. Any problems with anybody trying to shift this onto another patch, speak to me straight away. The body's on this patch, so the crime is on this patch. Right I've got to shift. Anything else?"

Curran now assumed the mantle of senior partner with Fenwick.

"Thing is, Boss, we think it would be a good idea to make a start straight away, with the initial enquiries. You never know, we might…"

Stanley standing up and reaching for his jacket, looked down in an almost paternalistic way. "Yes, yes, I'll authorise the overtime, but don't rip the arse out of it." He reached the door and looked back. "Well done lads. Remember this is our murder, it stays on this patch."

The two officers remained silent for a second or two. Both exhaled sharply and regarded each other. Fenwick was the first to break the brief silence. "Oh yes, oh yes my son, the overtime gravy train has just started, let's get on it. Right Inspector Curran, as senior hand, where do you think we should commence our enquiries?"

Curran put on a mock display of concentrated thinking. "Constable Fenwick, where was the last place where old Sam was seen before he left town more or less?"

"Let's see, he was at the chandler's, the newsagent's." He then feigned difficulty in trying to recall the final location. He snapped his fingers and looked heavenwards. "Of course, the pub."

"Yes, Constable Fenwick, the pub. I think we need to investigate the pub. You never know, there could be the crucial piece of evidence, the very piece of evidence that would solve this terrible crime. Shall we rattle the lad's cage for a while and then continue our enquiries at that very place?"

"Why not, why not indeed?"

"And, Constable Fenwick, do remember that this will be on overtime."

CHAPTER 4

Daniel had now been left in the interview room for, what seemed to him, hours. For all his life he had seen space. Out in the fields or at the farmyard itself, he had only to raise his head to see into the far distance down to where the sky and the earth came together. Even when inside the ransacked old farmhouse, the windows allowed for the same, although précised, view. Now he was in a gloomy box where the walls appeared intent in closing in on him. He could feel the tension pulsing through his veins.

He could hear people approaching the room, hollow footsteps in the empty corridor. Voices becoming more discernible, bubbling closer. It was Curran and Fenwick, he could hear Curran say, "There's a girl arrived from some duty solicitors, I think she's just a clerk or something. You want to see the state of it. That bloody spiky hair, them trousers with a dozen pockets in them, T shirt, what a bloody mess. Probably some kid on work experience. Let her in, if they want to send kids, that's their look out."

A young woman fitting that description approached the two officers. "Hello, I'm Tracey Williams from Baxter and Martin. I'm here in respect of Daniel Hamblin. Are you the officers involved?"

Curran's 'yes' was as curt and abrupt as a one word answer could be.

"Could I have your names and ranks please?"

As she was noting their details in a folder, Curran looked across to Fenwick, made a face of mock surprise and, with a slight wobble of his head, mouthed, "Tracey?" towards Fenwick.

"Why is he here?" She continued making entries into her folder.

Fenwick, in noting Curran's attitude, replied slowly with an over emphasised casualness.

"Well there has been a murder."

Without looking up from her notes she countered, "So it is murder." There was no reply. "You have already decided that it is not a case of manslaughter, but murder. Perhaps it was some sort of accident. May I ask what the evidence is that allows you at this stage to state with certainty that it is murder?"

"Well, he, he was killed by a shotgun and usually that means…"

"I see, is it Constable Fenwick, yes? Well Constable Fenwick, with such an incisive legal mind, I am certain you will progress very quickly in your chosen profession."

"It's a homicide."

"Thank you for that clarification, Inspector Curran. I understand that the victim was the father of Daniel Hamblin."

"Yes." This time Curran's reply was more circumspect.

"I understand that Daniel has certain learning difficulties and may be considered as being vulnerable?"

"Yes."

"Why is he here?"

Curran's reply contained considerable more caution than previously. "He is here to assist us with our enquiries into the death of his father."

"Is he under arrest?"

"No, but we thought that whilst matters were fresh in his mind we… "

"Has it been explained to him that he is under no obligation to be here and that he is free to leave at any time?"

"Well he didn't seem to mind when we told him."

"I see Constable Fenwick, it must be the 'He Didn't Seem To Mind' section of the Police and Criminal Evidence Act that deals with vulnerable persons that you have relied on. Well done, I can see your career going from strength to strength. Where is Daniel now?"

The two men remained silent, one waiting for the other to offer himself up. Eventually Curran replied in a manner that suggested he knew what response he would face. "At the moment he is in an interview room."

"I see, and how long has he been in the interview room? You will have made a note of the time." Her tone was flat and displayed no emotion.

"About an hour." Curran was not enjoying himself.

"About," the word was stressed. "An hour. Has he been accompanied during that hour?"

"No."

"Has he been offered any refreshments or asked if he needed to use the toilet?"

"No." Curran, although on a roll with his answers, was now regretting his sloppy approach. He tried an attack. "Can I ask if you are actually a solicitor?"

"Yes, you can ask." She still had not looked up from making notes. "Now, will you take Daniel out of the interview room immediately, ask him if he wants refreshments or needs to make use of the facilities. I want him taken to an office where I will speak to him in private. Do you think you can manage that?"

"Look, is it Miss? Ms? Williams. There has been a violent death and we are somewhat short on resources."

"Thank you, inspector. I think I have grasped the basic facts. Now, shall we look after Daniel?"

A room, acceptable to Tracey Williams, was allocated. She spent a period of time with Daniel, still making notes. She left the room to find Curran and Fenwick in the immediate vicinity. She addressed Curran, without making notes.

"Inspector, Mr. Hamblin does not recall actually being invited here or being told, in clear terms that, if he did not want to come to the police station he did not have to and he does not recall being told that he is under no obligation to remain here. In fact he feels that he was given no choice and had to accompany you here very much against his wishes. He tells me that he was told if he did not come to the police station, 'things would not look good for him,' and that he wasn't to 'bugger' Constable Fenwick about." She left the words hanging, the only show of emotion was the pen she was flicking between two fingers. The silence continued. Her pen flicked a bit faster. "Well, is Mr. Hamblin correct?"

Fenwick ventured tentatively. "Maybe he didn't quite understand, perhaps we could have made it clearer for him."

"Yes." The word was drawn out to the point where it tested to the extreme the tensile properties of the language. "Perhaps you could have." She paused, looking down at the floor. There was some slight shuffling from the two officers. "Of course you realise that your joint failures to act properly, especially considering Mr. Hamblin's perceived issues, leaves you open to claims of intimidation and harassment, if not false arrest and imprisonment. Right now he could confess to being Jack the Ripper, an armed bank robber and Yorkshire's most prolific poacher and no court in the land would even consider listening to either of you. Right, what do you propose now?"

With considerable circumspection, Curran put forward his proposal. "We would like to ask Daniel, Mr. Hamblin, some questions we hope will assist us in our enquiries into the death of his father."

"Do you really still say 'assist us with our enquiries'? How quaint. Well, I have spoken to Mr. Hamblin and explained that this is a serious matter and that he may be of some assistance, with 'your enquiries', and he has agreed, in order to help solve this matter, to answer some questions. These will not be questions under caution, nor will they be recorded by tape. It is not really necessary to say this, but anything Mr. Hamblin has said already cannot be used as evidence. I'm sure you agree with that. I am correct in saying that that is in accordance with the Police and Criminal Evidence Act, Constable Fenwick?"

Fenwick, who had, by this time, withdrawn from the exchange, was slightly taken aback. "Well, yes, yes it is, as you say, in accordance with the Act."

"Thank you so much, Constable, I do feel reassured. He would like a cup of tea."

In the room used for the interview, Tracey Williams sat beside Daniel. "Now, Daniel, these officers would like to talk to you about what happened today. They are doing this so that you can help them, so they tell me, with their enquiries. Now to be clear, you do not have to stay here if you do not want to, you can leave at any time. Also, you do not have to answer any questions if you do not want to. Now, Daniel, do you understand what I have told you?"

He looked at the faces in front of him then back to his legal representative. "They weren't very nice to me, they said I had to come here. I didn't want to. He said I had to get a taxi."

"Really, Daniel? If the officers did say that I am sure they didn't mean it and are very sorry to have upset you." She gave the two policemen a quizzical look. There was a slight coughing sound and an exchange of glances. Fenwick took his cue.

"Er, yes, Daniel, if we, or I have done anything that you didn't like, I am sorry, very sorry. I didn't mean it." He felt a slight kick on his leg from under the table. It was Curran's way of saying that the *mea culpa* speech had exceeded the requirements of the moment.

Tracey Williams gave a slight downward nod of her head so as to express her approval.

"Now, Daniel, I am here to help you, you must think of me as your friend. If the policemen ask a question that I think is unfair to you, I will tell you not to answer. You can ask me questions at any time. Remember that, if you want to, you can leave at any time. I understand that it has been arranged for you to stay with a local lady."

Curran spoke. "I assume that you will have no objection to constable Fenwick making a written note of what is said?"

"Provided I am given the opportunity to examine those notes before I leave and for me to sign them after the last entry."

"Yes, I think that would be in order." Curran was starting to climb back into the ring.

Tracy Williams gave a hint of a smile. "Good, obviously I will be making my own contemporaneous notes."

Curran commenced his interview. "Right, Daniel, can you tell us, in your own words…"

Tracy Williams exhaled sharply, her look towards Curran confirmed her growing impatience.

Curran tried again. "Daniel, can you tell us what happened today, how you came to find your father?"

Daniel looked at Tracy Williams. She nodded her approval to speak.

"Well, like I said before, I was down at the bottom of Little Acre field, digging out the ditches, it's for the drainage. Has to be done at least twice a year or it gets right blocked up."

"Yes, Daniel, what happened then, why did you go up to the farmhouse?"

"Well, I'd been down there for quite a while, I thought, 'I could do with a drink, a cup of tea.' I didn't know if me dad was back from the market, he always goes to that. Sometimes it's a bit late when he gets back. So I went up, then I saw dad. He was just lying there. I said, 'Dad, Dad, what you doing?' But he never moved. I could see all blood, I knew it was coming from him. I went over and shook him and shook him, and shouted at him, I kept saying, 'Dad, Dad what you doing?' But he never moved. It really scared me. I mean I wondered if he was really dead. I had a thought afterwards that was the first time I ever touched him, and he was dead. Funny that."

Tracey Williams reached across and gently squeezed his arm.

Curran stuck to his brief. "What happened then?"

"I got in the Land Rover to fetch Mr. Reece, he's in the next farm. Then he called the ambulance, then all the police turned up."

"Was Mr. Reece at his farm, is that where you found him?"

"That's right, when I got there he was in the big barn. I think he was trying to fix the bailer. He's had some trouble with that. I've helped him with it before, but it's still not right."

"How did you and Mr. Reece get to your farm?"

"He drove me in our Land Rover. He said I didn't look in a fit state to drive."

"Thank you, Daniel. That is helpful. Daniel, did your dad have a gun, a shotgun?"

"Yes, he has got that old one, mind you he's had it for years, for as long as I can remember."

"I see, Daniel. Could you tell me where he kept it?"

"It is usually on top of the dresser, he kept it handy. We used to have chickens on the other side of the yard. There was always foxes coming round. We don't have chickens anymore." Daniel's last sentence was delivered with a degree of earnestness.

Curran waited for a few moments for Fenwick to catch up with his note taking. "When you saw your dad today, lying on the floor, did you see his shotgun?"

"I never noticed." Daniel gave a quick look to Tracy Williams to see if his response was acceptable. She smiled her approval. Daniel continued. "I didn't think to look for it, should I have done? Is it not there now? Did you look on top of the dresser, the one in the kitchen?"

"Is that where he usually kept it?"

"Yes, on the dresser."

"Have you ever used your dad's shotgun, Daniel?"

"Oh yes, it's for the foxes, rabbits and crows when we have lambs. I'm better at it than me dad. He doesn't see so well now, well I mean he didn't. He had glasses, but he broke them or lost them, I'm not sure. If there was a fox about, he would tell me to get it. He never got them fixed, the glasses."

Curran continued. "When you were working, did you see anybody come to the farm? You didn't see a car did you?"

"No, when you are down at the bottom part, like Small Acre, you can't see the house or the drive up to it. It's quite a long way down. Dad tries to shout for me when I'm down there, but I can't hear him. Well most of the time I can't."

"Can you see the road from there?"

Daniel shook his head. "No."

Fenwick nodded to Curran that he had completed his note, Curran took his cue.

"Right, so you didn't see the gun. Did your dad have a wallet, did you ever see a wallet?"

"Oh, aye, he had a wallet alright. I never saw much of it."

"Where did he keep it?"

"When he was in, he locked it in a drawer, but if he was off into town he would take it with him."

"When he took it with him, where did he put it, how did he carry it?"

Daniel's left hand moved across his chest and he thought for a second. "I would say he put it in his jacket, in a pocket on the inside. That's right, I've seen him fasten it down with a safety pin."

"Do you know if he had any money in it today?"

"Oh, I never got to see in his wallet, he was proper careful of that. I don't think that he would have a lot of money, at least he always said he didn't have much."

"Daniel, have you any idea of what sort of things your father had in his wallet, you know bank cards, cheque cards, that sort of thing? Anything that would help us identify it."

"Like I said, he would never let me see his wallet. I don't have any idea what was in it, sorry, no."

"We have been told that your father was seen in possession of a large amount of cash. Do you know anything about that?"

Daniel sat upright. "Oh, had a large amount of cash, did he? Well how much was that then?" His tone was that of a scolding wife to an errant husband. "He never said anything to me. He never would. If I thought he had money on him, I would have told him to pay me what was mine for all the jobs I do. He never paid me. I should have had some of that money."

"Did you hear your father coming back from the market?"

"No, not really. I didn't hear him coming back. I wouldn't do if I was down at the bottom field. And probably the tractor or digger would have been going as well."

Having been able to give a positive response, Daniel was now starting to relax to the task.

"We understand that your dad sold some land recently, it's common knowledge round here. Do you know what he did with the money, do you know if he kept any of in his wallet?"

Daniel was feeling more comfortable, against his expectations he understood the questions. Now he was able to embellish this answer.

"I asked dad about how much he got for it but he wouldn't say. Anyway I knew how much he was asking, I saw it on the agent's advert that dad brought home. He left it on the table, it had a photo and everything on it. I think he forgot about it, but I saw it, I saw how much it was. It used to belong to his dad, I never saw him though. He died a long time ago. Oh, right, well I said to dad, now you've got a lot of money, perhaps you could give me some, for the jobs that I do at the farm. But he said that he had to pay the lawyers a lot, he didn't like them. They said they were going to take him to court because he wouldn't pay them. No he didn't like them."

A jolt of awareness hit him. Looking at Tracey Williams then at the desk, he said, "I'm sorry lady, you're a lawyer. I didn't mean you. My dad didn't like them other ones."

Tracey Williams turned and smiled at him, putting her hand up so as to prevent him tying more knots. "That is quite alright, Daniel. Some of them are not very nice."

His absolution granted, he smiled back and continued. "Where was I, oh that there was the lawyers, then he said he had to pay the agents and he owed the bank a lot. Well that's what he said. Said he didn't have a lot left. I know he had to pay for some supplies. He owed them as well."

"Did your dad have anybody who didn't like him, anybody he might have upset?"

Daniel could feel himself flagging now. The tension he initially felt was melting away. Apart from one or two neighbouring farmers, he was, probably for the first time in his adult life, interacting with people. He was the centre of attention, but now he was feeling pressure.

"Look, I didn't really meet any of the folk that dad talks to, them in town, so I don't know. There was never people coming up to the farm or anything like that. He spoke to some in town, but I don't know, I'm not sure."

Tracey Williams, sensing that her charge was becoming more uncomfortable, gave him a rest. "Are you saying the gun and wallet were not found at the farm?"

"No, they weren't, but could we ask you to keep that to yourself, it may form part of our…" He hesitated.

"Your enquiries, inspector? I assure you of the upmost discretion. So presumably, although you are not likely to find the gun but it's possible, but if you find somebody who has either the gun and or the wallet, or its contents, it is likely that whoever has them, is either the person you are looking for, or that person knows them. Perhaps trying to sell the gun in a pub. Daniel, do you understand what we are saying? It looks like the person that did this to your dad has gone off with his gun and his wallet. Could you describe the gun for the officers?"

"It was just an old gun, it's been there for years. He even had to put tape around the handle as it was getting a bit loose."

Tracey Williams was ignoring Curran's rather theatrical show of impatience owing to his position being usurped. She turned towards Daniel, who found her direct gaze difficult to deal with.

"Do you know what sort of things he kept in his wallet? Did he have bank cards or credit cards? It could be very important, it could help to catch whoever did this?"

"I don't ever recall seeing into his wallet, as I said he keeps it locked in his drawer. I don't know what he had in it. He would never let me see it."

She completed the notes in her pad, then looked at the officers. "I think Daniel has had quite enough for one day. He has been through a most distressing and harrowing set of circumstances. Unless there is any burning issue that you need to address, I think we should call it a day."

Fenwick rested his pen. Curran sat up. "I think that there are one or two more things we would like to put to Daniel."

Tracey William's repost was instant. "Such as?"

Curran thought for a moment. "Perhaps you are right. He has been through a lot and we have got to get him to Mr.s Knowles's guest house. We will need to take a witness statement though."

"Yes I understand inspector, but that can be done later and I will be present when Daniel is giving his statement. I can drop Daniel off at the guest house, I understand that it is only a mile or so."

Left alone in the interview room, Fenwick threw his pen down onto the desk. Curran stood up and stretched.

Fenwick left his chair and rested against the wall. "What did you think of her then?"

"The divine Tracey? A bit gobby, a bit full of herself. Usual young thing trying to make a name for herself. I seen worse, a lot worse than that. She will learn in time, when she comes looking for a favour for one of her clients. When she's been told to sod off a few times she'll come down a peg or two."

"I thought she was a right little bitch, smug, mouthy know it all. Probably a lezzer."

"Don't let it get to you, Barry. it's like this all the time. We are coppers and do things our way, if you played it by the book all the time you wouldn't get anything done. They come in here all Human Rights and legal procedures, it's a bit of a game. We get what we want, feel a few collars, they get what they want, smart arsed legal arguments in court so their clients can see them earning their crust. But round here the local magistrates will always back us up. Look, Barry, mate, don't let it worry you. You get used to it. What time is it? Nearly eight. The old overtime clock is still running, I think we should continue our investigations in the pub. Let's see what Sarah has got for us.

CHAPTER 5

The nose of the car dipped under braking and there was a crunch of gravel. It had stopped in the drive of a detached house of grey local stone. What would have been a somewhat morose construction was lifted by the neatly painted white window frames and an equally well decorated large front door. The lawns that bridged the house and the road some seventy feet distance were trim and clipped. They had the benefit of being restrained by flower beds whose garish colours had little to do with nature, but at least added emphasis to the boundary. Everything was neat. This wasn't lost on Daniel, who, after being encouraged to leave the car, stood not knowing what to do next. He was told that the lady was Mrs. Knowles. Although he did not know what to expect, for some reason he was slightly taken aback by, what was to his mind, the glamorous figure in front of him. What he saw was a tall, slim, elegant woman with shoulder-length blonde hair. He found her assured demeanour somewhat daunting. She smiled at him and nodded an initial greeting.

His awareness of his own appearance crept up on him like a pick pocket. He looked at his own garment and realising, for the first time, that although he was still in the white coveralls given to him by the police, that he could have been facing her in his usual grease adorned farmyard attire complete with baling string. Despite his discomfort, he noted that her clothes faithfully followed all of her feminine contours. He felt an unusual tightening in his throat. He thought that he had never seen such a beautiful lady, in fact he could not really recall ever being this close to a lady. He was intimidated and in awe. He remained silent. Tracey Williams introduced herself, then placing a hand on his shoulder, gently propelled him towards Mrs. Knowles.

"This is Daniel, I understand he will be staying with you for a few days until things get sorted out." With one hand still on Daniel, she offered him a small white card. "Daniel, this is my number. If you ever need to, or want to, contact me, do so at any time. If those policemen, or any policemen, say they want to talk to you, you must tell them to call me first." He turned as the car crunched over the gravel towards the road. He turned back to the woman, now alone his anguish increased in proportion to his vision of his own sartorial shortcomings and the yawning social gulf between them. She was old, but not as old as his dad. She smiled at him and nodded an initial greeting.

"Right, Daniel, you must be shattered. Come on in, Love, let's get you sorted. I'll put a brew on, I imagine you must be hungry." Then, almost as an afterthought, "Love, I'm so sorry to hear about your dad, it must have been an awful shock. Are you feeling alright? Malcolm, that's Inspector Curran, said he has arranged for a lady to come from social services to see if she can help you. Even though it's getting on a bit, she said she'll be here soon. It's Mrs. Jones, she is a very nice lady. You will find her very helpful."

She shepherded Daniel to a large slab floored kitchen. He still had not spoken. "I think, Lovey, that you would probably like a nice long bath?" She continued her appraisal of him. "And maybe you could give your hair a wash. That would make you feel better. I'll show you to your room, it's got its own bathroom in it, in fact all our rooms have. In Small Brook cottage we have five high quality rooms - we have in the past been awarded three stars. All are en suite and have complementary toiletries and tea and coffee making facilities." Too late, she realised that her well-practiced welcome speech had made contact with stony ground and that her target audience didn't speak that language.

"Now here's your room, you will notice that the window has a southerly aspect… well I think it is a very nice room. Don't you?"

Daniel nodded in open-mouthed amazement.

"Now, when you have had your bath, and washed your hair mind, there's a dressing gown for you. I think we will get rid of this boiler suit thing. The lady from social services - as I said that's Edith Jones, she's a friend of mine, married to Eric Jones who runs an insurance business, perhaps you know him - well she is bringing you some new clothes. Malcolm Curran told me what sort of build you were so I reckon I know what size will fit you."

Now alone, he looked around his temporary accommodation. He had never known such luxury, it was overwhelming, he wondered if all normal people had houses like this. Surely not, this must be a special place. His room did indeed have its own bathroom and after considerable hesitation and more urging from Mrs. Knowles, he luxuriated in deep, warm, soapy water, he felt protected. He dried with large white towels that had a softness he had never known. He determined there and then that when his father's money came - well it was his now - he would have a proper bathroom put in at the farm. When he came out of the bathroom, he realised that his white coveralls had gone. In their place was a selection of jeans, shirts and sweaters.

There was a knock on his door. "Have you finished with your bath, Love?"

He nodded.

"You did give your hair a good wash, didn't you Daniel? We will see Mr. Curtiss the barber tomorrow, with that mop you could be his greatest challenge, I hope he doesn't charge by the pound."

He nodded again.

"Those clothes on the bed… I say, can you hear me, Daniel?"

He nodded. There was a pause. "Yes, yes I can."

"Well those clothes are for you. You don't have to pay for them, Mrs. Jones got them for you from the charity shop in the High Street, the one next to the butchers, she got the lady to open up for you. The lady that runs it that is. She is a good friend of hers. It's not the first time. Just see what ones fit, then come down and we'll have a look at you."

He surveyed the bewildering array in front of him, looking from the clothes to the door then back again. There was even a holdall. Could they all really be just for him? From the collection, he tried on jeans a shirt and a sweater. They were clean and they fitted him, certainly a lot better than the garments he wore around the farm. He kept looking at himself in the mirror. He found it hard to comprehend the transformation, telling himself, repeatedly that he looked more normal; he wasn't so bad looking after all. Now, if he had some money, he could go into town. He wouldn't look so different from any of the other lads now. Never know, might even buy a girl a drink. You never know. He felt strange in his new clothes, but also excited. He thought about the events of the day. His father had only been dead a matter of hours, but look what has happened since then. He thought that he should be sad, or let people see that he was sad, but he wasn't. Maybe this was the very beginnings of a gradual dawning that he was free from the man, who although he may have kept him and fed him, regarded him no more than his personal property.

The overwhelming feeling of fear and apprehension that day's happenings had introduced and that had inhabited him, were slowly being diluted with the excitement of the possibilities that may wait for him. From his new wardrobe, he selected a pair of jeans, a blue check shirt with dark blue cuffs and breast pocket and a brown thick knit sweater. After convincing himself as to his new found sartorial talents, he opened his door, no more than an inch. An inspection of the area outside showed there were no impediments that would hinder further progress. He moved downstairs, taking the upmost care not to make any noise. He stood outside the kitchen door, he could hear the burble of conversation between his new landlady and, what he would find to be, Mrs. Jones from social services. After a few moments he coughed gently, then having received no reaction, a little louder.

"Come in, love come in, Daniel, come and see Mrs. Jones, let's have a look at you."

He entered the room stopping a few feet from where the women were sitting. The vision of Mrs. Jones struck him. Slim, slimmer than Mrs. Knowles even, she wore a dark blue jacket and skirt and a white blouse. Her dark hair shone, catching the light as it moved in a single wave. She smiled softly, but her eyes were smiling as well. She stood and offered her hand.

"Hello, Daniel." He thought she looked like a very kind lady. "Daniel, love, I wouldn't have recognised you. You do look nice. Come on let's have a proper look. This is Mrs. Jones, she brought you all those clothes. You do look nice. Mrs. Jones, I think we have a transformed young man here. Daniel, I can't get over how different you look." Daniel held his arms out at a slight downward angle away from his body in order to assist Mrs. Knowles in voicing her approval. He felt embarrassed and awkward. This was tempered by the attention he was receiving from those who did not seem to be only interested in what he could do for nothing. For the first time, as far back as he could remember, somebody was doing something for him and, without being asked to. They offered him a meal, but eating with strangers was unnerving. He pretended he wasn't hungry, but he was. Food was later left in his room where he enjoyed tastes and textures that he could not believe existed. His bed was warm and clean, but it seemed too good for him to get into. He kept looking at himself in the mirror, trying on a variety of shirts and sweaters, packing and unpacking his own holdall. His opinion of himself and his improving status, in the confines of his room, was growing. His life on the farm, up until now, was being viewed from the other end of the telescope.

Mrs. Jones, before she left, knocked on his door and sat on the end of his bed. She smelled of perfume, a sensation that he had not encountered before. She smiled at him gently and looked into his eyes. When she moved, her neat coordinated clothes made a soft swishing noise. If ever he felt pleasure by being with somebody it was now. She asked him about life on the farm, all the time making notes. She said that, in the short time she had available to check, there were no records available that showed any history, employment or otherwise, that related to Daniel. She said she saw that his father collected his state benefits for him. She asked about wages paid to him. His face reddened.

"I never got no money, he never gave me nothing. I haven't got any now, I don't know what to do. My dad said what I earned had to be paid for board and keep, my food and the like."

Mrs. Jones made further notes, finally when she put her pen down, she told him that as his father was his employer, but didn't pay even a minimum wage, she could authorise an immediate emergency payment of cash to him.

"Look, Daniel." As she spoke she touched his arm. His body throbbed. "It's the weekend now, so what I'll do, I will give you some cash now and then we can adjust it on Monday, how does that sound?"

"Can I keep it, or do I have to give it back?"

"No, Daniel, you keep it, it's yours and you do not have to give it back." Mrs. Jones read some forms out to him, she said he was probably a bit too tired and shocked from today's happenings to read it properly. He signed in a large scrawl. Then she gave him a hundred pounds. It took his breath away. He handled the notes as if they were hot stones.

"Daniel," she spoke as she was leaving his room."That is your money, you do what you like with it. Maybe you feel like walking into town tonight to buy yourself a drink, you know, to settle your nerves. You have been through a lot today."

He didn't go into town that night. But the next day he did. He had his first proper haircut and was dressed in clothes that meant he looked just the same as others. He had money in his pocket. As he first travelled through the town, he was surprised to be passed unnoticed. Nobody stopped and stared, there were no caustic remarks about being a tramp, about having 'mud on your boots'. He was beginning to feel part of the fabric of the place. He looked in at shop windows and noticed how casual the people were in selecting and making their purchases. He glanced through the doors of the local pubs observing drinkers just sitting there. Just sitting and doing nothing. Some were by themselves, others in groups, chatting casually. One day, he thought, one day.

After his weekend at the guest house, it was decided, for reasons not made entirely clear to him, that he should return, on a temporary basis, to the farm. It was something to do with collecting personal belongings or making sure that the police had not broken anything. He felt he wanted to say that he did not have any items that were just his or, that there was much that could be broken. However, on thinking about it, he realised that there were reasons why a return would resolve some issues.

He was taken back to the farm by a lady who said she was from Social Services, but it wasn't Mr.s Jones. He felt somewhat cheated at having to travel with somebody else. This lady drove her small car with a degree of ferocity, lurching into corners at speed. It was all he could do not to bump into her as she rattled the gravel on tight right hand bends. He hung onto his seatbelt with one hand and the dashboard with the other, dipping forwards under harsh braking and backwards when accelerating. She spoke to him, but there was no communication. She said things that did not invite a reply. She said that if he ever needed anything he was to 'phone her. He didn't think she really meant it. At the times she started to talk to him, she always seemed to have to take a call on her phone. She seemed much happier talking to those other people than to him. As the hedges became a blur, a call would come in. Often she let go of the steering wheel to change gear whilst her mobile was pressed to the side of her head. She kept calling everybody 'Sweedy'. "Hi, Sweedy." "Bye, Sweedy." When they arrived at the farm and his head catapulted forward for the last time, she handed him a little card that had her name and 'phone number on it. She started to explain that when he wanted to go back to town, he could call her. In fact he could call any time, as she spoke another call came in.

"Oh, hi Sweedy, no it's fine just dropping somebody off." He tried to tell her that he didn't have a phone, but she, still talking, further assaulted the accelerator then she and her little, car bounced and rocked away.

Left alone in the farmyard, he looked around. Nothing appeared to have changed, but it was somehow different. In the house where he last saw his father slumped and gaped mouth, somebody had tidied up. He walked around touching familiar objects. All the time he expected to see or hear his father. The silence rang in his ears. Although alone, he constantly looked about as he walked around the yard and buildings. He took a final glance and with heart thumping and stepping like a stag over stones, he went up to his hideout in the roof part of the old coach house. He saw that an area had been inspected by the police, but the scuff marks and new disarray stopped well short of his space. He pulled away the bits of furniture and equipment that covered the small doorway. He knew he didn't have to go there anymore. His father had gone, but it was still his private space. Nothing had changed, nobody had been in there. It had not been found. The police said they were going to search the farm, but they did not find his secret room, or considered it so remote from the incident that it was ruled out as being of any potential value. He sat for a while, looking out of the peep hole of a window, there was nobody around. It took him some time to assure himself that he was truly alone. He smiled and moved the plank that concealed the entrance to his private cache. He reached in and removed and fingered his old treasures. Slowly he put them back, then took out his most recent additions.

CHAPTER 6

Superintendent Stanley strode through police station with a heavy, measured step, nodding closed mouthed acknowledgments as he transited the corridors to his office. Before he had reached his chair, Fenwick and Curran followed him into his space. He threw his briefcase onto his desk and looked out of the window standing with his back to the two men. Taking his seat, he swivelled his chair slowly from side to side whilst affecting a pensive attitude as though deep in thought on a matter of some moment. He then regarded his men with an unspoken question, giving an indication that proceedings may now begin. His initial feigned indifference stuttered to a halt when he saw the urgent and triumphant faces of his officers. He reacted with an affected nonchalance. "What are you two buggers up to? Collared our murderer, have you?"

"No, Boss, but we've got a significant development."

"I see, a significant development. Significant development if you will. Well so have I. Got the initial coroner's report. Would you believe, old Sam died of a massive shotgun wound? Well, bugger me. But he was on his last knockings anyway. Apparently his heart was so diseased it was making medical history, he should have been dead months ago. Coroner said he didn't know what kept him going. Said he would be surprised if he had lasted another month or two. So lucky for us that our man of mystery blew him to the back of beyond. If he had put up more of a fight and had a heart attack when his wallet was being ripped off, which is what we would expect of him, we wouldn't even have got a manslaughter charge to stand. So, gentlemen, it is still murder." Being satisfied that he had asserted and demonstrated his authority, and still swivelling his chair, he now invited contributions from Fenwick and Curran. "So what have you two aces turned up?"

"Superintendent Stanley." The ponderous measurement of Curran's words could not hide the anxiety with which he wanted to project them. "We have turned up something of significance." He turned to Fenwick and addressed him with mock solemnity. "Constable Fenwick, would you say, in your vast experience of investigating crime, that this development was significant?"

"I would indeed, Inspector Curran, I would indeed."

Would you two buggers stop pissing about and get on with. You haven't got the twat that did it have you?" Stanley was rising from his chair as he spoke, remaining half standing.

"What we have got is most unusual."

"For Christ sake bloody get on with it." Stanley was now standing upright.

"Right, Boss." Curran made a slight downward chopping motion with both his hands. "You know old Sam spent some money in town, right, well one of the things he bought was a lottery ticket, from Seth Hunter's newsagents. He uses the same numbers every time, never varies."

"And?"

"He's only bloody won it, just over two million quid. Two bloody million. Old Sam."

Stanley slumped into his seat. "Are you buggers winding me up? You're not winding me up are you?"

"No way, absolutely, God's honest truth." Curran paused to ensure the message had registered. "Two frigging million. And the old bastard can't spend it. Well not now he can't."

Stanley gazed open mouthed at the two men looking from one to the other. The nod of his head indicated what his next question would be. "Are you sure, are you absolutely one hundred percent sure? I mean there's no mistake? You have checked it? You're not… Jesus Christ, two million?"

"Two million plus Boss," reassured Fenwick who referred to his notebook. "In fact two million one hundred and twenty-seven thousand six hundred and ninety-five pounds." With more energy that was actually required, he flipped his notebook shut and with a flourish that bordered on the ostentatious, he returned it to his pocket his head rocking slightly but stiffly. He stared hard at his superintendent, his look meant that, for this brief time, he had changed from the instructed to the instructor.

Stanley gasped, he look winded. "Well I'm… That can't be right, can it? More than two million you say." He looked up, realising that it was time to regain his composure and to show that he was the senior officer in charge. "Right tell me how have you confirmed it?" Curran aimed for an attitude of sang-froid which showed that his years of experience allowed him to deal with situations such as this, as nothing more than a development, a progression of events. He wasn't aware that his right leg from the knee down appeared to be gripped by a minor spasm causing an exaggerated shivering action.

"Spoke to the newsagent, Seth Hunter, where he bought it. Always does the same numbers. Hunter is one hundred and twenty percent positive. The lottery people have contacted him, they run security checks with amounts like this. It's absolutely certain, same numbers every week."

"Apart from Hunter, who knows about this, did you tell him not to discuss this under any circumstances?" Stanley was now getting back into his stride. The two officers did not rush to answer. This was a situation that had the possibility, one way or another, to create a partnership amongst the three men. Curran continued with his casual look, which was now beginning to feel comfortable.

"Look, obviously we told Seth to keep it quiet. He said that only other person that knows, outside the lottery officials, is his wife. We told him that this could be crucial evidence in the enquiry and if it was released, it could compromise a major and expensive investigation and that, from our point of view it would not reflect well on him if it got out. I think he got the message. We contacted the lottery senior security manager at head office and explained that this must be kept quiet. There is no problem with them. Hunter will not say a word. There's a couple of issues with him trying to flog counterfeit booze that we have left lying."

"Tasted like shit," interjected Fenwick. The muscles of his face cringed recalling the effect of imbibing the immature spirit. "Still it was OK for the odd Christmas present."

Stanley brushed the last contributions aside. "So, what have we got? Well what we haven't got is a ticket that's worth more than two million quid. What would happen if we found it, say in the effects of somebody who may have been, for a while, a suspect?" He continued without waiting for, or expecting, an answer. "At the moment, anybody who was found to have the ticket would be implicated in the dastardly and heinous murder of an old scrote." He swilled ideas around his head. The others in the office knew to say nothing. Curran stood up and closed the office door.

Stanley continued, although now he was really talking to himself. "Supposing, just supposing for the sake of an academic exercise, that a third party came into possession of said ticket, could he or she cash it in? Supposing they said, for instance, they found it in an old wallet that somebody had thrown away by accident and the original owner couldn't be traced."

"Won't work, the number is known. The security people are blocking it. It will be known to be the property of a murder victim. To let somebody benefit from it would be like allowing somebody to benefit from a crime. And, as we were taught on our training courses, you can't do that."

Stanley pushed himself upright staring in silence at Curran for moments. "Inspector Curran, I am most impressed, very impressed indeed. I didn't know we had a budding lawyer amongst us. You're quite right of course."

There were a few more moments of silence, each man finding something to look other than one of his colleagues. Reality flowed over Stanley, his shoulders relaxed, he smoothed his tie down. "Right gentlemen, that was most useful, I think it is a major step forward. All we have to do is wait for our villain to try to cash in his ill-gotten gains and we nick the bugger."

Fenwick sat forward and eventually spoke. "Of course it probably may never be cashed in. Really it's not likely to. We assume, and everything points towards the fact - that old Sam was done for the cash in his wallet. Whoever got it is likely to grab the cash out of it and sling the wallet. He's not going to hang on to it if it's likely. In the event of him being nicked, it would link him to Sam. I mean he's not going to go through it just in case he finds his Tufty club card with points on it. He's going to sling it. We know that's what every little toe rag does. Even if he knows the ticket is a winner, big time, what can he do? Try and claim two million, which he won't get, then go down for life. Mind you, you never know, some bozo may think it's worth a punt."

Curran joined in. "Oh yeah, some doom brain goes into Hunter's newsagents, like wearing a pair of dark glasses and a baseball cap..."

"And fake moustache," assisted Fenwick.

"Yeah, and fake moustache and he's like, 'Here's my ticket; can I have two million quid please, oh and a couple of pouches of baccy, some papers and yeah bottle of vodka, one of them big ones. Thank you, bye.' Do you know what, I wouldn't fall off my chair if that happened."

"Yes, well." Stanley was now regaining his authority. "That's as may be. But as the lottery people are putting a block on this, I want them to notify us if anybody tries to use it. I assume they've got CCTV at all their sales points. But we must keep it under wraps. And look, if after a few weeks this whole thing starts dying on its arse, I don't want anybody going to the press to flog this lottery ticket story. It is likely to be of interest, quite a twist. As it happens, I am acquainted with some of the guys from the nationals. Mail and Express and the like. Don't worry there'll be something for all of us. Bit of a drink at least."

The constable and inspector rose to leave the office, turned and walked to the door. There was something in the silence and stillness of the superintendent that caused them to halt at the threshold of the door. They turned looked at the still silent motionless Stanley. They looked at each other and back to the seated man, who with a slight movement of his hand and a pursing of his lips motioned the two men to return. They closed the door and resumed their seats, nobody spoke. The hush hung in the air, a prickly tension started forming like crystals of ice on a pane of glass. Stanley spoke, his voice lower than it had been. "Why do we assume that the ticket was in his wallet?"

Curran leaned forward. "It is an assumption on our part, but we know he kept his money in his wallet. Half the town knows that now. It is the likeliest place to keep it. It's either that or one of his pockets. As he didn't trust anyone, he would keep it in the safest place. We were at the farm when uniform listed his property, such that it was. The clothes he was wearing were searched; nothing there."

"You searched the entire farm? What did uniform turn up?"

Fenwick looked at Curran and took his cue. "Well uniform gave it a good going over, they were mainly looking for evidence of a break in, the shotgun, the old boy's wallet. As I said they didn't seem to turn anything up, when we were there, they would have said."

"Did you two have a good scout round, check the drive, the brook by the bridge in case the wallet had been dumped?"

"We did the usual, checked where the gun and wallet might have been slung over walls and hedges and the like, down beyond the entrance to the farm." Fenwick maintained his role as spokesman.

"So uniform didn't turn anything up? "

Inspector and constable nodded in unison.

"Scenes of crime, nothing?"

There was more affirmative nodding.

"Do you think that you two should have another look? It might be worth getting the lad in again, push him a bit; recent visitors, anybody his dad had a row with, outstanding debts, that sort of thing. Get back into town. We know he owed money at the chandlers. Have another word with the newsagent Hunter. He flogged him the ticket, find out exactly what the old boy did with it. Did he put it in his pocket, under his hat, whatever? He was in the pub, have a word in there. Find out what CCTV cameras there are. See if there was anyone taking an interest in him. And get the clothes he was wearing; check them again."

Curran took a deep breath. "What if we find the ticket behind a hedge or something, it's not likely to lead us to the gunman or anything, I mean…" His last words faded.

"Barry, I wonder if you would mind leaving me and Malcolm to have a bit of a word?"

Fenwick and Curran looked at each other, both gave a slight shrug. Fenwick slowly rose to his feet, as he left the room he quietly clicked the office door shut.

"Malcolm, how long have we known each other now? What, about fifteen years, ever since you first came here. We've been through a few things in that time. Been a bit, shall we say, enterprising at times, to our mutual benefit, so to speak. We know it isn't the best paid job in the world, so a little extra now and then always helps. It's never really harmed anybody, well not anybody who hasn't deserved it. I've always regarded you as a man of the world: pragmatic, sensible. You seem to have a realistic grasp of life in the force. I don't recall you as being adverse to the odd entrepreneurial venture. Can I take it that we are talking man to man here?"

Curran gave a shrug then nodded agreement.

Stanley continued, his voice sotto voce, a gently wagging finger added emphasis. "Right, what is said in here, stays in here. That's understood, isn't it? Listen, we know the lad's half-baked, he's got nobody now, no relations. If he does get that lottery money, and only he can get it, he's going to need friends who can give him financial advice. Look, I've got a mate who does investments, bonds, property portfolios and the like."

Curran interrupted. "Is he any good though?"

Stanley lowered his head to his chest and made a fist. "Is he any good?" The words were spoken with equal parts of exasperation and incredulity. "Is he any good? He's complete crap, useless. It's not six months since he walked out of a Crown Court fraud trial, only because Crown Prosecution made their usual bollocks and lost half the evidence. He was looking at five to seven years this time. He was flogging building plots on land that he had no rights to and where there was never a snowball's chance of getting planning permission anyway. He's in the Canaries now, just in case they find that evidence. But they won't. Look, if my mate gets the lad to make some cast iron investments, it's nothing to do with us. But I'm sure he would show his gratitude to anybody who puts a punter his way. Sort of commission, a finder's fee, if you get my drift. If he is remote from us, there cannot be any connection to this station, there would be nothing to tie us in with him. Now think about it, in or out, let me know. Nobody else gets a sniff of this OK."

"What about Barry, is he in on it?"

"That's a matter for you. Can you trust him? If you do let him in, you will never, and I mean never, discuss it or talk about any part of it in my company. You know the system. Does he have to know? Personally I think the fewer the better. It's better split two ways rather than three."

Curran started to speak, but then thought better of it.

Stanley concluded. "But before we do anything we have got to get that ticket. We're coppers, we should be able to find it. And remember." Now the finger wagging became more vigorous. "This is a robbery and murder, I don't want any accidental shooting or manslaughter. The old bugger was shot by somebody intent on stealing his wallet. All right?"

CHAPTER 7

Right, first things first." Curran addressed his colleague as they strode along the main street of the small town. "Stanley has made a point that we put all our effort into finding this bloody ticket. Says it is the one thing that will lead us in the right direction."

"What did he want to talk to you about in the office?"

Curran walked on in silence for some distance, furrow browed, tight-lipped. "I can't really say, I think he wants to try and pull some stroke. I don't want anything to do with it."

Fenwick stopped walking and grabbed Curran's arm at the elbow. "What's he going to do, get the ticket and cash it in? He can't do that. That's not going to work. What's he trying to do?"

"It's best you don't know, don't ask. Don't have anything to do with it."

"Do with what? If they find the ticket, lad claims it, goes into his bank account. Bosh, job done. How can anybody have anything to do with it?"

Curran closed up to Fenwick, staring directly into his eyes. "Whatever you do in this case, do it as per the book. Write up your notebook every day, make sure it is completely accurate. Especially if Stanley asks you to do something. Cover your backside. He can be a dangerous man, he's pulled some real iffy stunts. Watch him very closely."

Fenwick started to speak, but Curran raised his open palms as a silent order not to pursue this conversation. "Come on, we've got an enquiry to conduct. Let's start with Seth Hunter, let's get chapter and verse on the purchase of this ticket."

"Chapter and verse? He only bought a bloody ticket. He didn't enter into negotiations to buy rocket launchers."

The two men walked along the High Street maintaining a silence that was not comfortable. Curran could no longer hold the pressure of silence back. He spoke as they walked.

"Look, and mind you keep this under your hat, not a living soul. Stanley wants us to find this ticket so he can run some sort of scam. Don't ask me how, but he's got some weird idea. All we have to do, if we find this ticket, is hand it to him. It was his orders if anybody asks, remember that, always remember that. As far as you are concerned, in that briefing we've just had, his orders were, above everything else, to find the ticket, I will back you up. You have got to watch him, never ever trust him no matter what he says or does, he's more crooked than most of the punters we lock up."

Fenwick decided that now he could speak. "What do you mean, in what way?"

Curran gave a sigh that shook his shoulders. "Listen, I'm going to tell you something now. I want you to remember the names and details. If Stanley ever tries to drop you in it, I mean seriously drop you in it, you tell him that you are aware of his past rackets, and tell him, if it comes to push, you will start shouting. Right? He will know that it was me that told you, that doesn't worry me. He won't be able to complain or do anything about it. My promotion chances are long since gone."

Fenwick remained silent, not wishing to break the spell. Curran addressed him in a low whisper. "When I first came here, about fifteen years ago, Stanley had just been made up to chief inspector in Newcastle. I met him on a job we were doing. I think it was some Liverpool gang shooting across the motorway and screwing upmarket houses. He always had a reputation as a chancer. Fair enough, he always got away with it, but I've seen him pull some real iffy strokes, nothing like this though." Curran stopped and reflected on what he was about to reveal. Doubts crept in. He stalled for time. "Remember, we are making routine enquiries on the direct orders of our beloved super. Is your notebook up to date? You never know how these things are going to pan out, wheels do fall off." Fenwick automatically felt his pocket and half pulled out a notebook. "Well, more or less, I was going to write it up this evening at the nick."

"What you are going to do, Constable Fenwick old son, is cover your arse. I want you to send me an email asking me to confirm, no to clarify, that at the meeting Stanley instructed us to give priority to finding the lottery ticket. Say that you weren't quite sure, you could make the point that you think it would be better, more logical, to conduct the usual type of enquiry. If anybody asks me, I'll say that yes I asked you to do this as to cover any allegations that we went looking for this bloody lotto voucher rather than do routine enquiries. I have had problems in the past with that old bugger, when he's given me orders and when it all goes tits up, he denies it saying he cannot recall giving such an instruction and says he will 'take it up with me.' He's done that a couple of times over the years, leaves me looking like a right prat."

Fenwick was slightly taken aback at the abrupt change of direction.

"You were going to tell me about Stanley at the time when you first came here you said." Curran's narrowing eyes stared into the distance. He appeared to be reminding himself of events, rather than relating them to his younger colleague.

"I tell you that bloke has pulled some real strokes in his time, I don't know how but he always gets away with it. He jumps from one piece of thin ice to another. Believe me, he will be covering his arse, all we are doing is covering ours."

"What for, why are we covering our rear ends, what are you trying to tell me?" Fenwick's rapt attention was now giving way to impatience. "The story so far is that you and Stanley knew each over fifteen years ago."

Curran nodded. He had decided to continue.

"Right, Jack Marshall, you know him, he has just been made up to chief inspector. He does the admin role. Well, he was an inspector on Stanley's team in Newcastle. Jack is dead straight, couldn't stand Stanley, still can't. He came close to Stanley getting the heave ho. If you ever need to rely on anyone, go and see Jack."

Fenwick, in saying nothing, invited Curran to continue.

"Strictly between you and me, and I mean strictly, Jack got wind of this stunt being pulled. Stanley, as always, teamed up with some out of town ex-con, well not even an 'ex', some real Dumbo he had by the nuts for some attempted fraud. Stanley funded this con to set up an escort agency in some back street in Newcastle. So the con fronted it for him. It was just a rented room and a phone, punting out local tarts, high class mind, for visiting businessmen who were looking for a bit of company, you know, just somebody to talk to and to visit art galleries and museums."

"Oh, aye." The irony was not lost on Fenwick.

Curran inhaled slowly then exhaled sharply and continued. "Look, this has got to go no further than you and me, unless, as I said you need to use it. Anyway, when the punters collect the slapper of their dreams from the office, the con running the escort agency clocks the car registration. Stanley then got some old constable mate of his to check the car out on the PNC system telling the control room it was seen cruising in the red light district, even though they were miles away. All the results showed the names and addresses of the registered keeper. These were given to his business partner who would then, after a couple, of days 'phone the punter at home or at work, asked him if he had a fulfilling evening with the lovely Doreen, or whatever, then put the arm on him for a couple of grand to ensure that said slag would not start 'phoning, the punter's home to ask if he still loved her.

Worked a treat. The punters are not going to complain, and what if they did? What could they do? No connection to Stanley. Nice little earner."

"So, is he still doing it?"

"Not that one, not now. It went a bit wet and nasty. They did the usual number on this punter one night, the PNC went back to a company address, they gave him the usual bell, usual blag and bosh the wheels started to come off. The punter was, in fact, an undercover social security investigator checking up on the lasses who were on the agency's books. I mean they all claim for everything. The car was registered to an accommodation address because, and you'll love this, Social Security were having problems with coppers blowing them out, especially around housing estates. Worried that they might be checking up on some bobby's mum or dad for fiddling the social."

"Bloody hell, what happened?"

"It hit the fan. Social services complained of police involvement in a scam and of screwing up their investigations. He wasn't anywhere near the red light area. Questions were going to be asked in the House. They found out, for sure that the old bobby had requested the registration check, and were going to throw the book at him. He saw his pension going down the drain. He told Stanley that he was not taking this one by himself. Stanley told him to stick to his guns and insist the guy from Social Services was definitely cruising around the red light district and that he had seen him talking to a girl who got into his car. Above and beyond the needs of an investigation you might say. Stanley ends up speaking to his equivalent in Social Services, says he stands by what the bobby says and if they want to do anything about it, they would charge the investigator for importuning, real eyeball to eyeball stuff. Even said he could produce the lass involved and she would confirm that she conducted business with the investigator lad. He said if the address where the car was registered to was contacted, it was because the lass had found a business card in the car and she, whoever 'she' was, was just showing a bit of enterprising spirit. Also mentioned was the fact that the local stipendiary magistrate belonged to the same golf club and local chapter as Stanley. Collapse of stout party. Of course the guy fronting the scam disappeared, never to be seen again."

"Didn't our top brass get to hear about it, I mean it's a bit thin?"

Curran nodded vigorously, anticipating Fenwick's intervention. "Oh yeah, they heard, but Stanley got his retaliation in first. He got straight on to the Chief Super, I think it was Mickey Barnes at the time, yeah it was; not exactly whiter than white himself. Stanley tells Barnes that he had heard that Social Services were conducting enquires on his patch and did not have the decency to let the local force know. He said that the old bobby, I think he was Freddie Smith, dead now, did a great job in not only finding their investigator, but also caught him with his trousers down, in more ways than one. The investigator was carrying out a real in depth enquiry sort of thing. Now Social, being somewhat embarrassed, are trying to create a smoke screen. But not to worry dear Chief Super, I have sorted it and Social Services have backed right down. Basically nobody wanted to see all that dirty linen. Stanley won, he out eyeballed them. Like they say, never take a skunk on in a pissing competition."

"What was Jack Marshall's bit in all this then?"

"Well, Jack is a bit sharp. Stanley had been giving him a hard time, Jack wouldn't play ball with Stanley's various schemes. When it was kicking off and Jack could see what way it was going, he nipped over to Freddie Smith's house saying he heard Stanley in with the Chief Super and that Stanley is dropping old Freddie in it, saying it was nothing to do with him and that the records show that virtually all the vehicle checks have come from Freddie. So if there is a scam it must be down to him. He convinced him, never the sharpest, to give him all the details so that Jack could try to sort it out. You know, get hold of the front man to make sure he is got out of the way, find a girl who would back up the story that the investigator really was on the pull. He told him that if he had any cash from the scam to get rid of it because if he is nicked, his house would be searched and a stack of twenty pound notes would look a bit more than iffy. Freddie was bricking it, a complete wreck, he coughs the lot. The racket had been going for a couple of years, he used to meet up with Stanley to split the cash and so on. Of course Jack Marshall has a tape recorder running. He goes straight back to Stanley, fronts him up and says he is going to blow him out. Stanley starts calling Freddie Smith a liar, how dare Jack do this behind his back, can't we come to some sort of agreement. Long story short, Jack knows that old Freddie is up for retirement in weeks, his wife is in a bad way, if anything bad happened to Freddie, it would affect her very badly. Then the Chief Super Barnes has his ten penny worth. Suggests that he doesn't want to start a messy fight with Social Services that nobody is going to win, maintain good working relations and all that old horse feathers."

Curran stopped and turned towards the constable looking straight into his eyes, an act that would give greater weight to his next explanation. "See, Barnes and Stanley went back a long way, big mates. It has been suggested that Stanley learnt his trade from Barnes. He tells Jack what a good officer he is and how he could expect to progress through the ranks and that there is a promotion board coming up soon. Jack drops it, but obviously keeps the recording and tells Stanley that if he ever pisses him off at any time from now to retirement, the gaff will be well and truly blown. Jack duly gets his pips." Curran stopped to light a cigarette. Fenwick spent the time digesting the information. Curran blew a long jet of smoke out then turned to Fenwick. "Look, a few grand always comes in handy. But do not kid yourself, if Stanley needs to throw you and me to the wolves, he will not hesitate. And whatever anybody makes out of this, if anybody makes out of this, Stanley will scoop the pool. But remember, if it all goes tits up, we will be well in the soft and pungent. So if you want out, get out now."

"Am I in?"

"You are now, if you want it."

"What's the score, what's he going to do?"

"He's got a mate, a real villain, he reckons they can do a number on the lad to part him from his money." Anticipating Fenwick's next question, he added, "Don't ask."

The two men walked on in silence for some time. Fenwick's arms moved as though he was warming up to conduct a band. "How much do you reckon we could make? Would it be ten grand, like?"

"Could easily be that. If Stanley's mate does a good number on the lad, he could take him for hundreds of thousands. Bet your grandma's rice pudding, it will not be split evenly. Stanley and his mate will get the big chunk, we will get the scraps. Remember, he's due to retire in less than a year. If he makes a killing, he will be off with his pension and lump sum. Join his mates in Marbella or the Canaries no doubt. If we do this, we must make sure that, if push comes to shove, he carries the can. We must always back each other up."

"Well, what's the… err? I mean if he is collared for this, what's he done wrong? If his mate does all the leg work, and he doesn't finger Stanley, job's a good 'un. There nothing to tie his mate to Stanley. What has anybody got on him? What would he be doing wrong?" Fenwick was still conducting.

"Think about it, Constable Fenwick, conspiring with a villain to commit fraud against a lad that's not right in the head. That is theft; that is stealing. Any profit he makes would be money laundering as it is proceeds of crime. Let's see, theft, conspiracy to commit fraud, theft, malfeasance of a public office, conduct unbecoming. Yes, as a senior police officer entrusted with enforcing the law and protecting the public, he would go down for four to five I reckon." He paused, his next words were emphatic.

"Make no mistake, if you and I are caught with our fingers in the till, it will be much the same for us. Remember, his mate is a villain; a villain is always a villain. If he had to do a deal where he shops a senior copper so that he can pull a light sentence, he will. Maybe we should decide not to find this ticket."

Fenwick had stopped conducting. "What if we go along with Stanley, and say he turns up trumps, pockets a huge wodge, what is there to stop us putting the arm on him and shaking him down? I mean he can't complain to the chief con. The worst he could do would to give us crap annual reports."

"We get those already," assisted Curran.

"Yeah, I've been thinking, if this lad's a bit thick, won't they get somebody to act as his guardian so that he could be looked after?"

Curran pondered this last offering. "Yeah, they could do, probably would do, but it would take some time before all the quacks involved and the social services got their act together. Could take a year. Anyway how thick is he? Granted he's a sandwich short, but there's folk out there worse than him that looks after themselves. I tell you what I've known a few coppers that are probably worse than him. Right, it's eight thirty, let's give Seth half an hour, then how about a pint?"

CHAPTER 8

"Come on, Seth open up." Fenwick rapped the door of the newsagent's. "Come on Seth. Let's be having you."

"Let's be having you," mocked Curran. "Where did you get that from, the Sweeney?" As he spoke he held a mobile phone to his ear. "Alright, Seth, we're at your door, could you get down here and let us in. What, no it's not a shakedown, just make sure we don't see any of that Chinese whiskey that you've got. People are going blind drinking that stuff. Come on, move it."

The shopkeeper was a small delicate featured thin man who moved with precision. His taut skin seemed to shrink wrap his face, highlighting with a degree of clarity all aspects of his bone structure. He had small, dark, darting eyes that, together with a large, hawkish nose, gave him a bird-like appearance. He moved with the rapid and unnatural erectness that men of his stature often have. He escorted the two men into his drab lounge. Heavy curtains, which always remained three quarters closed, displayed their vintage as the original colours had faded to a ghost of the intended hue and had acquired a tinge, due mainly to them acting as a filter to retard the release of cigarette smoke onto the general population. The heavy grey nets acted as a backstop to deal with any wisps making a dash for freedom. This capture of cigarette smoke was not an act of kindness, but a desire of the occupants to keep the world at bay. The ambience set by the ancient drapes continued as a theme throughout the remaining living areas.

The police officers sat down without being invited. "Hello, Doris love, we just want a word with your old man. He's not in any trouble or anything, just helping us with our enquiries as they say. Perhaps you could put the kettle on. From previous experiences the woman realised that her presence will be an impediment and shuffled away throwing baleful looks at her still standing husband. The last thing those two wanted was tea.

"Grab a seat, Seth, it's alright, we just want to talk about old Sam Hamblin. I trust you haven't mentioned the lottery ticket to anyone at all. That could play a key part in our investigations, so Seth, not a word."

Fenwick nodded a silent approval of his fellow officer's approach. To show an assurance of his earnestness, the shopkeeper leant forward and displayed his best attentive attitude.

"Not a word, lads, on my life not a word." He indicated towards where his wife had been. "She knows. The lottery security people spoke to her when the numbers came up. She knows not to say anything. She daren't." He sucked heavily on a cigarette. It seemed to take major effort from his almost skeletal frame to do so.

Curran continued. "Seth, we've already established that old Sam bought a lottery ticket here, what did he do with it?"

"What do you mean?" He didn't exhale the tobacco smoke, rather he let it play around his mouth and allowed it find its own escape route.

"Where did he put it, Seth?" Fenwick felt that it was time he made a contribution to the proceedings. "In his trouser pocket, jacket pocket?"

"Oh I see." This time the cigarette smoke was exhaled, demonstrating his dexterity. "No, Sam, he always bought a lottery, always the same numbers. He always put it in his wallet, made a bit of a thing about it, as though it were a secret, but really, he drew attention to himself. No, he always put it in his wallet, tatty old thing. Kept inside his jacket. Mind you, this time, I couldn't help but notice that he had quite a wad. He's just sold his father's old place, he did alright from what I hear. Mind you, I thought he was taking a bit of a chance humping that wallet around, you never know somebody might... oh, they did, didn't they. Did they do it for his wallet? But Jesus, what a bummer, cops a big one on the lottery, then well, I suppose he cops it." Curran helped himself to a cigarette from a pack on the table and lit it. His question came out on the tail of the exhaled smoke. "Was there any talk in the town about old Sam and his bulging wallet? We know he was in a few places, shops and the pub. Anything come back from anybody?"

Now Fenwick helped himself to a cigarette. Hunter realised his omission. "Sorry, would you lads like a drink? Anything you like."

Curran slumped back in his chair. "Yeah, OK, I'll have a Scotch, as long as it's not that foreign fake crap - what was it called, Highland Bonnet? Tasted more like it came from under a highland kilt."

"No, lads, no I've got the real stuff, proper brands."

"Have you still got the number of the lorry it came off, I mean we can check the invoices if you want?" Fenwick's enquiry was not in the line of official business. Whether Hunter's face crumpled out of concern over the provenance of what he was offering, or by calling into question his integrity, was not pursued. A bottle was produced and generous measures poured into tumblers. Hunter resumed the conversation. "What can I say? I wouldn't say he was flashing his wodge, but he made such a fuss about getting his cash out from his wallet, that he drew attention to himself, like he was trying to hide it. I could see that there was a fair amount in it. I mean you could see a thick roll of twenties, a real thick roll. But I haven't heard anybody say he was flashing it, but everyone knew he had a fair amount. The whole town knows that he had just sold his dad's land, and old Sam was never one to put his money in the bank if he could help it. I think he had a few debtors, he didn't want to put it in a place where they could get access, if you know what I mean. So no, he wasn't flashing it about, but we all reckoned that he was carrying a fair amount." Curran took a sip from his glass, pursed his lips to savour the spirit then swallowed. He did not disapprove. Fenwick noting his senior officer's unspoken approval, gave a slight nod to concur. "Were there any likely looking blokes from out of town? It's a fairly big market, there must be some standard undesirable types from out of the area."

"There's always those types, they come and go. Most folk around here have got an idea who they are and keep an eye on them. But I don't know that there was anyone that stood out. I thought that you lads would have kept your eyes peeled."

"Wish we could," offered Fenwick. "Do you know how many staff we've got and how big the area is? It must have been alright in the old days, chasing poachers and checking shotgun licences and the like. All changed now, but now it is all cut backs and time sheets, too busy ticking boxes to go out feeling collars."

Hunter's facial expression changed to show a considerable amount of sympathy, or he hoped it did.

Curran sipped his drink. "There's nothing else you can tell us about Sam Hamblin? Any enemies serious enough to top him, anything like that?"

"What, old Sam? No, he was a miserable old sod, tight as a shark's arse at fifty fathoms. I would never give him credit, if I did, I would have a job getting paid. But we all knew what he was like. More or less kept himself to himself."

The two officers rose and drained their glasses. Fenwick smacked his lips noisily.

"Right we'll be off then, thanks, Seth. Nice drop of Scotch that, yes very nice indeed. Wouldn't you agree, inspector?"

"I would indeed agree, constable, very nice, very tasty."

The look of sympathy drained from Hunter's face. "Oh, right, yes, right, that's not a problem, I'll just fetch you one."

"Each," offered Fenwick. Hunter nodded with his eyes shut, then paused and waited, anticipating next line. "I seem to be getting short on fags." Fenwick added with an expression of exaggerated innocence.

Hunter nodded slowly as if to accept the inevitability of the situation and shuffled off to his storeroom.

In the pub, the two officers found a table at the back of the room with seats that faced outwards towards the door. It wasn't busy and there no one close to them. Each sipped his beer in silence. After a few moments Fenwick turned to Curran. He glanced around, satisfied that no conversation between them would reach any of the other patrons, he lowered his head towards the older man. Responding to the signals given out, Curran inclined slightly towards Fenwick. His look invited the question that had now reached the end of its gestation time.

Fenwick spoke in a low, soft voice. "You know that subject we were talking about, you know the ticket and our boss's mate who might be in a position to benefit our good selves? Yeah, well it's all well and good, but there is a big, big flaw in the general scheme."

"What's that then?"

Fenwick looked around again, satisfied that conversation would still be inviolate. He looked back and continued. "If we do get any proceeds from this, it has got to be in cash, right?"

"Right."

"How do we handle that? Apart from sticking it underneath a mattress, which, from what you say, could make it rather lumpy, what else could you do with it?"

Curran took a draught of his beer, slowly put the glass back on the table and then looked at it as though it was a piece of art.

"Put it in the bank." Spoken with precision, the words were spaced out evenly.

"In the bank?" After checking, Fenwick realised that his alarmed reply had not reached anyone else in the room. "Put it in the bank, isn't that a good place for the rubber heel squad to look for dodgy payments? Isn't that the first place they would look?"

"Not if it is in my bank." It was Curran's turn to check the acoustics. "Not in my bank."

He left the mystery there on the table in front of Fenwick. He took another casual gulp of beer. Fenwick stared at him. There was no clarification. In the silence that followed, Fenwick's curiosity ballooned like bubbles of air coming up from the deep. "How do you mean, what's your bank?"

Curran granted his silence a further extension. "Yeah, my bank. What shall I say?" He paused. "When I was in London, it was no holds barred. In those days quite often there wasn't a cigarette paper between us and the villains. Half the blokes I worked with had brothers doing time. We were the untouchables, who was going to investigate the Met? Each other's backs were well and truly scratched. Quite a few of them retired to Spain or Portugal. A fair few decided that taking early retirement was a better option than facing a disciplinary charge. Get the money and get out. Can't touch you then. So they're all out there in the Costas or whatever, mixing with the blokes that, when they were working, they were meant to be feeling their collars. Now they are all mates.

When the tourists are having their summer holiday, they are a gift from heaven. Lots of them go out there, straight into the nearest bar and stay there. A lot of them, especially the Brits, go there for the cheap booze, out of their trees most of the time. They get a bit careless with their belongings, wallets and the like. So there is a trade in borrowed passports, wallets and the like."

"Borrowed, don't you mean nicked?"

"No, borrowed. Nicking is against the law - wouldn't be involved in that sort of thing."

Fenwick's brow furrowed slightly, then he shook his head. "You've lost me, go on then, explain."

"Look, Mr. Average Brit goes on holiday to Spain, even the best of them get tanked up. To some of them it's a major hobby. Sometimes they get so pissed that they couldn't bite their fingers. If it is late afternoon or early evening and they are careless enough to, shall we say, allow access, to their personal effects, things are liable to be borrowed from them. Quite often they keep all their bits and pieces in the wife's handbag. If they are in a bar, or in hotel lounge, a bit worse for wear and they present the opportunity they can 'lose' bags and wallets. Or, if they are going for a day's excursion, and they leave their stuff in the safe in the room, well that can be borrowed as well. Courtesy of the hotel staff of course, usually the maids or managers." Conversation was temporarily halted when a patron walked past their table. Satisfied he was out of earshot, Curran continued.

"All that happens is that their passports and driving licences are photocopied. First thing you do is to apply for another passport in the same name using the photocopied details. Lots of businessmen who travel a lot carry two passports, quite legitimately. If they have to send off a passport to apply for a visa, they can still use the other one to travel with. Some countries can be a bit awkward if you present a passport with a Lebanese stamp one week and an Israeli the next, you could spend a lot of time talking to the immigration officer. There's never a problem. There are, shall we say, connections with passport offices here and with embassy staff abroad. They will either want a bung or a want some substance that they enjoy relaxing with. Of course once they're in, they stay in, they are not allowed to leave. If they try to get out, they are presented with an envelope with photos of them enjoying themselves. You know, doing the business with some local tart or with a straw up their left nostril. Or there's recordings of meetings where favours have been exchanged. You know, the usual. Some of our boys were well trained in surveillance techniques, still got the touch. Everybody has got a price." The patron walked back past their table and out the door, they assumed he was looking for a friend.

"The beauty of a separate passport, is that you can use it. It's never been reported stolen. When it's put through a scanner, it's not going to come up as being used at the same time at another airport. Safe, safe as houses. Driving licences, not a problem. There are a few places where you can have a licence and ID cards, 'made', don't cost that much all things considered. As they say, 'if a man can make it, a man can fake it.'"

Fenwick was now engrossed and ignoring his drink.

"Once you have got somebody's passport and driving licence, it is dead easy to open a bank account in that name. You tell the bank that you have bought an apartment in Spain and that a Euro account would be very handy. The banks over there are quite happy, they don't ask too many questions, some of them even work on a 'commission' basis. Usually they are happy to get the business."

Fenwick's eyes showed that his brain had comprehended the details.

"Nice one. And if it all goes belly up, it can't be traced to the 'new' account holder."

"Spot on, constable. They have an alternative ID. They call it their 'holiday name', it allows them a certain freedom, y ou are ahead of the game. It's all sorted. My man, shall we call him 'George', you never know you might actually know him. Anyway George is well in with the concierge of a large apartment block in Marbella. That's where my account is registered to. Any mail that comes for me, he posts it to me here. If I have to sign any bank documents, I send them back to him, he sticks a Spanish stamp on an envelope, job done. If I want any cash, I give George a bell, he draws it out from cash points, bungs it in an envelope and sends it to me. Less his fee, five percent of any transaction. Works a treat."

Fenwick suddenly sat up straight. "Bloody hell, what a stroke." He realised that his exuberance was likely to attract unwelcome attention. To nullify it, he found Curran's ear, and in a whisper repeated, "Bloody hell, what a stroke."

Curran's initial concern at disclosing such sensitive material was waning. His attitude started to border on casualness. "I know some Met blokes have got a few. There is one, he was a chief super, who has got a fist full. There are Irish accounts, German, French, you name it. Usually, the blokes who live in Portugal have accounts in Spain and the ones in Spain use Portuguese banks. It's a bit more remote. Thing is, if the wheel does come off, they are untraceable. You keep out of the bank as much as possible. Use cash points. "

"Why would they want more than one account?"

"They rent them out. If somebody has got some cash that is a bit warm, they can use one of these accounts. Usual charge is ten percent of the balance."

Fenwick ran all this round his head, the look of approval showed, his eyes registered comprehension.

"So, your mate in Spain has access to your account and draws out cash for you when you want it?"

"That's right."

"What would happen if this bloke decided to clean you out? Go round all the cash machines and draw it all out?"

"You see, I am not George's only customer, in fact I am one of quite a few. He rakes off five percent of each transaction. He is on a nice little earner for doing not much and for no risk. If he did try to do a runner, he wouldn't get far anyway. There are quite a few ex-Met over there, they keep an eye on him, on the just in case basis. It's a sort of insurance policy. We all watch each other."

"So you really don't trust George?"

"George is a nice bloke. He has looked after all his clients very well. He knows that if he had it on his toes, well he probably wouldn't have any toes, that is if he was lucky and the boys were in a good mood. No I don't trust him."

"Where does the money come from? The stuff in this account in Spain?"

"Ah, my slush fund. Shall we say it comes from investments, various investments? Mind you, the investment opportunities up here are nothing like down in London."

Fenwick raised his glass to his lips, then lowered it again without taking a drink.

"What if George was sending you money over here and it got intercepted, say by customs?"

Curran nodded an approval of the question. "Well, that could be a bit of a problem, if it came to my address. But it doesn't come to my address. Obviously it does not have my name on it. I have an accommodation here in town with somebody, it goes to their address, it's a business where people come and go. The most there would ever be in a packet is two to three thousand Euros, customs are not interested in amounts like that. George always puts a note inside to his 'grandson' and hopes the money included helps to buy the car he wanted. If customs want to make a noise about it and they go to where it has been addressed to, the person there says they have got no idea where it came from, they don't recognise the name and it must be incorrectly addressed."

"Nice one, do you think that, if this stroke that Stanley is talking about came off, could we, I mean me, use your account in Spain?"

"For five percent, yeah. But then George would expect his five percent on top of that for any transactions, but it is bomb proof. The only traceability is George and he is not going to blow just one person out because he then loses all credibility and probably a lot more. No, he keeps his nose clean. A very nice little earner in his retirement." Fenwick downed the remainder of his pint in one go. "I tell you what, we are going to have to find that lottery ticket. You having another one?"

"Let me think about that, costable. Do you know, I think I will?"

CHAPTER 9

Daniel was now into his fifth day at Mr.s Knowles guest house. In this short time the extremes of his unease due to living a strange life that gave him luxury that, a few days ago, he would not believe existed, were being eroded. He was beginning to understand the routine, when he should be present for breakfast and evening meal. It was beyond his comprehension as to why Mr.s Knowles expected him to wear freshly laundered clothes each day. He succumbed to her urging to shower on, what he thought, was an all too regular basis. It all seemed very strange, but he accepted the new rules. Perhaps this is what other people did, but he wasn't convinced. However, the ingrained strictures he had been subject to for all of his life ran as deep and as permanent as the growth rings in a tree. The superficial gloss he now showed, was tempered by deep rooted distrust. He had visitors. Tracey Williams showed up and asked him to sign some more forms. She reinforced her previous dictum and told him that, if the police ever want to talk to him, either at the guest house, or at the police station, he must contact her.

She made him rehearse the lines, "I wish to co-operate, but I want my lawyer to be here."

Mr.s Jones from social services saw him three times. Most of the time she just talked to him, mainly about his father and life on the farm, what his jobs were, did he receive any form of pay. All the time writing down everything he said. He liked Mr.s Jones, she smiled at him and spoke softly and in a way that he could understand. She always wore nice, pretty clothes and smelt of perfume. When she left she always shook his hand. After she had gone he would stay where he had been sitting until the shadows of her perfume had started to fade. In her last talk with him she told him that it might be better if he left the farm. She had looked at the situation and thought that it was too much for one person to manage. As it was, from what she could find out, the farm wasn't making enough money to pay all the bills. But whatever happened, the social services would look after him, make sure that he had a home, perhaps a small flat. She gave him a book where he could go to the post office each week where they would give him money. He continued his stay at Mr.s Knowles's guest house. The police had told him that the enquiries at the farm were now complete and that he could, if he wanted, go back. But Mr.s Jones said that that was unreasonable, for a variety of reasons, mainly because she judged the accommodation to be uninhabitable. She suggested that, for the immediate future he should stay with Mr.s Knowles.

It was a surprise to Daniel and a relief when Mr. Reece came to see him. In the past he had been very good to Daniel and always seemed pleased to see him. Now he treated Daniel differently, more like he was a proper fellow farmer. Reece sat in a chair in the lounge indicating to Daniel to do the same. After expressing his sympathy for his father but faltering somewhat when he tried to say he wasn't a bad sort really, he leaned forward and stroked his face and neck as though trying to smooth down an errant beard.

"Daniel, you know that round here we look after our own, and your dad, well although he was a bit sort of, well he kept to himself a bit, he was still from one of the old farming families from these parts. But as I always said, we look after our own and we would like to help you. So, I've had a word with Bill Pearson from Morley's farm, it used to be his father-in-law's, married Lorna Morley years back. Anyway, me and Bill have agreed, if it's alright with you, Daniel, to mind your dad's farm, keep it going till things get sorted. We will do the milking, well, what's left of it now, look after the livestock, such as it is. Just keep an eye on the place, keep it ticking over. Mind, we may have to pay for some labour and there will be expenses. What we was thinking was that we would keep our costs from milk yields and whatever crops you might have in. To be honest with you, Daniel, I don't think there is going to be much for you in the way of profits, but at least you should not be running at much of a loss. We might get something back on subsidies and the like, anything left over, we would pay direct to you. It would all be above board. Bill and me think you ought to have a word with Whelan, your dad's solicitor, just to make sure it's all straight." He sat back in his chair, stroking his hair and lightly scratching his head. His silence invited a reply. The stillness of Daniel's face belied the frantic activity of his mind. He knew what was being said, it meant that he could leave matters to somebody else. The concept pushed its way up to the front of his mind. Not only did he find the proposal agreeable, he really, by now, didn't care too much about running the farm. He was adjusting to being in civilised surroundings, he had new clean clothes that other people would wear and he was given money each week.

"That sound like a good idea, Mr. Reece, but could I still live there? I don't know how long I can stay here, they want me to stop somewhere else. If I have to leave here, if it's alright with you, could I stay at the farm?"

"Of course you can, Daniel, it is your farm now, you own it. But I have to say this, from what I understand, your dad wasn't too good looking after the finances. He just wouldn't invest in it, things started to slip. We know he paid the bank with some of the money from the sale of his father's land, but I think there's still a far bit that he owes."

He could see Daniel wrestling with the information he had just received. "What I'm saying is, well if you were to sell it, there wouldn't be a lot of money to come, the bank is due a fair whack of it. But if you were thinking about selling, I would ask you to let me know first. I could give a fair price and you and I have known each other for a long time. I wouldn't mess you about. If I did buy it, there would always be a job for you. You could stay for as long as you liked. But, that is a matter for you. If you did go down that road, I think you must talk it over with the solicitors so that it will be all above board." Reece's words about selling the farm were a bit too much to take in.

"If I could stay at the farm, I could still fix your machinery and things, and Mr. Pearson's. I'm good at that, well you seen me do it."

"Ay lad, you can still fix things." Daniel watched Reece's vehicle turn out of the drive of the guest house and join the traffic.

The effect of having the responsibility of running the farm removed and actually making the decision to agree to it brought a slightly dizzying although enjoyable sensation. A burden he did not realise he had, had been lifted. And he could still go to the farm. What had become increasingly clear to him, was that he wanted to go back there. In the time since he was left alone in the world, he had had just one brief visit when he had the nightmare ride in the furious little car. In his mind, he could not remember being away from it for more than a day and those occasions were so far distant that the milestones of memory and time had become a blur. He thought of market days when his father would leave the farm in the morning and not return until early afternoon, quite often later, much later. Usually he was more mellow and quieter and would have a strong smell of the local beer. It was his habit to have a meal of whatever was to hand then to slump into his chair and sleep. His guts would rumble like a rough fed heifer and bouts of snoring would erupt, climax and subside on a frequent but irregular basis. Daniel had stopped asking to go with his father a long time ago. There was always an angry reflex refusal.

"No, boy, no. You got to stay here and look after things. Farm can't run itself, now make sure you do them jobs I set."

Years ago, when he was just in his teens, he was at the next farm attending to Mr. Reece's baler. He nodded a good day to Mr. Pearson who had come to see his neighbour. The visitor asked him if he had seen the new space war film in the little cinema, which the town boasted in those days. He said that his son had desperately wanted to see it and didn't stop talking about the rocket ships and space battles with the astronauts. His son was much the same age as Daniel, but he attended the local grammar school. Although he had seen Pearson's son from time to time, he backed away from any idea of an acquaintance. Pearson said that his son and Daniel should go into town and see the movie together. Daniel mumbled about his dad and being busy on the farm and how he had to look after it. He didn't really know if he would like films anyway. When he had finished the maintenance work, Pearson told Daniel that he would take him back to the farm. He ushered him into his jeep for the short journey. At the farm Pearson was out of the vehicle before the boy.

"Sam, Sam, you there, Sam?"

Eventually the old man scuffed his way across the yard with a look that was a mixture of suspicion and questioning. "Bill, everything alright? He's not broken anything has he? If he has, I can get him to fix it."

"Hello, Sam." The old man felt Pearson's direct gaze like a spotlight on an escapee. "No, Daniel has done a good job, a really good job, like he always does."

The old man's tenseness melted a little. "That's good. He does do a good job. Good value as well. Would cost you a lot more to get the garage to come out."

Pearson continued. His direct stare was almost blinding now. "Look, Sam, my lad is going to the cinema tomorrow, some space rocket film. I think Daniel should go with him. Tell you what, I can pick him up about noon, that will be OK won't it, Sam?"

Inwardly Daniel recoiled. Would he be in trouble? He was sure he would incur his father's anger for bringing about this situation. The spotlight on the old man was now driving him backwards. "Well he has got things to do and…"

"He's a lad Sam, he can't work all the time. Now as he has done such a good job for me, it'll be my treat." He turned to Daniel. "It's a reward for all the things you have done for me. I really do appreciate it. It's a way of saying thank you. So that's not a problem, Sam, is it?"

"No, that's not a problem. No. I just thought that…"

"You thought what, Sam?"

"No, nothing, that'll be fine. Like you say, it will do the boy some good to have a bit of a break, provided when he gets back…"

"He what, Sam? Provided he what, Sam?"

"Oh, nothing, nothing."

Pearson was, by now, almost standing on the old man's toes, staring him in the eye. The old man flinched, half putting his arm up for protection and looking away as if in expectation of a blow to the head. "See you tomorrow, Sam. We will probably be asking Daniel to come with us again. I don't think that will be a bother to you. I would be very disappointed to hear that Daniel couldn't come or that he had extra work to do because of it. Is that clear, Sam, is it?"

The old man was beaten. He gave a slight nod and slouched in silence back to the barn. Daniel did go to the cinema again that summer, in fact he went several times. He sat in the gloom in his farm matured coverall and his old tweed jacket and was transfixed. At moments of high drama his chest would heave as it seemed it would never suck in enough air. His eyes would bulge and his mouth would gape. When the tension was subsiding, he would scan the audience as though seeking assurance that the danger had passed. The ticket stubs from the cinema were kept. Then, after the discovery of his hideout, they formed part of his collection of memorabilia. The collection grew with the addition of a few books and comics given to him by Pearson's son, all placed in safe keeping.

For days after his cinema attendance, he would replay the plot in his head, going over how, when all seemed lost, the hero was always able to turn the tables on the villain and win the day. He would learn that real life is not like that. The next summer Pearson's son went to boarding school and, despite reassurances that the outings would continue, they didn't. That was something else he learned, to realise that promises are easily made and just as easily broken, was almost reassuring. It confirmed that, perhaps, his father was right and the approach to life he was in the process of absorbing, was right. At the same time he wondered what it would be like if he had been better dressed or his dad got on with people and they liked him or he had spent more time at school and could talk to people properly.

CHAPTER 10

Stanley had his reading glasses perched towards the end of his nose. After the slight rap on his door he looked up to see Curran and Fenwick viewing him from the other side of the threshold. He shuffled some papers, perused one with overplayed seriousness, then he applied his signature with a grave flourish.

"Come in, shut the door." The last piece of paper held his attention, there was a frown and another flourished signature. Curran, who had long ago acquired the very necessary skill of reading paper work when it was upside down, saw the heading. He didn't need to read it. He recognised the heading, it was the usual note from the canteen showing next week's menu.

He removed his glasses and looked up. "Right, gentlemen, an update from old Sam's shooting, what, more than a week ago today. What have we got?"

Curran took the stand. "Not much more than we had before." His attitude was relaxed. That in turn was noted by Stanley.

"Oh really, that's not very encouraging is it? I thought there would be developments." Curran was not in a hurry to expand his opening statement.

"We've got a body, we've got some tyre marks and we've got a missing shotgun and we've got a missing lottery ticket. We have checked every CCTV camera around, all that shows is old Sam driving home, half pissed, by himself. There is no footage of anybody following him. There are only a couple of roads going out of town in the direction of the farm, but there is nothing to indicate that he was been followed. We considered that somebody may have clocked the bulging wallet, knew where he lived and went out to wait for him. That means he knows Sam, knows where he lives. That in turn means that he would probably be aware of the lad. So he would be taking a chance hanging around; grabbed the gun and the wallet and legged it. It does suggest that he was aware of the layout of the farm, in that if he knew the lad was down at the lower end, he wouldn't be seen and with the lad's tractor, or whatever he was using, making a noise, he wouldn't be heard."

Stanley made a slight grunt. "So it could be a local with knowledge of the place."

"Could be." Curran didn't seem to be totally absorbed with the subject. He wondered if or when Stanley would cut to the chase.

"What about the tyres, the impressions in the mud? One had a split in it."

Fenwick spoke up. "We had uniform check as many local farms as possible. You chased up your oppos in the surrounding areas, there hasn't been anything that ties in. The lad said he was working down at one of the lower fields clearing drainage ditches. I went down there, got covered in mud, and, like the lad said, his digger was there and there were the signs to show that he had actually been working on what he told us he was doing."

Curran took over. "There is one thing that may be of interest, but it is a bit thin. The girl who represented the lad when we spoke to him, right gobby little bitch, she called me yesterday to ask if we were going to speak to him again soon because she was going away for a couple of days for some conference or something. She mentioned that when she was speaking to Sam's son at the bed and breakfast, he asked her about selling the farm. He said that Bill Reece, he's the neighbouring farmer, had been to see the lad to ask if he would sell the farm to him. The lad wanted advice from a solicitor, but she said that she didn't do that type of work and that the lad should see the solicitor his dad used when he sold that piece of land. I know it is stretching a bit, but we know that Reece has got a fierce temper. It's just about possible that he was asking old Sam to sell the place, there was a row, gun was grabbed, went off. Possible."

Fenwick asked. "What about the tyre tracks? Apparently they were made that day, very distinctive."

Curran considered this. "Yeah, well it is possible they may be a bit of a red herring. Maybe somebody, for whatever reason, drove up the path to the yard. Maybe they wanted to buy something, sell something or nick something. Drove in then drove out again."

Stanley peering over the top of his glasses, pronounced, "It is possible, but it is too much of a coincidence. Nobody goes up there. Why would they on this day? From what we can ascertain, there are hardly any visitors, of any type, to the farm. It's too much of a coincidence that, on the day of the shooting there are tyre tracks, probably from an old type Land Rover. From the state of the tyres, it is probably knackered, it's unlikely to have an MOT. Sounds typical of the sort of banger that you could find round here." His two officers concurred in silence.

Stanley tapped his pen on hi desk. "What about the neighbour wanting to buy the place him buying it? Is it worth anything? Have we looked into that?"

Fenwick, referring to his notebook. "Yes, spoke to a couple of the local agents. They are of the opinion that old Sam's place is well run down. The land has not been looked after and the buildings on it, well you have got to see them to believe it, on the verge of collapsing, most of them. A right dump. What the agents say, and they all say this, the farm might and only might be worth buying, especially if it's adjoining one. If Reece stuck it onto his farm, he would have a place about twice the size of what he has now. But it wouldn't need twice the work, or expense, and there could be better returns, more profit. At the moment it is only good for rough grazing.

Curran chipped in, "In time it could be improved, especially on the dairy side, which has gone right down the tubes with old Sam. But, and this is the interesting bit, a lot of farms round here are struggling to earn their keep. Some, nearer Newcastle are starting to make money by getting planning permission to develop the land for barn conversions and the like. Apparently you could knock down and rebuild the farmhouse itself without planning permission as it is already a dwelling. But what these agents are saying is that if the house was rebuilt to a good standard and planning permission was granted to convert the outhouses and barns, it could be worth a fortune."

Stanley sat up. "Do many folk round here know about conversions and the like? Has anybody else been asking old Sam about buying his place? I mean this could give us a whole new motive. How much do you think it would fetch, with planning permission that is?"

Fenwick continued. "Apparently it depends on certain things. How close is it to a major town? Is there good access to a reasonable road? Is it in an area that has already been developed, or is it an area that has potential. Will it affect the surrounding area?" According to the agents, well the ones we spoke to, the old boy's place could have potential. It's close to a good road, handy for Newcastle. And the land itself could be rented off to farmers for grazing or even as paddocks for horses. But - and it's big 'but' - planning permission can be very difficult to get and there's no certainty that it will be granted. Unless you know the right people."

Stanley was stroking his chin firmly and rapidly, his hand moved down as if to loosen his collar. "Bloody hell. Do many folk know about this?"

Fenwick was eager to demonstrate his recently acquired expertise in land development. "It doesn't look like many, or that any developers have targeted this particular farm, but there are always some sniffing around, looking for opportunities. They reckon there could be a bit of a rush for this place. Because of the state of the buildings, it could go cheap. But they say it is very difficult to put a value on these places. If was just for farming, it wouldn't be worth much. If it was likely to get planning permission, well it would go to the highest bidder."

Stanley looked at both men in turn. "This business about the lad selling and planning permission and all that, does not need to go any further than this room. I don't want to start rumours and set hares running, it could bugger up this investigation."

"I take there is no news on the lottery ticket. I mean you two have searched everywhere. It's got to be somewhere. Why did the bastard that did this hang onto the bloody wallet? Why didn't he sling it like he was supposed to? What do they teach them at thieving school these days? In my day a proper villain had the decency to sling a wallet or a handbag over the nearest hedge. Not these modern day clowns, no they have got to hang on to it. Why for Christ sake, why?"

Stanley threw his pen down onto his desk to register his displeasure. He continued. "Look this land business, let's get Reece in and give him a bit of a seeing to, let's shake him up a bit."

Curran sat up. "Do you know what he is like? A bloody barrack room lawyer, stroppy as hell. Look, Boss he was the one who caused all that carry-on with the obs team on his farm. If we give him grief, the first thing he is going to do is get a brief and sue us, again."

"Oh that prat." Stanley reflected. "Look, he hasn't done a witness statement yet. Could we get him for that? Or even go up to his farm and while you are taking his statement, just sound him out about what he knows about the possibility of Sam's farm being sold. Just say we've heard rumours and he's the one who could fill our inside straight?"

Fenwick looked at Curran and took a deep breath. "I don't suppose that even he could object to a statement, especially if it was to help catch his neighbour's killer."

Stanley tidied up a sheaf of papers. "So, at the moment, what we've got is a lad that is daft, but, at a push it is possible that he could be in the frame."

Curran and Fenwick shot each other a glance, both noting the unexpected change of tack by Stanley.

"But, Boss," appealed Curran. "I thought we were to…"

"I know, I know. But this bloody ticket is not going to turn up now. On the 'just in case basis', get the lad in again, and push him a bit this time. As it stands I suppose he could be a suspect."

Curran came back. "On the face of it, forensics have ruled him out. They say, and we all know, that if he did it, he would be covered in blood. And he wasn't. Why would he kill the bloke, his father that has looked after him all his life? It just doesn't add up."

"You are an inspector, you should know that it doesn't always add up. Now get him in. If we could show accidental homicide, he could still cash in that ticket. Suppose he was larking around with the gun and it just went off?"

"Except we haven't got his gun, or the wallet. So the story is, a lad with more legs than IQ accidently shoots his father, nicks his wallet and disposes of it and the gun, washes all trace of the blood that would have spattered all over him, calls the police and fools everybody?" By now Curran, half-way out of his seat, realised that perhaps it was inappropriate to harangue his boss. He resumed his seat. Before Stanley could formulate a reply, Curran tried to deflect any response that may not have been to his liking. "Anyway, his brief is a right dog. Everything has to be by the book, doesn't let you get a word in edgeways."

Stanley's impatience went up a notch. "You are coppers for Christ sake, deal with it. Since when has a smart arsed lawyer ever been a problem to you? They have only learned their stuff from a book, you blokes have learnt it from the streets, by dealing with real villains, getting them through the system to court. You deal with the real world, these bloody lawyers spend hours debating how many angels can dance on the head of a pin. It's all theory, not practical."

The discussion halted. Stanley looked towards Fenwick. "Constable, would you mind leaving me and Inspector Curran, we have a few things to clarify." The last word was spoken only after being considered then carefully selected.

As the door shut, Stanley addressed Curran. "This lottery thing, I've been checking a few things out. Basically, if a ticket is lost, a claim can be made by the purchaser within thirty days. If it's after that they won't pay out. There was a court case, a young couple lost a couple of million quid because they left it too late. So if a claim is to be made on the basis of a lost ticket we had better get a move on, the clock is ticking. It is vital that the lad gets the money, the sooner the better. Then we can arrange for his assets to be 'enhanced', shall we say."

Curran remained impassive. The chief superintendent regained his thread. "What is likely to happen if a claim is made for a lost ticket and it is accepted, it could go into old Sam's estate then it's all sorted out according to his will."

Curran sat back in his chair, Stanley allowed him his thinking time. "Thing is, Boss, it's doubtful that he made a will. Even if he did, he may not have left anything to the boy. I thought he looked after the lad, took care of him. Now I'm hearing that things may not have been so rosy. He was married, but his wife died years ago. He might leave it to her relatives."

"Yes, I thought it wasn't that likely that he would have made a will. It's all a bit messy, too uncertain. Our best bet, if, whether we find this sodding ticket or not, is to say that it was a joint venture between the old boy and the lad. I take it, it wouldn't be a problem getting your shopkeeper mate to state that it was made clear to him, by old Sam, that the ticket was bought for both of them? That old Sam, him and the lad both paid towards it. That means the winnings will go to the boy."

Curran shrugged, "Can't see that as being a problem at all, especially if he thinks he might get a bung."

Waving his pen in a slow horizontal arc, Stanley addressed both men, "Good, the lad's not going to be a problem, he will do as we tell him, just you make sure that he does. Tell him he can have flash cars and that he will have women chasing him. He's bound to fall for all that sort of stuff."

"Yeah, could work, Boss, but, if we want to collar the bloke that did this, the ticket has got to be found. I reckon that, especially with those tyre tracks, that whoever did it, just grabbed the gun and the wallet, chucked them into the car and made off. He may not have stopped for another sixty or seventy miles, then slung them over a bridge, or in a skip. If he has done some distance, he would have more time to think as to how to get rid of the wallet without it being found. If he gets caught, he's got a lot to lose."

Stanley, hand across his mouth, thought for a few seconds. "You're right of course, absolutely right. If it doesn't turn up, and I appreciate the odds are not in our favour, as I said, we will have get the lad to make a claim on the basis it is lost and see what happens. I don't think we can do much more than that."

CHAPTER 11

On the street outside the police station, Curran pushed open the sleeve of a packet of cigarettes. The packet was proffered to Fenwick who, with an upturned palm, declined the offer. Curran lit up and inhaled deeply, he exhaled through tight lips then examined the glowing end of the white tube.

"Well, what's first, grabbing the lad or chatting to that nice Mr. Reece?"

Fenwick, with his hands thrust deep into his trouser pockets, remained silent, staring at the pavement. He looked up. "What shall we do with Reece? I reckon, as it is a witness statement, we should call him and ask him if he wants to see us at the nick or at his place. I suppose we had better play it friendly, good cop and good cop."

Curran was becoming more fortified with nicotine. "I reckon he will want to see us at his place, if he will see us at all."

Fenwick rocked on his heels. "What about the lad, didn't you say his brief, or whatever she is, is away for a couple of days. Wouldn't we need to arrange for somebody else to hold his hand when we speak to him?"

"Sod that, we just happened to be passing the guest house and dropped in to see Mr.s Knowles. We would just be having a friendly chat. Do you know something, I don't think he is as daft as he lets on. He seemed to work his way through the interview, even if he did have the acceptable face of punk to lean on. Well, toss a coin, who's first?"

"Let's sort out Reece, give him a bell; arrange to see him. It's bound to be at his place, it would take too much time for him to come into town. We can get hold of the lad any time."

Curran took a last draw on that particular cigarette, threw the remains to the pavement and dealt its final blow with the sole of his shoe. He flipped the cover of his phone.

"Mr. Reece, its Inspector Curran here, how are you? Good." He turned to Fenwick with a look of pleasant surprise. "Obviously I'm calling in respect of the death of your neighbour Sam Hamblin. There are some routine matters that we would ask your cooperation on. As you were acquainted with him for a long time. I'd hope that we could ask you for a witness statement. No, I can't compel you to give one, it is entirely voluntary. But in the event of a court case, it may mean that you won't have to attend as a witness. Your statement can be read to the court. Well, whatever is convenient to you, we could come to your place, unless you particularly want to come into the station."

Again he turned to Fenwick and gave a shrug. "You mean Constable Fenwick, yes I see. No I suppose you could have had a better introduction, right, right, OK. No, there are not any other police officers who can take the statement. We are the investigating officers in this case." Curran shook his head in a demonstration of impatience and dismay.

"I appreciate that we did not get off to a good start, but I thought, despite your opinion of the police, which of course you are entitled to, you would want to help us find the person that killed your neighbour. As it is, we don't know if the person that did this, is targeting the farming community."

Curran raised his head upwards and sighed deeply then turned his 'phone off.

There was a silence. Fenwick posed the question. "Well, is he going to give us a statement?"

"I don't think so, unless 'bollocks' means 'yes officer please do pop over here and I'll answer all your questions.' Do you think it does?"

"I have to admit that it doesn't sound much like it. Do you think he could be in the frame for this one? I mean he could have gone over to see the old boy about buying the farm, had a barny and just lost it. It's possible that Sam was waving the gun around, Reece grabbed it and 'bang' welcome to the big ploughing competition in the sky. And he's got a motive, the old boy is out of the way, he can work on the lad with a view to buying the farm cheap."

Curran weighed his constable's words, "Possible, possible. He's got a short enough fuse, and old Sam was a crotchety old sod. He wouldn't be too happy if Reece was trying to strong arm him into selling. From what I hear, Sam Hamblin had lost it, although he came from a farming background, these past ten years or so, he's been letting things go to rat shit. He's not been investing in stock or equipment, not been doing whatever farmers are meant to with fields and fertilisers and all that. Basically, as a business, it was going, or had gone, downhill. Some say it was the stress of looking after his lad all the time. So it seems he wasn't making any money, therefore he couldn't invest so he was just losing more and more. Of course, the local vultures knew all this and were waiting to pounce."

Fenwick pursed his lips and nodded his head slowly as if considering his inspector's explanation.

"Do vultures actually pounce? I thought they just flew down and waddled up to a carcass?" The question was put with considerable gravitas. He continued. "Tigers pounce and probably leopards do as well, but I 'm not so sure if your average greater spotted hairy toed vulture is into pouncing, I could be wrong, I'll admit to that."

"Alright Jungle Jim, alright, vultures may not pounce but inspectors do boot constables up the jacksy and make them get their round in. Anyway, let's consider Reece as a possible."

Fenwick puffed his cheeks out. "How do we progress that? There's nothing that we could nick him for, well not just now. There isn't any evidence to link him in, currently he's a good guy. All we've got is a rumour that he wants to buy the farm. I suppose anybody in that situation would do the same."

Curran lit another cigarette, Fenwick indicating he did not want to join him. "Yeah, you're right, can't bring him in. Can't search his place. He won't even talk to us. At the moment he's bomb proof. We would have to associate him with the shooting."

"But there is the little matter of him not being splattered with blood. Whoever did it would have been covered in it."

Curran sucked then exhaled. "He could have got changed, farmers are not noted for being slaves to fashion. He could have gone back, taken off one set of overalls, had a shower and put a fresh set on. How long would that take, ten minutes? No blood, no gun powder residue."

"I know what you are saying, but did you notice if his overalls looked like they had just been laundered? There was such a lot going on, I mean I don't remember him being all neat and clean. I think it's a long shot saying he could have done it, a real long shot. I would still go for somebody who clocked old Sam in town with his wallet and came out here to do it."

Curran stood silent, staring into the far distance. "Do you know what we have got to do? We have got to stop pratting about, worrying about what Reece thinks of us or what he is going to do if we piss him off, and go out there and shake him up a bit. Never mind the bloody rules, let's do some proper old-fashioned police work. Let's pretend we are coppers for a change."

At Reece's farm the two officers exited their car without haste and with a slow and deliberate pace, they crossed the yard. They found Reece in an outhouse where he was stacking sacks of animal feed. As he became aware of their presence, he half looked over towards them, then continued with his task ignoring his visitors. Curran and Fenwick walked to within six feet of where he was working and stood in silence watching the farmer going about his chores. Reece was the first to break.

"Well, what do you two jokers want?" He spat the words over his shoulder as he continued stacking. Fenwick moved to respond, but an arm with an upheld palm placed in front of his chest from Curran made him swallow the words. The silence continued, the officers not moving and Reece still working but giving a bit more concern about how the bags were arranged. He stood up and turned around.

"Well, what is it? Have I dropped some litter or parked on yellow lines?"

"No, Mr. Reece, it's murder. We've come to talk about a murder, like we said on the phone." Curran's tone was almost jovial. "Perhaps you remember it, about a week ago, your neighbour, old Sam blasted to buggery. Are you not bothered about it?"

"Don't come the smart arse with me, any bloody nonsense and I'll have you, I'll have the bloody pair of you. I told you not to bother coming out here. You two can get off my land now, or I'll ……"

"Or you will what, see us banged up for life? Watch us as we swing from a gibbet? That's right, you've got us in the palm of your hand. We're terrified, quite terrified."

Reece was watching his own hand being played against him. He stalled momentarily weighing up the challenge, trying to guess what the next move would be. He decided to take the initiative. He tilted his head up and approached the policemen. There was something less positive in his actions now, a slight hesitation as he seemed to sniff the air.

"I've told you two already, clear off, get off my land now, or so help me I'll, I'll……."

Curran did not try to help him finish his words. He was sensing the ebbing of bravado. In a slow and deliberate tone he ended the brief lull.

"Or you will what? That's right, you are going to have us for, let me remember, drinking after hours, taking free drinks, cheap meals, drunken driving. I think you also called into question the state of my marriage. Now then, Mr. Reece, have you got anything else up your sleeve to terrify us with? Perhaps a bit of gun running, drug smuggling, knocking on doors and running away? Well, have you?"

Reece started towards the main building. "Right, bloody right, you asked for this, I'm getting it sorted and I'm getting it sorted now." There was a slight stiffness in his movements as he approached the door to the house, and he started to slow down. He turned towards his protagonists. "Well are you off, or do I make a call?"

Curran and Fenwick remained immobile, adopting an attitude of insouciance. Curran made a theatrical shrug then relaxed his shoulders.

Reece was now static. "I mean it. I bloody mean it. I'll make that call."

This is what Curran was waiting for. He stared at the ground then back up to Reece. "Go ahead, don't let me stop you. Make that call." He paused, then sauntered slowly towards Reece. "Who are you going to call? The police? We are already here. Is there something you want to tell us? Go on, we are all ears."

The certainty that Reece had initially shown was now draining like a tide from a creek. What, to him, had been previously regarded as a shield of protection was now evaporating. Now that he tried to act on what he had seen as flaws and failings of the two officers, the reaction he was expecting did not materialize, quite the opposite. Instead of seeking shelter from a storm of career threatening arrows, they just stood their ground, unconcerned, unruffled. It wasn't meant to be like this. What was happening?

Curran now scented victory. "Are going to make that call, or are we all going to stand here like three dummies? Thing is, Reece, you are just shooting the breeze. All those wrongs, all those heinous offences you have been shouting your mouth off about, don't exist, well not for you they don't."

"Don't they, don't they just, well you just watch me."

"Reece, blow it out your arse, OK? What are you going to do, blow the gaff about having a drink with some friends? Well listen, luvvey, if you think that any one of those landlords would say a word against us, you are wrong, very wrong. Not for your reasons. Most of the landlords don't mind, it goes with the territory, they know any little problems they may have, we can help them sort it. Can you imagine what would happen if they gave evidence against us to prop you up, you who have hardly ever set foot in any of the pubs round here. Are they going to tell the magistrates, 'Oh yes Sir, we have after hours drinking, happens all the time?' Do you think they are going to put their licences on the line just to suit you? Think again Old Luv, think again."

Reece was recoiling, open-mouthed; he had given up on trying to show a semblance of control.

Curran was enjoying himself. "What else was there? Let's see. Right, drunken driving. No doubt you have got really solid evidence to support that. Not the sort of thing you should go around shouting your mouth off about without evidence. A very serious allegation to make, especially against police officers. What sort of evidence do you have, breathalysers, witnesses, signed confessions? Or just the ramblings of a bitter and twisted farmer who is on the record as hating the police?"

Reece was now standing still with Curran circling him, his head jutting forward nipping at the farmer's crumbling defence. "Well, what else have we got? Ah that's right, apparently I am having 'relations' with a local lady. No doubt you have all the details confirmed, irrefutable. You being the clever man that you are would know all about the laws of defamation."

"No doubt you have possession of the clearest evidence that I am committing a malfeasance of a public office. So let me see, if you are going to make all this public and you do not produce any evidence, you are going to face a defamation case from me and, I presume the lady. I am assuming that the lady in question is married, is that right? I don't think that she, whoever she is, would be too happy to be branded as adulterous."

Fenwick, realising that he was a mere spectator, was now leaning on his car with arms crossed. Once or twice Reece shot a glance at him. Whether it was for mercy or assistance, he wasn't sure. He didn't care. He watched as Curran appeared to grow taller over the cowering farmer. Curran was not letting up.

"I do hope you have a minimum of a hundred grand or so to spare. That is what you risk losing if you do not win your case, but then you are a man of substance, a man of integrity. Risking a fortune to get one over on a bent copper would be well worth it to you." Curran stood up straight. Now he barked at the farmer. "Now then, what are you going to do? As they say, in the very best of circles, start pissing or get off the pot. Make the call or shut up."

Reece was a beaten man. Like so many who save up ideas and feed them with growing efficacy in the vacuum of time, they find they are no more than mischievous dreams that fade away and dissolve with their promises when called upon to pay up. Within a matter of minutes he had had his rehearsed defence against authority torn up and thrown in his face. It may have been his farm, but it was Curran's territory.

Curran made his last thrust. "When we had that little discussion before, at the time of Hamblin's death, you asked me what could I do to you if you had a go at me? I think you mentioned parking tickets or road tax. Not in your dreams, not in your wildest dreams. I've got plans for you that even scare me. You thought you could destroy me. I know I can destroy you. Do you understand? Do you understand what I am saying?"

Reece was unable to speak, Curran knew his lack of an answer was acquiescence. "Right, constable Fenwick, I think we will take Mr. Reece's statement, where, Mr. Reece, you will explain, in detail, what happened on the day of Sam Hamblin's death. You will explain your relationship with the deceased, how long you have known him, how you got on with him, if you had rows or disagreements."

Reece now released from the onslaught resorted to the luxury of rage. "You bastard, you absolute bastard!"

Curran walking towards the car gave a little snort of a laugh. "Got it in one, got it in one." He turned to face Reece pointing his finger at him. "If I ever hear you slagging me off again in public, or word gets to me, it won't be burning your barn down or putting sand in the fuel of your tractors, I'll take you to court, I'll put you in the dock. Make it legal, show you for the prat that you are. You've got a big mouth when you are in front of an audience, but when it's man to man, you are just wind and piss." He paused, letting the heat drain from his assault. Staring the farmer in the eye, he calmly and quietly continued. "I will destroy you. I will destroy you."

Fenwick, who was now deciding whether to admire Curran or damn him, had remained a motionless onlooker who, at times, had felt the blows directed towards Reece almost as punches aimed at him. He shot a questioning glance towards Curran. He didn't know if he had been given a lesson or a warning.

Curran returned his glance indicating that he knew what Fenwick was thinking, but a gentle wave of his hand indicated that he knew what was being considered, but it was all part of the act.

"Now then, Reece, you will tell constable Fenwick here just exactly what you were doing on the day old Sam was so brutally and horribly murdered. You will give him every little detail, nothing will be left out. Is that clear?"

An awareness struck Reece and trembled through him. "You don't think… you're not saying you think I did it? You're not saying that are you?"

Curran was now resting, allowing his adrenalin levels to return to normal. Fenwick having been instructed now took up the reins. "Well, we don't know, you might have done. You had the opportunity, just nip a mile or so down the lane. You've got the motive, we hear that you would like to get your hands on old Sam's place, apparently it could go for a song. He's not even in his grave and you are tapping his lad, his half daft lad, to see if you could buy it."

"I was doing the lad a favour, it was to all above board. It was for the lad." The levels of tension in his voice were matched by the eye bulging twisted look on his face.

"Yeah, right, you would have still got it cheap though, wouldn't you?"

"It was a favour for the lad, it was just a suggestion. I told him to see his lawyer, it was to be all proper."

Fenwick, in depriving him of the comfort of an explanation, moved on.

"Do you know of, or do you have any idea where Sam's gun and wallet are? Have you seen them since the time of his death?"

Reece slumped. "Why should I? Why should I have seen his gun or his wallet? Why should I? No I haven't seen anything, I haven't got anything."

"So that's a 'no' then? In that case you won't mind us having a look around your place. It's for your own good, shows you are co-operating and, when we find nothing, it supports your story."

"My story, what do you mean? You don't seriously think I did it? I've never been in trouble in my life, never. I'm not under suspicion, you don't think that do you?"

"As we said, we don't know. So shall we have a look around? Start with your house, OK?"

In ten minutes Reece had gone from regarding himself as a confident, assertive person who could speak his mind, to a shattered shell now fearing being caught up in a murder. He would realise, in time, that he was a confident, assertive person, but in future the desire to speak his mind would be tempered by the mauling he had just received.

"Yes, yes, look round the house look anywhere you like. You won't find anything. Look as much as you like."

Fenwick indicated that the farmer should go with him into the house. "First I would like to see where you keep your overalls, both clean ones and any that you might have in the laundry."

The unofficial search was not undertaken with a great deal of enthusiasm and was limited to living areas, barns and outhouses and waste disposal. Following the inspection, Reece signed a statement that outlined his actions on the day of the shooting. He was beginning to regain his composure and felt stupid and angry for allowing himself to walk into a situation, mostly of his own making, where he was not able to raise a glove in defence. Curran, outside leaning on the car, was making a 'phone call, which appeared to be intense but not requiring any animation. Fenwick eyed the farmer without speaking. Making use of his senior officer's distraction, he looked the farmer straight in the eye. "What is of considerable importance to this enquiry, is old Sam's wallet. The gun is important as well, but it could all hinge on the wallet. What I am saying is, if you know where that wallet is, I would appreciate, really appreciate, if you let me know. In of all this, things get mixed up, it all starts off with a bang, well it did in this case, but I mean the investigation. I realise that things get overlooked or forgotten in the heat of the moment. What I am saying to you, and this is just between me and you and absolutely nobody else, that if you are aware of the wallet and tell me, I can say I found it. There would be no reference to you. I assure you it will be between you and me and nobody else at all. But it could be vital to solving this. Do you have any idea where it might be?"

"Wallet, what bloody wallet. You want me to give you his wallet on the quiet so you can catch whoever did this. It's not ten minutes since you said I could be a suspect." Reece was now recovering from the recent working over from Curran. He may have lost that battle, but it wasn't over yet.

"I haven't seen any bloody wallet and if I did I'm bloody sure I wouldn't give it to you two thugs." The more his voice rose with anger, the more Fenwick tried to flag it down. "All I am saying is, if you find the wallet, just call me and nobody else." As he spoke, he made sure that his colleague was still engaged in his 'phone conversation.

"If you do hand it in to me, I can assure you that anything he said," Fenwick half pointed to indicate his inspector, "Won't happen, all those threats, nothing will happen. He was bang out of order anyway."

Reece was not sure what was happening, but something was. Maybe he was acquiring more ammunition against the local constabulary.

As the two officers drove down the lane from the farm to the road, they slowed for a car coming from the opposite direction. The driver, a woman, wound her window down and smiled.

"Hello, you are the police officers dealing with poor Sam's death. Have you been talking to my husband? I hope he was alright with you, he can get a bit grumpy, but he's alright underneath it all. Did he offer you a cup of tea?" The men indicated that they had not been given refreshments.

"Oh he is naughty, I shall tell him off for you."

Curran gripped the wheel and looked across. "Mr.s Reece, is it? I wouldn't tell him off if I were you. He's feeling a bit upset, I think Sam's death has got to him."

CHAPTER 12

Daniel was walking the four miles or so from town to the farm. He did this once or twice a week. Although his present accommodation was infinitely more comfortable than the farm, he found it hard to break the ties of a lifetime. Also he was away for the best part of the day, which meant he didn't have to engage with people from the town. As the news of the death of his father seeped out, he was subjected to more pressures. The local press was chasing him in order that the headlines that trumpeted lines such as 'Local Farmer Brutally Slain. Mystery Man Sought' could be given, what he was told, would be the 'human touch'. He didn't want to talk to people from the newspapers, he didn't know if he was allowed. Others nudged each other in the street and pointed him out. Complete strangers fought back the tears in expressing their sorrow. What had previously held him back and kept him away from all that he thought he wanted, now was his sanctuary. This was his own time. He felt awkward being with any form of company. Being at the farm would allow him time to reflect on what was happening around him.

After two weeks, he was becoming used to staying with Mr.s Knowles. She smiled at him a lot, he helped around the house, mainly in the garden. She never said that he did anything wrong, but he never discounted the possibility. Mr.s Jones from the social services said that he could extend his stay until she was satisfied that proper provision had been made for him. At meAt the guest house different people came and went every day. Some wore suits, some were dressed as he was in jeans. It was usually men, occasionally women. The men tended to ignore him, sometimes there was a 'good morning', but not much more. The women were different. Once Mr.s Jones introduced him to a lady who was staying there.

"This is Daniel," she said. He couldn't think of anything to say, so he just smiled at her. Her reaction was to look slightly alarmed and to clutch her hand bag closer to her generous bosom. He wasn't sure if he had done something wrong, something that was not accepted by people. Mr.s Knowles saw his look of embarrassment and shame.

When the woman had left, Mr.s Knowles said to him, "You don't want to take any notice of her, Daniel, I think she is very rude. I'm glad she's gone, I don't think I will let her come back here."

"I don't think she liked me, Mr.s Knowles, I didn't mean no harm. Just when you said 'This is Daniel,' I didn't know if I should have to speak to her. Should I have said something?"

"No, Love, not at all you should just do what you think is right. If I introduce you again, if I were you, I would just smile and say 'hello'. No she's not very nice that one. Look, Daniel love, just remember you are a very nice young man, and now that your all done up in nice clothes, you are very presentable." He frowned at the last word. "I mean you are a nice looking lad. I know you have had a hard time, being stuck on that farm all the time and never mixing properly with anybody, but you will get over that, you will change. Why, I can see it in you already. Do you remember that first day you came here, you wouldn't say a word to anyone? You had hair like a crow's nest. Well that was only two weeks ago, and look at you now. A proper young man. Do you know what, I wouldn't be surprised if someday soon, you would come back with a young lady friend." The last comment caused him alarm, embarrassment and a frisson of excitement in equal measures. He blushed deeply. "I mean it, Daniel, I think you would be quite a catch."

He liked Mr.s Knowles, except when she put her arms around him. But she was kind and kept telling him to go out and mix with others of his own age. He would walk into town just because now he could. Cafes and bars did not look so daunting to now, although, as yet he never ventured inside. But he told himself, he would.

Mr.s Jones was really nice, she spoke to him softly and let him have plenty of time to think what he wanted to say. When she spoke, she gazed directly at him. She made sure he got his money, which he was saving, and tried to get him to go to the church youth club. She also took care of paying for his stay at the guest house. She never rushed away, and made certain she had time for any questions that may have been fermenting within.

The police had told him that his father's old Land Rover was not taxed or insured. It did not have an MOT, nor was it likely, without a considerable outlay, to be granted one. Also there was the matter of a driving licence. It was suggested that he apply for one. He intended to, but the array of official forms, having to read about theories of driving and learning the Highway Code was daunting. Maybe Mr.s Jones could help him.

It was late June, with a clear blue sky free from the blemishes of clouds. The narrow lanes leading back to the farm rolled underneath his feet. The day was still and hot, the air almost seemed to tick in the dry heat. Overhead a squadron of stiff, crescent-curved, winged swifts quartered the sky in an aerial dogfight; sharp silhouettes, flashing turns and dives, screaming out their intent, one minute hedge-hopping the next soaring just to take advantage of the blue backdrop then down again weaving their airy wake with weft and warp. Pods of gorse seeds cracked and clicked, the still air held its light coconut scent as an offering to an empty stage.

In the hill tumbling weeks since his father's death, he seemed to be falling through a dream of people. All his life had been spent, more or less in isolation. The chance to practice and hone social skills were met with blunt rejection from his father. He had often wondered what it would be like to be part of something, to be able to walk out of the door and talk, casually and easily, with friends. Now he felt he had been snatched from his own existence and dashed into what he had always wanted. Now he wasn't sure if he if it was really for him. Too many people, too much rushing. When they had finished what they wanted to say, they just stopped and walked away, he didn't get his chance to form a reply. Now, on these walks to the farm he had time to run things through his mind, to reduce matters to a pace of his own choosing. He had to see official people, once or twice it was some sort of doctor who just wanted to talk to him. He asked him about his father, did he remember his mother? What did he think about living on the farm, what did he want to do with his life? Daniel knew what it was all about, they were checking to see if he was daft or not. He wasn't sure what to say, maybe the wrong answer would get him into trouble. So he kept his replies to what he thought were simple one liners. His most frequent replies were, 'I don't know,' and 'It was alright I suppose.' There were stupid questions like, did he love his dad? 'Well no, he was just my dad.' Did he miss his dad? 'Well, I suppose so.' He didn't want to give replies that meant he might have to go and stay in some home for people like him.

The bank manager spoke to him about mortgages and beneficiaries of wills, he wasn't quite sure what it all meant, but he realised that when all the fuss died down, he would be the next owner of the farm.

The bank manager said, "Well yes, you will be the owner of the farm, but there are certain things we should talk about. There are a number of loans granted by the bank in respect of the property, but we will cross that bridge when we come to it. I understand that Mr. Whelan is the family solicitor. When the time comes he will help you, as will I."

The road rolled on, as he started to crest the hill just beyond the boundaries of the farm, he could see the roofs of the buildings gradually rise into view. At the brow of the hill, some three hundred yards from his home, he stopped. He held one of the fence stakes that bordered the field that ran down to the yard and scanned the horizon. He stood in silence for a few minutes before he moved on.

He muttered to himself, "It's right, you can't see into the bottom of

Small Acre field from here." He stopped and looked again. He was right, the field rose in a gentle swelling before it tumbled down to where he had been working that day.

As he reached the farm gate, birds feeding in front of the grain barn, on becoming aware of his approach, flew off in the order of panic proper to their species. This was his second visit, the first was with the crazy woman driver who spent all of her time on the phone. Now the farm had time to settle and was quiet, but not like it was quiet before. There was a stillness that hung over the place like a light veil. Without thinking about it, he knew that he would not hear a door slam, or scuffing feet going through the yard. There would not be a growling rumbling voice stretched with impatience giving orders and counter orders. It was still. He walked over to the doorway into the house. He remembered that day when he stood here at this spot, he looked down on the frame of his dead father who looked, with his glassy eyed fixed gaze as though he was staring with alarm into the far corner of the room behind. He had never seen a body before, he thought it would be neat and orderly. Instead it was almost formless, those outlines that define beings were gone. Instead a shape that owed more to a bag of laundry sprawled away from him.

By the door red and white plastic tape, endorsed with warnings from the police not to cross, hung broken and listless. He had no interest in entering the house anyway. There was nothing of any material value or use for him there. It was not of interest to him. There was no pull to lure him, there was no emotion. Instead he walked towards the old coach house. At the threshold, as was his habit, he spun around slowly, he shoes quietly scrunching the gravel beneath him. He paused, there was no one there, it was all clear. Inside he made his way up the dry wooden treads and along the jumbled collection of forgotten wooden furniture and discarded farmyard implements towards his door. There was no police tape up here. As before, the only signs any of disturbance did not go beyond the first two or three yards. All was as he left it, the police search had not intruded this far. Before pushing away the small door that screened off the entrance to his space, another glance over his shoulder. Inside he looked down through the small piece of window. Just stillness outside.

For a long time he sat and watched, drinking in the solitude. Now he was back, the feeling of release from a lifelong burden started to soak into his bones. Another scan through the window showed that he was still quite alone. He slid and lifted the floorboard and watched over his hoard, his growing collection, items were removed and inspected. Now he had the luxury of being able to arrange the various items along the floor. There was no risk of a barking command or footsteps nearing to cause apprehension. He was appreciating a new dimension to his recent status. Time was his own, stopping and starting were issues of his choice.

Eventually he thought about returning to the guest house so, with care, he replaced his cache and the floorboard. The view from the window indicated that nothing had changed. Had he made his observations from the window a minute or so earlier, he may have seen, from a raised copse half a mile or so distant, sunlight reflected in small flashes from glass. On his way back to town the warm evening sun was on his back. He wondered if tonight he might chance going into one of the pubs. He had watched others strolling casually in and out of these places there didn't seem to be any action required other than walking in. He wasn't sure what was expected of him once inside. The only times he had seen the inside of any pub, was on the rare occasion he accompanied his father into town on market day. He would watch as the town was emptying of tradesmen and customers, the noise and bustle slowly sliding away. At the Golden Fleece, he would stand half in the door and hiss at his father to come out. Rosy-faced and loosened with drink, his father would dismiss the beckoning of his son.

"I'll come when I'm good and ready so just you wait. I'll be out before long." Other drinkers would admonish him. "You shouldn't talk to your boy like that, Sam. Be fair, he's only trying to get you home. You should think about him for a change." Some of the patrons would try to encourage the lad to come in for a drink. Any communication directed towards the boy would fly past him unheard into the street.

"Dad, dad." He wanted the words to be loud enough for his target to hear them, but no one else. When his embarrassment reached a peak, he would withdraw to the old Land Rover and wait until the pub door clattered open and the slowly progressing figure of his father would collide with the sunlight.

As he approached the guest house, without knowing why, he tried to make his approach as silent and as unnoticeable as possible. His aim was to arrive at his room without attracting the attention of Mr.s Knowles. Whereas she always seemed pleased to see him, he found it difficult and awkward to pick up and run with the threads of conversation. His replies to any of her questions tended to be hesitant and stumbling, using as few words as possible. He was worried that his answers may not be the correct ones, that somehow they were inappropriate. He could never recall giving a response that was satisfactory. In his life on the farm, he could not bring to mind an exchange of words that did not take a downward path into bickering. After a life time of criticism of being informed that, whatever he had done, it was wrong or could have been done better, he still waited for that blow. If he tried to justify his actions to his father by explaining why he had performed a task in a certain way, he had come to realise, that a well-practiced negative response countering his claims would be thrust angrily forward and the encounter terminated by his father's departure from the scene. Mr.s Knowles had been very proper towards him, respectful even. So far. He didn't know if she would argue or make fun of him, but it is best to be prepared and not let your guard slip.

He was about six feet short of reaching the front door when he heard the sound of tyres on the gravel. He turned to observe Inspector Curran and after the death of his father. His chest tightened, his back straightened, there was an almost audible intake of air. He stood still facing the car. What was the right thing to do? Should he stay or perhaps acknowledge them with a wave and continue with his original journey? His breath was coming in short sharp sniffs.

"Hello, Mr. Hamblin, how are you today?" The mantra given to him by the lawyer Tracey Williams was spinning around his head in fragments. "You are looking well, see you've scrubbed up nicely, really smart. Isn't he smart Constable?"

"Yes indeed, smart as a new pin."

The words in his head were starting to join up. "That lady lawyer said that I wasn't to talk to you unless she was here." For emphasis he added, "She said that when you were there, at the police station." He looked inside the door. Sanctuary was so close. Both officers smiled with their mouths but not with their eyes.

"Mr. Hamblin, Daniel, if we may." Curran was by now inches from the boy. He gazed slack-jawed at the young man. "What she meant was at the police station, yes, only at the police station and only if it was official business." Daniel stepped back out of Curran's shadow and bumped into the door.

"She said I wasn't to talk to you, I think she meant away from the police station as well." He was now finding her words. "She said that I want to co-operate, help you like, but she must be here with me, that's what she said." He hesitated. "And you heard her."

Curran placed his hand on the boy's shoulder. "We did indeed, Daniel, we did. But look, we are not here to talk to you, although it is good to see you and see that you are coping well. No we are here to see Mr.s Knowles, we have dropped in for a bit of a chat with her. A bit of a chat and, with a bit of luck, a cup of tea. So we are not working at the moment, it is a sort of rest period, so it's nothing official. We have got to have some time off, Daniel, we can't work all the time." With his hand still on the boy's shoulder he gave him a gentle shake. "Right, is Mr.s Knowles in at the moment?"

"I'm not sure, I've just got here. I've been up to the farm." He stopped abruptly. Was he giving too much away, what would the lawyer say to him? Fenwick touched Curran's sleeve.

"Been to the farm have you? That's a fair step, how long did it take you, must have been just over an hour?" As he spoke a shadow of a question passed over Curran's face.

Daniel looked away. "I suppose so, I wasn't checking."

Curran rang the bell. As they waited, both officers stood in silence with their arms down and hands crossed. Curran turned towards the boy. "Sounds like she's not in. Never mind, we can wait for her. That's alright with you, Constable?"

Fenwick nodded his approval. "Right. Daniel, you will have a key, you can let us in. We can all wait for her inside, that's alright with you isn't it Daniel?"

He felt his pocket where he kept the key. "So you have got a key," observed Fenwick. "Right, Daniel, off you go, let us in."

"I don't think… I mean I don't know that I'm allowed. It's not my house see, Mr.s Knowles might not like…"

Curran shook Daniel's shoulder, "For goodness sake, Daniel, we've been friends, very good friends of Mr.s Knowles for a long time now. She has never minded us coming in when she is not here. She trusts us, we are policemen." Now Fenwick was also resting his hand on Daniel's shoulder. "It's never been a problem before."

There was a brief silence. Daniel spoke. "Then why haven't you got a key then?"

Curran's smile, such as it was, was now stretched tightly across his lips. "OK, Daniel, let's give her a call." He flipped his 'phone open and dialled a number. "Yeah, hi, you alright? Good, good. Look I am at your place with Barry and Daniel. I've said to Daniel that you have no objection to letting us in with his key while we wait for you." There was a pause during which time he started to nod his head. "No, it was just a social call to have a chat with you and a cup of tea." Another pause. He turned his back to the two others at the door. "Yes, well I see, can we talk about that later? Right I'll put him on. Here you are, Daniel, Mr.s Knowles wants a word with you. She says it's OK." He handed the instrument over.

"Hello." The introduction from Daniel was tentative and cautious. He listened. "Alright, thank you, thank you." He handed it back to Curran, who switched it off and slipped it into his pocket.

"There you are, told you, Daniel. She said go on in, make yourself at home. I think we will get Constable Fenwick to put the kettle on."

Inside the premises, Daniel edged his way towards the stairs. "Don't go, Daniel, come into the lounge, stay and have a chat, tell us how you are getting on. It must have been a real shock, that happening to your dad. Still, you look like you have landed on your feet here, very nice place. Comfy is it? To your liking?" No replies to the questions were given or expected. He indicated that Daniel should sit down. The two men sat in silence. Curran taking an interest in the traffic running past the bottom of the garden. Daniel sat to attention looking around as though in hope of a rescue. He tried to remain motionless but small twists and turns demonstrated his level of unease. Fenwick returned with a tray of tea. He picked up a motoring magazine from the coffee table and started to flick through it. Daniel did not look at the tea placed by his side. Curran, cradling the cup in his hand, opened.

"Actually, Daniel, we have made a bit of progress with the investigation. We've established some leads."

"I don't think I'm allowed to talk to you. I'll be in trouble with that lawyer. I think I should go up to my room."

"You can't get into trouble with your lawyer, you are in charge of her. Even though you don't have to give her any money, through the government, you are paying her. You are in charge, not her. You don't want to take too much notice of her. People like that, the more she speaks the more she gets paid. Anyway, we are not talking about you now, we are not investigating. As I said, we are on our break. We have just come to see Mr.s Knowles."

"What do you want to see her for? Is it about me?"

"No, lad, no. We drop in from time to time for a chat, just, like we are having now. Just a chat, that's all."

Daniel turned to look through the window. No rescue there. Fenwick flicked the pages of his magazine. Curran persisted. "As I was saying, I think we have some good leads. Look, Daniel, I can't say too much, but we think it's probably somebody who saw your dad on that market day when he was flashing a large wad of money. They knew where he lived tried to grab the money and in the scuffle, well, bang."

"The money?" mouthed Daniel, He recovered his composure. "Oh, the money, he always kept hold of his money." Fenwick put down his motoring magazine tucked his chin into his neck.

"Daniel." He looked up. "Daniel, my old son, there is one line of enquiry, which we cannot, well should not, disclose to you. But you, you are the main witness in this case, you have already helped us a lot; you really have. Daniel, not only are our enquiries now taking place across several force areas, we are also working with a major financial institution."

"A major national financial institution." Curran stressed. "National."

"What do you mean, national, major, financial what's that? Do you mean me dad is tied up with a national institution, what do you mean? I don't understand."

Curran bent forward lowering his head and his voice. Fenwick put the magazine down to watch the conversation unfold. "I know I can trust you, we want to find your dad's murderer as much as you do. So what I am going to say is strictly between us, nobody else should know, not even that lady lawyer."

Daniel's unease was now making room for intrigue. He leaned forward towards Curran. "Thing is we believe that your dad bought a lottery ticket."

"A lottery ticket, me dad?" His face showed he was struggling to comprehend. "He never spent on anything, except beer. Are you saying he bought one of them lottery tickets? I don't think so. Dad was never one to waste money on them things."

Curran batted Daniel's intervention aside. "Well he did, we know this for a fact. We have got witnesses. Daniel, it is beyond doubt that your dad did buy a lottery ticket." In the belief that the officer was practising upon his credibility, Daniel slumped back into his chair.

"Me dad would never do that."

"Look, Daniel, not only did he buy one, he won; he won a lot of money."

Daniel felt as though he was on a verbal roller coaster. "No." The boy's reaction was loud and drawn out tapering to an end only when the air was expelled from his lungs. "Where is it then, this money? How much is it?"

Fenwick stood up and delivered his lines in the manner of a vicar giving a blessing. "It's more than two million." He confirmed the amount in a slow hoarse whisper. "More than two million." Curran looked up at the figure standing over him with annoyed exasperation.

"I thought we agreed not to mention the amount. Did I not say that we would leave that out?" Fenwick gave nonchalant shrug and resumed his seat. Daniel, now overloaded with information and new concepts, sat open mouthed before finding his voice.

"What did he do with it, where is it now? Was it in his jacket or maybe the Land Rover? Have you found it? Have you found this ticket?"

Curran, rubbing the flat palms of his hands together, then clasping them into a prayer like attitude, continued. "That's the problem. That is the problem. At the moment we don't know where it is. We think, well we are pretty sure, like we said in the police station, that if we find somebody with your dad's wallet, then we have found our killer. But it's not always as easy as that. Quite often, when these people do these things, they throw the wallet away, it makes it harder for them to get caught if they do. What we want to know, what we need to know is, have you seen your dad's wallet since the shooting? Or have you seen the lottery ticket?"

Fenwick interjected. "We really need to find that ticket, it is very important."

Curran's glance towards his junior suggested impatience. He turned again to Daniel. "Have you seen that lottery ticket, Daniel, or the wallet?"

The boy's failure to grasp adequately what was being played out in front of him caused bubbles of agitation to well up with increasing intensity. "No, no I haven't, I haven't. I don't think so, what does it look like?"

"It's pink, small with numbers on it. Just a small slip of pink paper." Fenwick was overstepping the mark again.

Curran was now ignoring the constable. "That's right, small and pink with numbers on it. Thing is, Daniel, that stands to make you a very rich young man, because if your dad can't have it, then you should have it. It's over two million, think what you could do with that. Nice house, nice car, any car you ever wanted."

"I don't want a car, they say I haven't got a licence, I'm not to drive."

"Well, we can sort all that out for you, but we need this ticket. Are you sure you haven't seen it?"

"No, I'm telling you, I don't even know what it looks like. I didn't think he would buy things like that. No, he wouldn't, not him, never."

Fenwick, although he realised he had been, in effect, gagged by his inspector, found himself compelled to enforce his boss's message.

"It is very, very important, to find the person who shot your dad, and, also, it could make you a lot, an awful lot of money. You would be able to buy anything you want. His wallet might be behind a hedge on the farm, or it may be in the house somewhere where we haven't found it. Did you dad have a hiding place? Or it might have fallen between floor boards. It could be anywhere."

Daniel was absorbing the information now, he sat, elbows resting on the arms of his chair staring downward. Nobody in the room spoke or moved. He looked up, the movement of his eyes suggested he had something to say.

"If you catch this bloke, the man that shot my dad, what will happen to him?"

Curran, in a voice dripping with reassurance, met the boy's gaze. "Daniel, he will go to prison for a very long time. He will be locked up for years and years in a small cell. Daniel, this ticket, isn't it right to say that you and your dad both paid for it? Wasn't it like a little game you played, both paying for the ticket, because if that's what happened, you would be sure to get all that money. Daniel, it is an awful lot of money, all you have to say is that you and your dad bought it between you. If you did that, it might help us to catch the person that did this to your dad."

"How could I, he never gave me no money. I didn't have any. If I did I wouldn't buy a stupid ticket with it. He never told me he was buying those things, never did." Daniel was very still. He knew he was being pushed into saying something he didn't want to say. In a calm and definite tone he delivered his reply. "I've not seen that ticket."

Fenwick's request was urgent and impatient. "Look, all you have to say is that you and your dad always paid half each, that's all. There's nothing wrong in that. People do that all the time." He puffed out his exasperation, took a breath then continued in a didactic tone. "Thing is, Daniel, if you say that you paid for half of the ticket, you will get half the prize straight away, that's over a million. You just tell the lottery people you paid half and you will get all that money. We will tell them it is lost and, because we are policemen, they will pay you. The other half goes to your dad, well his estate. When that is sorted, you will get the lot. You have more money than you have ever dreamed of."

"I don't think I've ever dreamed about a lot of money. I only want what he should have paid me, my wages, that's all."

Fenwick was not backing down. "You will look for it, won't you? You will look for it?"

"I tell you, I've not seen a ticket, I don't know about it."

Curran and Fenwick, noting Daniel's definitive response, regarded each other both with an unspoken question. "Daniel, we have got to go now. We know you have tried hard to help us, and we appreciate that, we really do. But it would help us to catch the person who shot your dad if we had that ticket so that we could get you the money." Curran's plea was sotto voce.

"Do you not want the gun then?" Daniel's question caught the officers off guard.

"Why yes, of course we do, it's just that, well," Fenwick looked towards his inspector for support and was assisted only by a shrug. "Well, the ticket is more important. But the gun would help, yes that would help too, but the ticket is the thing."

Daniel watched as the two officers walked to their car then drove towards the road. He slumped into his seat. He felt clammy and slightly sick.

CHAPTER 13

In his room in the guest house, Daniel had combed his hair for the fifth time within a half hour period. He had tried on different pairs of jeans and four shirts lay crumpled on his bed in a violent clash of colours. Even though it was a warm still evening, he considered a variety of options of sweaters together with how they would look with or without his denim jacket. The varying sartorial effects were examined at length in his dressing table mirror, at times bending his knees in order that his upper frame could be assessed for fashionable acceptance. Eventually he settled for a green and white striped shirt, sleeves buttoned at the cuffs. He sat on his bed reflecting on his encounter with the police officers earlier that day. He had felt anger as he was sure they were making a fool of him. He didn't know what to make of this story about a lottery ticket and all that money, maybe the police were trying to trick him. He was due to have another meeting with the lawyer, he would ask her about it. But now there was a much bigger issue to deal with. He was going into town and was definitely going into a pub just like normal people.

He dwelt on the plan, then whispered to himself, "Perhaps I could go in tomorrow." No, it had to be today, this evening. He checked his appearance again. He undertook the same action with a ten and twenty pound note that he, again, pushed down into the bottom of the front pocket of his jeans. The front door key was still in his other pocket. He stood, smoothed down his shirt and opened his door.

He went down to the kitchen of the house and stood outside the door. He listened. Hearing movement from inside, he gently knocked on the door, nothing happened. He tried again with a degree or two of more force.

Looking at the door he swallowed and in a soft hesitant voice called, "Mr.s Knowles, Mr.s Knowles, it's me, Daniel, Mr.s Knowles." The abruptness of the door opening made him stand back.

"Hello, Daniel, love, all right, are you? Well, let me have a look at you. You do look handsome, you really do. Very posh. Are you off out? Going into town?"

He reddened, his hands went into then out of his pockets. "Yes, I am. I thought I would go in tonight."

"Good for you, Daniel, it'll be a nice break for you."

"Mr.s Knowles?" He paused with a serious and concerned face.

"Yes, love."

"I thought that I might, well I thought I would, you know…"

"What, love. What did you think you might do? Mind I've got an idea what you might do."

He appeared slightly alarmed.

"Were you thinking of going for a drink into one of the pubs."

He nodded towards her.

"Good for you, Daniel. It won't do you any harm. You need a break and maybe meet some company, some lads and lasses your own age."

"So you don't mind, it's alright if I go into a pub and have a drink of something like beer?"

"You go and enjoy yourself. Are you not used to drinking, no? In that case take it steady, if I were you I definitely wouldn't have more than two or three pints at the most, otherwise you will make yourself ill, and I don't want to have to clean up after you."

"Mr.s Knowles?"

"Yes, Daniel."

"How much does beer cost?"

"I'm not sure to be honest, I would think about three pound a pint."

"Three pounds, just for one pint of beer? Is that what my dad was spending?"

"I imagine so. It's not a lot of money really. As I said, if you just have one or two pints, it won't cost you much."

"And do you just go in and say what you want?"

"That's right, you go in walk up to the bar and say to the person serving, 'Could I have a pint of bitter please?' Mind you, you might be better drinking mild, just ask for a pint of mild. Then you can either stay standing at the bar or find a seat. It's probably better if you can get a seat, you can have your drink in peace. And don't rush to drink it, make it last."

"Right. 'A pint of mild please.'"

"That's it. You would be best going to the Golden Fleece, that's the one your dad used to go into by all accounts. It should be quiet in there. Here, hang on minute before you go. Let's have a look at those sleeves. I think they look better if the cuff is folded up a couple of times, more casual." She folded his cuffs back and stood back to admire her handy work. "You go and enjoy yourself, God knows you need it."

He trudged towards town in the warm and still evening air. As he closed in on the centre, his footsteps became heavier and slower, occasionally he glanced over his shoulder in case somebody was calling him to return to the guest house.

In the distance, the sign of the Golden Fleece became visible, as it closed in on him, he felt his heart pumping and legs getting heavier. The pavements were now much busier. Small groups, some engaged in subdued but earnest conversation, others with teeth bearing snorting laughs, pushed an easy path to pass him. He closed up on the pub, where, in previous times he had urged his father, now with glowing chops and filmy out of focus eyes, to believe that yesterday's boiled ham was a better option than refilling a cherished mug the contents of which had the ability to wash his life with a happy colour.

The open door allowed a view of business being conducted. At the entrance he slowed, he turned to face the interior, but his legs, of their own accord, dragged him beyond its reach. He found a position where he could observe the very little activity within. Then, at almost a charge, he was in and heading straight for the bar with a ten pound note thrust to the fore. Rapid and timely de acceleration brought him to the working part of the pub. He presented himself to the barman.

"Could I have a pint of mild beer please?"

"Yes, of course, sir, just as soon as I have finished serving this customer."

For a second he was stunned. As it became apparent that his lack of local etiquette did not have any noticeable adverse effect, his consideration for making for the door and the exit waned.

"Now then, sir, a pint of mild was it?"

He selected a seat in an area at the back of the room. There were two or three empty tables and having his back to the wall gave him an extra degree of security. His sipped the dark beer. It tasted like his dad's breath when he came home on a market day. A second swallow and the initial bitterness mellowed slightly. He remembered Mr.s Knowles's advice not to drink too quickly. He wasn't going to anyway, not at more than three pounds a pint. Eventually he drained his glass. He thought about buying another. Before he arrived he had a figure of two or three pints in mind, but, in all honesty, he couldn't see what the fuss was about, the taste was a bit strange to start off with, but it sort of mellowed. Then there was the price. More on the basis that he wanted to develop his purchasing technique, than anything else he approached the bar. This time he made sure he was not queue jumping, he knew what to ask for and how much it cost. This approach to the bar was more measured. He was about to speak.

"Same again?"

"What?"

"Do you want the same again? Another pint of mild?" The barman took the trouble to keep his voice lowered. He smiled pleasantly at Daniel. Hearing no objection, he produced another glass of mild. "You're Sam Hamblin's lad aren't you? I've seen you trying to fetch him out. You are a dead spit of him. Oh, I was real sorry to hear what happened to him, a complete shock; nasty business. He was…" There was a slight pause. "A real character. A bit quiet to start off with, but once he had a couple of pints he was alright."

He returned to his seat feeling more comfortable. The barman disappeared, returning moments later with the landlady. As he became aware that she was approaching his table, a slight panic rose through the beer he had consumed. She sat facing him.

"Hello, I'm Sarah, I'm the landlady here. You're Sam's lad aren't you? You look just like him. When I heard what happened to your dad, I felt awful about it. He was a good customer liked his beer, no trouble though, never a bit of trouble."

Daniel's calm was reseating itself. "Oh, I see."

"What's your name? It seems strange that I've known your dad all these years, and I seen you from time to time waiting outside, but I don't even know what you are called."

He cleared his throat slightly. "Daniel, me name is Daniel."

"Well, look, Daniel, I know it's a horrible time for you, but it's nice to see you here. You come any time you like. We will always be pleased to see you here. You probably need to get out at the moment. It must be very stressful. I've got to be off now, I'm serving in the lounge, but you come back." As she walked through the room, she nodded towards the barman. Later he came over to Daniel's table with a fresh pint in his hand.

"Here you are." He could see the uncertainty in Daniel's eyes. "This is from Sarah - on the house." He could see that further explanation was required. "It's Daniel isn't it? I'm Olly. Sarah has bought this for you, so you don't have to pay for it."

"Oh, I see. Thank you, thank you very much."

"No problem, Daniel, enjoy."

He regarded the object of the landlady's largess with some concern.

Now he had had two pints and was feeling very full. He wasn't sure if another would fit in. However, he imagined that to leave it may not be the done thing. He looked at it for some time. He was about to embark on an episode that would push the boundaries in more than one way. He raised the glass, as he did, the door burst open. A noise that, a few minutes ago, he had started to become aware of had been growing louder. It was mainly shouting, angry shouting and people making strange hooting sounds and female cackling laughter like a chattering magpie. It was laughter that had nothing to do with being amused, rather it was an announcement that the owners of the bray did not regard the society they were moving through as being anything other than deserving of contempt. That sound arrived at the door and seconds later, was inside the pub. Three young men and two girls continued with the cacophony. Their mode of dress and hairstyles demonstrated that there was no desire to conform with convention. Various items of metalwork that invaded differing parts of their bodies in generous quantities were set off by dense tattoos. He noticed that two of them had metal rings that started in one nostril and continued through to the other.

'Just like you put on bulls,' he thought. Two of the men, tall but pasty faced, made for a pair of quiet drinkers, men in their early sixties.

"Oi, you two, you got hats on, you don't wear hats inside." The two girls laughed fiercely, mouths wide agape, teeth and tonsils open to view.

One of them shouted, "You don't wear hats inside you daft old twats."

Olly the barman shouted, "I've told you lot before, get out or I'll call the police."

"Piss off. Ooh the police, look I'm shaking." This allowed the girls another excuse to display the finer points of their oral cavities. One of the boys thrust his face to within an inch or so of one of the drinker's.

"I said no hats." With that he snatched the offending headgear and threw it onto the floor. The two men drinkers blinked the blink of hopelessness. One of the gang spied Daniel. "Hello, what have we got here then? All on your own, sonny? Nobody to talk to. You can talk to us."

The barman barked, "Leave him alone, just leave it, he's doing no harm."

"Stuff it, I thought you were calling the police, well get on with it. Now then, sonny who are you? Come on, speak up. I can't hear you." The last four words were sung out. "Listen mate, when I ask you a question, you answer it, understand?"

Daniel did not move. Not a muscle. He stared straight back. "What you looking at, eh? You looking at me? Oops, sorry I've spilled all your beer.

How clumsy."

Daniel did not flinch.

"Mate, I'm getting pissed off with you." He leant across the table, grabbed Daniel by the hair and pulled him out of his seat. "Now you can speak to me."

Daniel's punch came out of nowhere, a short right into the yob's lower ribs that landed like a train hitting the buffers, then it moved up to his jaw. He went down as though he had just been instantly filleted. The expression of pain was trapped in his throat. He fought for breath and when it eventually came he gave voice to the intense discomfort he had only very recently inherited.

Daniel stood, arms by his sides, looking, without showing any emotion, at the remnant lying on the floor clearly in a distressed state. One girl started screaming, the other provided support.

"You bastard, you bastard, what have you done to him. He was only having a laugh, he didn't mean anything. We'll get the police on you for this. You bastard. What have you done to him? There was no need for that. We'll have the police, I'm telling you."

The other two men had knelt down to attend to their companion who, as his head cleared, became even more aware of the growing ache. In unison, they turned to face Daniel and stood. They crouched slightly, stepping carefully towards him as though trying not to make a noise, unblinking eyes fixed on him. Daniel remained impassive. Then, what they realised with their unblinking eyes, was that Daniel, although shorter than both of them, was head to toe muscle. The years of toiling in all weathers, lifting, carrying, heaving and pulling had defined his stocky frame. As one they abandoned the crouching, stalking posture and stood up. Daniel did not flinch, seemingly totally relaxed. The two men decided to defer the attack to a later date, pointing and jabbing fingers.

"We will get you for this, yeah, we'll have you. We'll bloody have you. Just you wait."

Olly the barman came around from the bar. "Right you lot, pick Hercules up and get out of here, or I will call the police. Now out."

The girls, by now, had adjusted their crying to a simpering whimper. The two young men attempted to lift the wounded coMr.ade, but he was a dead weight unable to assist them, movement intensified his acute agony. The victim's associates addressed themselves to the barman.

"Can you give us a hand? He's hurt bad. I think he might need an ambulance."

Olly looked on, not without some degree of compassion. "Not as much as he needs a wash. Now get out all of you and do not think about ever coming back."

The commotion had attracted the attention of Sarah the landlady and a few from the lounge bar. The two mature drinkers had recovered their headgear. One of them, dusting of his cap, nodded towards Sarah.

"That lad deserves a medal, the way he sorted that gang of layabouts. I've never seen anything like it. Well done, lad."

Daniel looked at Sarah then Olly and decided to address himself to the barman. "I'm very sorry about the beer being spilled, I can clean it up for you. I didn't mean to make a mess."

Sarah and Olly looked at Daniel. They looked for some time, their thinking was along similar lines.

Sarah asked him, "Daniel, are you not bothered? I mean about that lad. Does it not, you know, make you feel a bit agitated? You have just been in a fight, you laid out a lad much bigger than you, you've scared off his mates. I mean, they have been a nuisance around town for ages now, everybody is sick of them and you have sorted it in a minute. But it's not taken a feather out of you, are you really not bothered?"

Daniel struggled with comprehending the landlady's concerns. His face wrinkled to a question.

"Bothered, no, I mean should I be? He was just a lad. Did I do something wrong? I'm sorry if I did, and I am sorry about the beer. I will clean it up."

"No you won't, you'll have another one on us. Olly, fetch Daniel another pint."

One of the cloth capped men, still dusting his headwear, shouted over, "Aye, and when he's finished that, we're getting him one in."

Sarah tried to smile, but there was something she found troubling.

When Daniel did take to the street that night, he noticed that the sodium lights in the town had a haze around them that he had never seen before and the pavement was more uneven than he remembered. Although townsfolk passed by close to him, their voices sounded muffled. Now, at least, he knew what to do in a pub, but he was not going to make a habit of, not at those prices. He recalled the incident with the lad that spilled his beer and pulled his hair. He thought the people in the pub made a deal more of it than it was worth. It was much the same as if a bullock got a bit too lively, it just needs a bit of a slap to calm it down.

CHAPTER 14

The doorbell to his apartment rang. Fenwick's mind travelled up through the layers of consciousness until he was almost fully awake. He rubbed his face with his hands as though to pull away the cobwebs of sleep. His watch showed it was after ten in the evening. The bell went again. He turned down the volume on the television, the program he had been watching before he succumbed to the siren call of slumber, had now finished. At the door stood his boss and colleague, Curran.

"Oh, it's you."

"Your powers of observation never fail to amaze me."

"Come in, what do I owe the pleasure to?"

"Just a social call, to see if you were in. Thought you might have been galloping your maggot round Newcastle."

"Not tonight, having a nice quiet night in. I was watching the match on the telly, must have nodded off, tells you how good it was. Fancy a drink? I was having a glass of wine before I dropped off."

"I didn't know you were a wine buff, bit of a connoisseur then?"

"Not really, just like a glass of plonk now and then. Want one?"

"I'll have a Scotch if you've got one, as long as it not that crap from Hunter's newsagents."

Curran had never seen his constable in anything other than business attire. The T shirt and jeans he was now wearing seemed strange. Fenwick made off towards the kitchen, he stopped and turned; "Well, it is from Hunter's, but it's not that crap. It's what he very generously insisted on giving us when we had that talk with him."

"You still got yours? I finished mine already." Fenwick disappeared into the kitchen.

Curran shouted after him, "Nice place this, must have cost a packet, a bit tasty for a constable, if you don't mine me saying." He walked to the full length windows, which opened onto a small balcony overlooking open countryside. The lounge had the appearance of being a bright, modern, tastefully appointed room. The furniture was new and not cheap. What surprised him was the fact that everywhere was neat and tidy. Not at all what he expected from his younger partner. No empty beer bottles or last night's abandoned takeaway cartons.

Fenwick reappeared with a bottle and two glasses. "Most of this is courtesy of my mum. She's loaded, I'm the only boy in her life, so she spoils me rotten. Good old girl though. Grab a seat, social call you say?"

"Yeah, just to shoot the breeze. Is this one or two bedrooms?"

"Two."

"Very tasty, very nice. You say your mum forked out for this?"

"Yeah." The word was drawn out and inflected upwards towards its end.

Curran stood with his hands in his pockets surveying the area taking in any details he may have missed on the first sweep.

"What does she do, your mum, how come she's loaded? I wouldn't say you came from inherited wealth. You are a bit posh at times, when you're not paying attention, that is. Not from the streets like me."

Fenwick hesitated slightly, the unannounced arrival was out of character, and now an interest in his background, which in the year or so they had worked together had never been a topic of conversation. He noted that Curran was still in his working suit, which suggested to Fenwick that he had not been home, despite the fact they had finished their duties shortly after six earlier that evening He didn't appear to have been drinking.

"My, Mum?" The words brought him back. "She started off as a secretary in this massive company, electrical components or something, export stuff all over the world. She worked her way up, becomes PA to the managing director, then gets into the buying side and now she is some sort of director." He placed two glasses onto the coffee table and pulled the cork out of the whiskey bottle.

"She never married. She always said her one night of madness gave her a lifetime of happiness." He held his hands up in mock surrender. "I know, I know, it is really yucky, but that is what she says. Good as gold. I never knew my dad, she dragged me up by herself. I keep saying to her that she should find a nice bloke, have somebody else in her life, she says she's not interested."

"If she ever becomes interested in worn out knackered old coppers, do me a favour, give me a shout."

Fenwick's look towards his inspector suggested that he did not find that particularly amusing. He poured two large measures of whiskey.

Curran gave a slight inward shrug. "So, your mum, what does she think of you being in the job? Didn't she want you to go into the company she works for? I mean she could have given you a leg up. You wouldn't be scrabbling around at all hours dealing with the dregs of humanity for crap pay. You could be swanning around the world, travelling first class, stay at the best hotels."

Fenwick savoured a generous swig of the scotch and gave a gentle laugh. "She did offer me a job, starting in the mail room, she said I would get no favours, I would have to start at the bottom and, if I deserved it, I would move on to the next step. Looking back, I think I was a bloody fool not to take it."

Curran, in an economy of movement, raised his eyebrows and his glass at the same time.

"So, what do you think of this job, being a copper? How is it going, how you getting on in the job? This is your first year out of uniform." Curran took a deep slug of the whiskey. "You only did just over two years in uniform, that's pretty quick. Somebody must like you. Can't imagine who."

"Thanks, you say the nicest things. It's alright, I suppose. Not what I thought it would be, quite boring for a lot of the time. I've got to say, I find it hard to put up with Stanley, I realise he is a superintendent, but he's a puffed up bag of wind and not all that bright. How did he get so far in the job?"

"I'm with you on the bag of wind thing. He got to where he is today by playing the system. By finding a boss who you can suck up to, then follow him around. Go to the right parties, sing from the same sheet; learn the right hand shake. Being bright or good doesn't count for much in the promotion stakes."

Fenwick was still wondering about the visit, he had his suspicions. There was the odd half rumour, but there were plenty of those on all sorts of issues. But Curran, when he dialled Mr.s Knowles's guest house, had the number on his phone's list, he did not have to look it up. And when they went to the guest house to 'accidently' bump into Daniel Hamblin, he noted that his inspector knew which door off a corridor with several doors, was the one that opened into the large kitchen. When he and Mr.s Knowles spoke, there was too much direct eye contact, there was an ease, a familiarity to the conversation, half smiles for no reason. There and then, Fenwick made a small bet with himself.

"I thought, while we are here, we could have a chat about Sam Hamblin's demise." Although an acceptable subject, Fenwick still wasn't convinced that this was either a social visit, or that old Sam's demise was such a burning issue that it had to be discussed now.

Fenwick turned the television off and decided to play along. "It's funny you should say that, I've been thinking about it and, like they say on the telly 'something just doesn't add up.' Apart from the track of that split tyre, there is nothing else to suggest that anybody visited that farm. I keep coming back to either the lad or laughing boy Reece."

Curran took another sip, kicked his shoes off. "I don't think so. Like I said before, that lad is not up to it, not without leaving a string of clues. Yeah, Reece is a gob on legs, but he's always kept his nose clean, he's not suddenly, at his age, going to take up murder as a hobby."

"What about buying Hamblin's farm?"

"That farm is dog rough, not much more than rough grazing. If Reece wanted more space, there are plenty of places round here that he could get for about the same price per acre that would suit him better. If he did buy it, I mean look at the outbuildings and barns, they are in a hell of a state, most of them would have to come down, that takes time and money. He would have it if it was really cheap. I reckon when he spoke to the lad about it, he was keeping his options open and wasn't really that interested unless he could do some sort of deal."

Fenwick topped up the glasses. "Well, I still say that there is very little, almost nothing to show that somebody from town, either followed him out to the farm or was waiting for him. There is nothing on CCTV. I know it looks like the gun was taken, and the wallet." Fenwick slowed then faltered.

He looked at Curran, who was looking at the carpet through the bottom of his glass and showing no interest in Fenwick's powers of deduction. He looked up at the younger man.

"I wasn't thinking along those lines, who did it, who didn't do it. I don't know. Don't actually care all that much, according to the medical report, he would have been dead within a couple of months anyway. Mind, the overtime is still ticking up nicely, you can claim a couple of hours for this meeting now." Fenwick raised his glass to salute the god of overtime. Curran continued, "I was thinking of getting my retaliation in before our beloved super." Both men imbibed at the same time. Fenwick asked the obvious. "What do you mean?"

"I mean that that fat toad will try and rip off the lad for the lottery money. He will make sure that if the wheel comes off, his hands will be clean and, more than likely, that we are in the frame for it. If it does work out, he will make sure that we get the scrapings. He will scoop the pool and add it to his retirement fund. I tell you, if we get a couple of grand apiece, we will be very lucky, so, bollocks to it, I thought we could cut out the middle man and do it ourselves."

Nothing was said. Fenwick's chair creaked as he shifted in it. "Go on then, what did you have in mind?"

Curran rolled the tumbler of spirits between his hands. "Land development, buildings, planning permission. All that sort of stuff."

"How does that all work?"

"Right, the lad gets the money from the ticket. It is suggested to him that an excellent way of increasing his fortune is to develop the farm, knock everything down, build a new house, convert the barns. Turn the outhouses into apartments or offices. All that sort of stuff."

It was Fenwick's turn to examine the carpet. "So, how does this all work? First catch your hare?"

"What?"

"First catch your hare. It's from an old cook book. There's a recipe for hare pie, or something, and at the start of the recipe says, 'First, catch your hare.'"

Curran shook his head. "Sometimes I worry about your generation."

Fenwick interjected. "What I am saying is, to get the show on the road, we, or somebody, has to get the money to the lad. How do we do that?"

Curran brightened up. "Easy. We don't, his solicitor, madam big gob, does. Stanley is faffing around, ducking and diving, trying to get the winnings to the lad without anybody else knowing. Why not do it the easy way?"

"The easy way being?"

"We tell Tracey that his father had a winning ticket, that it was bought by the old boy, but as he now cannot collect on it, unless they do a special delivery to the underworld, the money will automatically go to the son. She, or somebody from her firm, will chase it up. Then we are the good guys for telling his lawyer all about it. As long as a claim is made for a lost ticket within thirty days, they should pay up. We can prove, or rather it can be proved that old Sam bought the ticket at that newsagents, at that time with the winning numbers, the same numbers he uses every week."

Fenwick was now sitting opposite Curran looking a little flushed, which was not all the result of the whiskey. "Won't the solicitors be a bit suspicious? Is it the type of thing they would do?"

"Listen, who are the greediest bastards on earth? Lawyers. They used to say, if there was a row over the ownership of a cow and one party was pulling its horns and the other its tail, who was the person in the middle milking it? The lawyer. If they see fees, large fees, they will stop at nothing."

Fenwick was becoming more animated. "Right, so the money goes into the lad's account, what next. How is it of use to us?"

"Variation on a theme. Stanley wanted his mate to flog him duff financial investments and split the takings. What I was thinking, we, or somebody, tells the lad the way to make easy money is to develop his land, barns and house and all that."

"And?"

"Well, like Stanley, we use a middle man, keeps us remote from any activity. We sort out a local builder and architect. They work for the lad, but screw him rotten on the bills. There is land clearance, that's more than a few grand, architect's fees, builder's costs, the cost of bricks, cable, heating boilers, all that sort of stuff. I reckon to clear the site and build houses and whatever, you are talking six to eight hundred thousand, add twenty percent, that's up to one hundred and sixty grand. OK, we have to split it, but we would get a lot more than if we went in with Stanley. And the lad now owns some very nice property. If we box a bit clever, there will be no connection to us. And what is a right or wrong bill from an architect or builder? Who knows?"

Fenwick gave thought to the proposed enterprise. "It seems like a lot of fingers in a lot of pies to me. A lot of mouths to keep quiet."

"What you are forgetting is that I've been an inspector round here for fifteen years. I have already had, shall we say, some experience in the building trade. There has been more than one occasion when a councillor has turned down planning permission on a plot of land up for sale, then see it sell for buttons, when, blow me, six or nine months later, the same plot gets permission granted and it quadruples in price. Except of course, it is now owned by the councillor's wife or girlfriend or dog or cat, sheer coincidence of course."

Fenwick softly tapped the side of his glass. "So it can be done? You've got the contacts?"

"Absolutely it can be done, and yes, I have got the contacts. What we would be doing has been done before; it's being done now, on a smaller scale I grant you. It won't be a problem, no problem at all. Why do you think I've got a Mickey Mouse bank account in Spain for?"

Fenwick was looking more flushed now, the room was warm. "What about Stanley, how are you going to handle him?"

"As I said, get my retaliation in first. When he finds out, and he will find out, there is no point pretending he won't, he will go ape, but there is not a lot he can do. What are his options? Is he going to report us for misconduct, give us a written warning? I don't think so, I've got too much on him. He is just as much a part of this system as we are. It starts when you see him with his hand ferreting around somebody's pocket, then he throws you a morsel to keep you on his side. Then he's not your boss anymore, not your senior officer. He's just another grubby official, as we are, who is on the make. We all know where the others keep their dirty linen. Anyway, he is due to retire in just over a year, he won't risk getting caught up in a mudslinging competition. What can he do? He can no longer beat up the locals and call in favours, he's going, he's yesterday's man. They won't want to know him and what can he prove? He's the master of keeping these schemes at arm's length, I learnt that from him. For him to do anything, there must be evidence that we are involved in something very iffy, some illegality and then present it to the powers that be. A dangerous thing to do unless you have rock solid proof and you yourself are squeaky clean. Then he will have to accuse the businesses involved with some sort of fraud. If he does and he can't prove it, he leaves himself open to defamation action. Over the years, he has been in bed with quite a lot of the business people from around here, they will have their insurance policies tucked away. No, he has got no room to move."

Fenwick walked to the window and looked at the night sky. "Why me? Why are you including me? You have got all the contacts, it seems you have a history with them, so there is mutual, er, I suppose you would call it trust. I've got nothing, you could do all this stuff and I wouldn't have a clue that it was going on. Why throw money at me?"

"Good point. First you will be a junior partner in all this. It will be my contacts and my knowhow that will put this together. So the split between you and me won't be fifty-fifty, more like seventy-thirty. You won't have to do much, probably a bit of fetching and carrying, nothing too heavy. Thing is, in trade terms, you are my jockey, I run the job, you help. One day, you will be the main earner and I will collect from you. So for me it's an investment, we've all got to start somewhere. If I carried on without having you on board, then you wouldn't involve me. Worse still, you might shop me. So it's an investment and an insurance policy."

Fenwick walked back to where Curran was sitting and, standing over him, asked, "What's to stop me shopping you now? How do you know that you can trust me?"

Curran scrutinised his glass, then, with raised eyebrows and a tight-lipped smile that suggested the question was naïve, he looked up.

"Barry, old love, you don't go into these ventures unless you have all the angles covered. It's got nothing to do with trust. Since you have been here, you have had the odd little dabble. That fake booze for instance."

"That wasn't much, a couple of cases, you said it was alright, even

Stanley had some off me. You can't say that was a big deal."

"Really, let's see, four cases of scotch, that's forty-eight bottles. What is the duty on spirits? They were litre bottles weren't they, say twelve quid a bottle, what's that? Well, forty-eight tens is four hundred and eighty, plus forty-eight two pounds; that is ninety-six. Call that total six hundred, round it up a bit. So you have screwed the customs man for six hundred quid of smuggled booze, and that booze itself is illegal as it is fake. If they knew, they would not like that at all, not one bit. They could come round here and tear this place to bits if they knew. But they don't. Of course, if it was, let me see, ten, no, twenty cases, it would be a lot worse."

"But there were only four cases." He paused, this game was getting a bit serious. "And you need proof, you have got to have proof."

"Barry, it can be any number I want it to be. Of course you need proof. That can be supplied, no problem." He took stock of how Fenwick was handling this implied threat. "Look, I wouldn't worry about it, you are in the system." He allowed the message to settle. "Around here, at least, quite a lot of us are. Those that are on the outside, so to speak, know that it is a tradition if you like, and they know that if they tried to throw a spanner in, they would not survive. You are either in or out, you can't be a little bit pregnant. You cannot shop me, I can't shop you and Stanley can't shop either of us. That's why, when he gets a sniff of what we are doing, he will flip his lid, but that is all. I've got him by the shorts. What can he do? Arrest us? I don't think so, we are bomb proof, absolutely bomb proof."

Fenwick sat down and digested Curran's words. His heartbeat, now relieved of its stimulus, was starting to find a less vigorous rhythm. Curran's smile asked the question. Fenwick broke the silence. "Well, if you think it is a goer, then count me in. When do we start?"

"Now is a good time. We have got to block any planning applications for the farm, we don't need investors killing the golden goose. I can see to that. It's unlikely that there will be anybody interested at the moment. Nobody knows about the lottery money. All the locals will assume that the lad will either try to run the farm, or sell it. It is not going to attract much attention. I think we have persuaded Reece not to upset us. Then we have to make sure the lad gets the money. We know that Stanley is after it, but he is going all around the houses, it's a bit too messy. There are thirty days in which to make a claim for lost or stolen ticket or, if you still have it, a hundred and eighty days. Old Sam got done nearly two weeks ago. I reckon we shouldn't leave it too much longer. I will speak to his lawyer tomorrow. I'll tell her that we accidently bumped into him at Mr.s Knowles's place, we had a chat, all informal, unofficial, no notes taken. Then I'll drop it on her about the ticket and that she should make a claim on behalf of the lad. She can make the application, he gets the money, job done."

Curran stared at his colleague waiting for a response. "What if…" Fenwick scratched his chin. "What if he gets the money and doesn't listen to us? The lawyers, sniffing all that loot, might throw a ring around him and keep us out?"

"That's something we have to consider. Not all of these exercises come off, some do some don't. If we speak to his lawyer, the lovely Tracey Williams, and ask her to sort it out, right, well she's a criminal lawyer. If she gets the money for him, more than likely it will be Whelan, his dad's old solicitor, who will want to advise him. Whelan is not easy, but he can be handled."

Fenwick looked up. "Another cut of the share?"

"Possible."

Fenwick swirled the whiskey around his glass. "If that land, the farm, could end up being valuable, that is if it got planning permission, why don't we buy it as it is now, then either sell it with planning permission, or develop it ourselves. Wouldn't we make more doing that?"

"It's a thought, but I think you should stick to what you know, what you do best. If you go down the road of buying or developing, everything you do can be connected to you. If you buy that farm, it's pretty rough, say a thousand plus per acre, maybe more and I reckon there is about a hundred acres; call it a hundred grand. How do you explain to the rubber heel squad how you came to have that sort of money lying around? Plus the fact you would be buying it from, what some would say, is a vulnerable kid whose father has just been murdered and you were the investigating officer. Then you buy it with no building consent, then suddenly it's granted. Too messy, it would stink." Fenwick seemed to accept the message.

Curran swirled his drink around his glass. "No, stick to your trade. We are facilitators, we put things together. We connect the right people to do the right deal. Keep it at arm's length so there is no comeback. No, we are fixers, it's done me well since I've been here, and Stanley too. He will have a very nice nest egg by the time he hangs his boots up. Right, what's the time, nearly eleven? Can I just use your 'phone to call the wife?"

Fenwick nodded towards the one on the wall by the kitchen.

"Hello, love, look sorry I'm a bit late, but I dropped in to see Barry, Barry Fenwick, yes, that's right, I'm with him right now. Oh ages ago, afraid we got carried away talking about this murder case. I should be home in fifteen minutes or so, bye."

Fenwick sipped his drink and smiled. He had just won his bet with himself.

CHAPTER 15

Curran checked that those in the office in front of him were occupied either with reports or 'phone calls, or were not doing anything, but were trying to create an impression of being industrious. He quietly closed the door to his office and returned to his desk. He dialled a number, then spun his chair around to face away from the workplace beyond his door and looked out of his window.

"Hello, could I speak to Tracey Williams please? Yes, I am Inspector Curran." He checked over his shoulder to make sure that none of those occupied had found the time or inclination to visit him. "Hello, Ms Williams? I'm sorry, is it Miss or Ms? I don't wish to make assumptions."

A clipped voice retorted, "Ms will do."

"Thank you Ms Williams." He winced slightly as, perhaps, the 'Ms' might have been over emphasised. "I realise that you are at some sort of conference at the moment. Is it OK to speak?"

"Yes, I have some time, we are between speakers, just waiting for the next one."

"Ms Williams, I thought that I should call you to explain our actions yesterday - that is, of Constable Fenwick and myself." His words fell into a void of silence. "OK, well, Constable Fenwick and I encountered your client, Mr. Hamblin, yesterday, purely by chance. It was at Mr.s Knowles's guest house. We had dropped in to see her, nothing to do with this case, and, well, Mr. Hamblin happened to be there and we had a chat while we were waiting for her to turn up. We did have a general discussion about this and that, but we made sure we did not talk about the case, nor did we make any notes of what was said."

"I see. Did either you or Constable Fenwick subsequently make notes?"

"No, not at all, I can assure you there will be no record of the meeting."

"I see, Inspector. I take it that you have reported this, shall we say, chance encounter, to your senior officer?"

"Yes, we will notify him just to make sure it is all above board."

"So you haven't spoken to him yet?"

"Not had the chance, Ms Williams, we are both very busy people, but I assure you that I will as soon as possible."

"I am pleased to hear it."

"What time did this 'accidental' meeting take place?"

"As far as I can remember it was about two o'clock."

"So, unless it was your day off and the constable's day off, you were both on duty yesterday."

"Yes we were, we were indeed, but, even police officers are entitled to a meal break once in a while. I assure you that it was just a social call to see Mr.s. Knowles."

"I see, Inspector. How long did you stay there?"

"Oh, not much more than fifteen to twenty minutes."

"So, if you had the conversation with Mr.. Hamblin, as you have described it, you didn't leave yourself a great deal of time for your meeting with Mr.s. Knowles."

"No, not really. Talking to Mr.. Hamblin took up more time than we thought. We had a meeting we had to go to." Curran, paused and continued in a lower voice than he had been using.

"Ms Williams, there is one matter that we did touch on yesterday, which I think you should be aware of."

"Really, and what is that, Inspector?"

"Well, Ms Williams, in the course of our enquiries, we have established that Mr.. Hamblin, the deceased Mr.. Hamblin, bought a lottery ticket on the Friday not long before he was shot. Apparently he bought one every week, using the same numbers."

"Mr. Curran, I don't wish to appear rude, but the speaker is about to start."

"I will be as quick as I can, but I do think this is important. It seems it was the practice that father and son contributed equally to the purchase of the ticket, a joint enterprise. Well, anyway, it is a winner. It has won rather a large amount."

"I see. Do you know what value this 'winner' has?"

"Yes, yes I do, although we have been asking those that we disclose it to, to keep it to themselves as it might have a bearing on the investigation."

"I see."

"Yes, well the amount involved is over two million pounds. That could make a substantial difference to Mr. Hamblin's lifestyle."

"I imagine it would." There was a pause. "Is there a point to this?"

"I wouldn't want Daniel, Mr.. Hamblin, that is, to miss out. I thought as you are his legal representative, you might be able to assist him in making a claim to the lottery people Apparently, as it a lost or stolen ticket, there is a thirty day period in which to make a claim. As you are aware, we are assuming the ticket was in his wallet and that it was taken by whoever shot him. It would be unfortunate if he missed out. Mind you, it would take him out of the legal aid bracket. That may even be a benefit to you."

"Yes, I see. Thank you for that, Inspector."

"That's a pleasure Ms Williams."

"Oh, just before you go, Inspector, is it safe to say that Mr.. Hamblin could still be considered a suspect in his father's death?"

"Nothing ruled in, nothing ruled out. We are still considering all options, still making enquiries, and, while I accept it is unlikely that Daniel was responsible for is father's shooting, we won't really know until it has been concluded and somebody has been charged and found guilty or the case is closed. So there could well be a lot more fees coming your way."

"Thank you, Inspector. That has been most enlightening, most enlightening indeed."

"A pleasure, Ms Williams. Please, if there is anything I can do, please do not hesitate to get in touch. Will you let me know how you get on with the claim for the ticket?"

"Oh, I wouldn't worry about that, you will definitely hear about it. Good bye, Inspector, thank you."

The 'phone clicked into its cradle. Curran put his hands flat on the desk. "Oh, yes, oh yes, my son, the money is on its way." He made his next call slightly hunched over the 'phone with his hand guarding the mouth piece. "Malcolm, I've just put the call in to Ms bloody smart arse lawyer. She's going to chase up the ticket."

"Are you sure?"

"I did happen to point out that if the lad cops for over two million quid, she won't be dealing with him on legal aid, but on her normal extortionate rates. She even asked me if he is a suspect. I said yes and that he had not been ruled out. You could almost see the pound signs in her eyes. She will drag it out for as long as she can now. She will be straight in to her senior partner looking for a rise."

"Perhaps we should ask her for a cut."

"Good point, now you are thinking. Where are you now?"

"I'm over by the farm, thought I would take a long walk along the hedges and walls just in case, you know, the wallet turns up. I must have done a couple of miles by now. All this walking about is a bit knackering. But, there is nothing so far."

"That's what I like, dedication to duty. I think for all your hard work you deserve a pint when you get back."

"Only if you insist." Fenwick slipped his 'phone back into his pocket, then raised the binoculars to his eyes. It was a warm day and the spot where he had been for the past few hours was not too uncomfortable. From the small wooded area, he had a clear view of the farm.

Tracey Williams clicked her 'phone off and reflected on the conversation she had with Inspector Curran. She tapped the number for her office. "Mr. Carter, I need to see Daniel Hamblin as soon as possible, preferably away from the prying eyes of our pair of detectives. I should be back tomorrow morning. I will want somebody to accompany me, who is available?"

CHAPTER 16

Curran listened to the radio as he waited in his car. His watch showed ten thirty. Night had swept its cloak over the fields and trees and the darkness was now almost complete. The car park he was in was for the use of forestry workers. It wasn't much more than a clearing in the trees and was off limits to the public, but long ago he had acquired a key for the padlock to the gate some six or seven hundred yards back along the path. It was a place he had visited several times before, although not usually alone. Through the trees he saw lights which indicated a vehicle was approaching his position. Bit of a shame he thought, the radio was playing Ramsay Lewis's Wade in the Water, one of his favourites. A very muddy BMW four by four pulled up alongside his Ford. When its lights were turned off, the night appeared even darker. He waited a few seconds, then left his vehicle and climbed into the front passenger seat of the BMW. As his eyes adjusted to the light conditions, the outline of the driver morphed into his vision. It was of a very large man, massively overweight. The soft glow from the dashboard allowed him to make out the dark trousers and voluminous sweater. He could not see the stains on the clothing, which he knew were always there, as was the flat cap. However, the smell of motor oil mixed with diesel, confirmed the driver's signature odour.

"Right, what is it this time?" The voice was surprisingly high for such a big man. The flatness of his vowels and the blunt directness of his approach suggested he had paid scant heed to any form of education that he may have been exposed to and that it was very unlikely that he would regard any man as being his better. Now Curran could see the man's fingers, as thick as his accent, constantly gripping and twisting around the steering wheel.

"You're not wearing a wire are you?"

"You bloody what, wearing a wire? What, Lenny, may I ask do you think this is? Bloody James Bond? Am I wearing a wire, for Christ's sake. Lenny, just what do you think I am doing here, I'm running a bloody scam. Am I going to record myself in case I need the evidence? Jesus Christ."

The steering wheel was grabbed tighter. "All right, all right, don't go on about it. You can't be too careful these days. There was that lass in Newcastle, she got caught when your lot bugged her."

"That daft cow, she was going round, pissed out of her brains and with more coke up her nose than your weekly ration of pies asking if anybody could shoot her old man for her. Yes she was recorded by a copper wearing a 'wire' as you put it. That is not surprising as she might as well put an ad in the local rag, 'Hit man wanted for elimination of husband, must have his own gun. References required.' I think our meeting tonight between you and me is in a different category. I don't want you to shoot anybody, well not yet. What I want is for you to use your very considerable influence with them that matter round here, to push a deal through. It shouldn't be too difficult seeing as you own half the town and most of the folk in it."

"Right, and watch your mouth. I don't need you and your crummy little deals. I could buy all the police here with small change."

"Right, Lenny, I'm sorry, but when you start with all that crap, I can't help it."

The grip on the wheel had now loosened, but the fingers were still constantly working gripping and twisting.

"What is it, what you got for me?"

"Land development, property - building. You still own that construction company don't you?"

"Last time I looked, yes."

Curran breathed in and out deeply so as to marshal his thoughts. "I have become aware of somebody who has a large piece of land that is ripe for developing. This same person also has access to all the money needed, and a lot more, to prepare the area and build on it. What this person needs, and he doesn't know it yet, is somebody to push through the necessary planning consent and a reliable builder to do the work for him. You do not have to lay out a penny, simply charge him for the work."

"Go on." The words were grunted.

Curran sighed deeply at the interruption. "As I was saying, this person has got the land, got the money, but hasn't got the brains. Lucky for us, he is somewhat lacking in that area."

"What do you mean, 'lacking in that area'?"

"He's as thick as pig shit. He doesn't know which way is up. If it could be sold to him that to build on this land he has just inherited would be a sound investment for the future, then we could guide him along that path."

"Who is this bloke then, is he local?"

All in good time, Lenny. Let's agree the basics first. What I was thinking was that I could go for a finder's fee. If I give you this punter, he's all yours. I can give you the details, then leave it up to you. If it goes tits up, that's your problem. You have to sort out the planning and get him to agree to the work. I will take a one off payment, I was thinking fifty grand. Then I'm gone. I keep that, no matter what. Or, I could go in with you on the basis that if it does get off the ground, I take a rake off of your bills. I mean the topped up amount. I reckon you up them by about thirty percent. I would take a cut of that, say half."

"Thirty percent, that's about normal, these big national firms do it, but they call it 'a premium'. If folk don't understand the trade, that's their look out."

"I can assure you, Lenny, this one hasn't got the faintest."

"I would have to know what we are talking about. I would have to see the land, make sure it's alright to build on, road access, that sort of stuff. I can't do anything until I see what it's like."

"Look, Lenny, if this works, all you have to do is stick up a couple of your jerry built sheds. There is no outlay for you. Apart from back handing a couple of local councillors and that."

"Aye, and they don't come cheap these days, greedy bastards."

"I'm sure you can sort them out in your usual way. Just a thought, you couldn't fill my inside straight on who is doing what to who in the town? It's just that it's useful for work at times. Ever since that council treasurer suddenly retired to Greece, or wherever it was, I've been a bit short of punters I can lean on for the odd favour. The doctor who was selling prescriptions did a runner. He came up with some good stuff when he was here."

"I can tell you, Barry, it's not easy these days. Folk just clam up, nothing seems to be going on. I don't know what the place is coming to, I really don't."

"Know what you mean, Lenny. Not good is it? Do you remember the accountant's place on the High Street, the one next to the chemist shop?"

"Oh, aye, I do. Didn't some old feller own that? Hasn't he retired since?"

"He has now, poor old bastard. We got him for flashing in the park at night. Not that it bothered any of the women round here, not that easily shocked, a lot felt sorry for him. We asked one lass for a description, all she could say was that the lining of his coat was coming away. Anyway, we collared him. We actually thought of getting him to cough to a string of shop lifting charges instead of the flashing on the grounds it would be less embarrassing for him. And it meant we could have cleared up twelve or fourteen cases instead of his one flashing number. Crown Prosecution wouldn't touch it, so we had to drop the flashing charge as well. He's gone a bit loopy since then, or he pretends to have done. Still, he might come in useful one day, you never know."

Lenny yawned and looked at his dashboard clock. "Right, I'll be off then. What are we going to do about this land job? What do you want, a one off, or a cut of the bill? You fill me in on what it's all about and I will let you know."

"OK, there are a few loose ends, but I will be in touch. A word before we go, that prat Stanley, my boss, may come knocking on your door for the same sort of thing. Remember, I was here first and remember who has pulled you out of the shit on more than one occasion. Think on, Stanley will be gone in a year and I won't. Do not trust that man."

Lenny gunned the engine. "He's alright, he's never stiffed me. Always got on OK with him."

"I'm telling you, Lenny, watch him. I would never trust him."

CHAPTER 17

"Well, Superintendent Stanley, if I may say so, that was a good round, a very good round. Well played. I think you are well up on me now. Been quite a time since I've come out on top, still I'm watching and learning, it won't be long before I get even."

"It was a struggle, Phil, you were really pushing me all the way especially on the last four holes. I had a couple of lucky putts and I think you had a couple of unlucky putts. It could have gone either way. There is always next week, you can get your own back then."

As the two men tugged their golf trolleys to the club house, a warm summer breeze pushed and plucked at their clothes. "Shall I get the usual in for you, you always take ages putting your stuff away?"

"Very kind of you, Nigel, as always. Seeing as it's you, I have a large one."

"As always, I'm only a poor copper you know, struggling along on a basic wage. Not like you wealthy businessmen, rolling in it. I think I've got enough small change in my purse to run to a double for you."

"I keep telling you, Nigel, I'd swap with you any day. Regular wage, guaranteed pension, fixed working hours, a gang of staff to do your work for you. I bet you don't know what to do with yourself during the day, just sit behind your desk hoping for a nice bank robbery or something. Just what do you do each day?"

"I delegate and manage. I don't 'do' things. But you see, Phil, as I keep telling you, I'm paid for what I know, not what I do. It's me that soaks up all the pressure. That crowd of cowboys who answer to me, don't know they're born. I just wind them up and point them in the right direction. Go on, get your kit put away. See you inside."

Stanley's partner found his way to the table that overlooked the sweep of the course where straggling players could be seen engaged in swings of various rhythms and efficacy and giving pursuit to their assorted efforts.

Phil took his seat beside him so that they both faced the playing area and had their backs to the bar. He poured a mixer into his gin, the ethereal bubbles of the tonic effervesced to the top then surrendered themselves to the atmosphere.

Stanley opened. "So how is the estate agent business? Still extorting money for old rope?"

"Absolutely, take it while you can. Is that what you really think? You see you servants of the Crown, or whatever you are, just turn up for work, sit around have a coffee. If the work doesn't come in you don't lose your bonus, you don't lose sales. Your salary comes in month after month no matter if there isn't a crime wave or mass murdering going on."

"I suppose there is something in that, but you are a wealthy man, posh car, beautiful suits. I imagine you will have another mansion once your divorce is sorted out. How is that going by the way?"

The other man gave a half- hearted grimace and a slight shrug of his shoulders.

"It goes on, it's going on what can I say? She wants her pound of flesh. The bugger of it is, I've built that business up over twenty-five years, worked all the hours, gone without holidays, nearly lost it a couple of times when things were rough. Then when it all comes good, bang, she's off. You know I employed her, that's how we met. Give her her due, she was a bloody hard worker, good on sales. But she came in when the business was on the up, she didn't see all the graft and all the times when we nearly went under. It's no fun having to lay off staff who have been with you for years and who have been very loyal and supportive. It hurts when you have to do that, really hurts. Mind you, when things improved I was able to offer some of them their old jobs back. She didn't see all that, now she expects half, or as near as damn it. She hasn't earned half, nowhere near it." He took a decent sip of his gin and stared into his glass.

"Yes, it seems a bit of a mess, bit of a sticky situation. Is there anything you can do?"

"Well, if she stays on as a partner with me, she can still draw her fees, which, I suppose, I can live with. But if she wants me to buy her out for fifty percent of the value of the company, it is going to hurt, hurt a lot. Actually she's not being unreasonable. It's these bloody solicitors winding her up, egging her on to grab everything that's going. They are not interested in equitable solutions, they just want their fees to keep rolling in, and they are eye watering to say the least."

Stanley's attention wandered to two fellow guests, whose sporting attire boasted most colours of the rainbow, the various shades of which paid little heed to subtlety. As they passed he mouthed greetings, his nod and wave to them were similarly muted. "John, David." He returned to the conversation. "Oh, yeah, solicitors, bloody nuisance most of them, twisting every rule in the book to try and get some ruffian or thief off the hook.

There are blokes walking the streets who should be locked up. Makes my blood boil, it really does."

His companion abandoned the salute that would have brought his drink and lips together and slowly returned his glass to the table. "Don't tell me, Nigel that you disapprove of our legal set up? Surely you believe in a robust system? If the rules were ignored or 'twisted' as you say, wouldn't that lead to miscarriages of justice? I'm no lawyer, but if your lot plumped for the easy option all the time, wouldn't that completely devalue the process of law? I'm not suggesting that your band of men would get up to no good, but look at what went on in the seventies in London and Manchester, the police were fitting up people all the time. A very good friend of mine, a respectable businessman, was sent to prison for handling stolen property, some office equipment, more or less purely on the word of the police officers involved in the case. At the retrial, when the police notebooks were examined, it was found that they had been falsified. Apparently some pages had been removed by opening the staples, and re-written ones put back in their place. Trouble was the police forgot the pages were numbered and had the date the books were printed, on them. The page numbers were not in sequence and one book had been printed on two separate dates. In the end, he got sent down, but nothing happened to the officers involved."

Stanley's reply showed signs of impatience. "He would not have been sent down for a first offence, or it would be most unlikely. He must have had a previous record."

This observation made his companion sit up and blink. After a moment's reflection he asked, "Is that really the case? He would not have had a prison sentence for a first offence?"

Stanley looked at his companion and slowly blinked his eyes. He said nothing.

His companion sat back and fixed his gaze at a slight upward angle. Then, more as if he was talking to himself than to Stanley, in no more than a loud whisper he said, "That explains it, that explains a lot."

Stanley was now back on home ground. "You don't go down for a first offence and probably not for the third or fourth, unless you have nicked the Crown jewels. Your friend must have had a fair old record to pull a custodial. Judging from your reaction it would seem that now you believe he was up to no good at some time when you knew him. See him much these days?"

"Well, no. After he got out, he left the country, went to Cyprus as far as I know, never heard from him again."

Stanley clinked the ice in his glass against the sides. "I'm not being funny, Phil, but if we always went by the rules, I mean strictly by the rules, most of the villains in the country would never see the inside of a cell, and they would probably never be worried about being locked up. I know what you mean, if we always took shortcuts and 'fitted up' as you so succinctly put it, of course the legal system would be devalued, there would be chaos. I agree that it has to be a robust system. If it loses its integrity, it has lost everything. But how would you feel if somebody broke into your offices or your house, stole your possessions, not just valuables, but mementos of your life, school prizes that your kids won, things that your parents left you. Then they trash your place, just for something to do? How would you feel if we said that we know who has done it, a regular offender? There is evidence, he's been seen leaving your house, caught on CCTV, been found handling your stuff. But in court a defence brief winds the witness up so much they don't whether they are coming or going and the evidence is thrown out. He gets one of his mates to say that they found all the items from your house behind a hedge and they were actually on their way to the police station to hand them in. How would you feel about that? You can have the law, or you can have justice." He realised that to add emphasis to his theory, he was now leaning well forward in his seat. He sat back into the winged chair.

"I hear what you are saying, but I think, even after what you have said, and I take your point, I would rather have the law. Once you start to bend the rules, where does it stop? You may well exercise a degree of caution, or discretion shall we say, and I'm not suggesting that you personally use these methods, but surely once it becomes an accepted practice, where does it stop? Wouldn't we end up like some banana republic?"

Stanley was now more relaxed. "Well, maybe you are right, maybe that was the bad old days. It wouldn't do to play fast and loose with the rules. Anyway, under the circumstances, I'm surprised to hear you come out on the side of our coppers, if you don't mind me saying?"

"No, I don't mind. I suppose there is no chance of you getting him posted. It's bad enough going through a divorce without PC Plod cleaning his boots on my door mat. I accept he is not the cause of the break up, but it does hurt, God knows why, when I see his car outside her place at night. Couldn't you do him for misuse of police property? Is he allowed to use his police car for that sort of thing?"

"There's not much I can do, he is permitted to take the car home and use it locally in case he gets a call out."

"Pity. Do you think he is serious about her, he is married isn't he?"

"Yes, he is married, second time around. And no, I don't think he is serious, he has always had a reputation for having difficulty keeping it in his pocket."

"I don't know whether I think that is a good thing or a bad thing. Even though we are splitting up, I don't particularly want to see her getting hurt. By the way, there is something I think I ought to mention to you, I don't know if it is of any significance, but when I have dropped in to see her from time to time, occasionally I have seen packages, postal packages with Spanish stamps on them. Twice now. The address is her place, but the names they are addressed to are nobody I know. I mentioned it to her once, she became quite defensive, saying they are addressed to previous guests and she posts them on. But I cannot imagine that separate former guests get packages from Spain. I'm certain that I saw him carry one to his car. To be honest, I didn't see him pick it up, but I am sure that is what he was carrying to his car. Look, I would hate it to think that she may be being dragged into something, well, not quite right. Thing is, I'm pretty sure that she keeps them for your Mr. Plod. It couldn't be drugs could it? Surely not. Perhaps I shouldn't have let you know. But as the police are already involved, I am hopeful that it is nothing serious. If something was going on, is there any way in which you could sort of help her?"

Stanley smiled knowingly. "What were you just saying about sticking to the law no matter what? I wouldn't worry about it. You are right, they do come from Marbella. It is one of his investments. No drugs, nothing like that. In fact, you would be doing me a favour if you just left it alone. I give you my assurance your lady wife, she is still your wife isn't she, has absolutely nothing to worry about. Are you having another one before you go?"

"No thanks, I'm driving, don't want your boys breathing down my neck."

"I wouldn't worry about that, when I come here, I make sure that I send them to patrol the other side of the county, I can guarantee you will not see any of my boys anywhere near here today."

"I see, thanks for the offer, I owe you one, but you never know, one of them may get lost. I'll just stick to the one."

"Phil, just before you go, I heard of a place that might be coming onto the market, a farm."

"Is that old Sam Hamblin's place? I thought it might be coming up. I don't think his lad would be able to maintain it as a business, I mean Sam just about kept his head above water, bit of an awkward old rascal. Mind you, he wasn't always like that, well he's never been the life and sole of the party, always had a reputation for hanging on to his money. Had some bad times though. He used to run that farm reasonably efficiently, but that was a long while back."

Stanley drained his glass. "So you don't think the lad could run it?"

"I doubt it. Sam never let him mix with others, lads of his own age. Hardly ever let him go to school, said he was teaching the boy himself at home. He never did, don't think he could, he just used the boy as cheap labour from what I hear. Sam ran everything. The boy never was involved in any aspect of managing or running the place." He looked at his watch, then reached for his car keys. "Nasty business. Sam wasn't the most popular of men, but who would do that to him? What would they gain? Have you any idea who has done it?"

"We are working on a few leads, but nothing definite yet."

Stanley looked around trying to catch the eye of the steward. "I had heard that the lad is a bit lacking, a bit simple."

Phil flicked his car keys in his hand, "I don't know about that, maybe not the sharpest knife in the box, but being isolated and intimidated by Sam doesn't help. Anyway, the farm is not the most attractive property, very run down, not much more than rough grazing, a load of muddy fields."

"Could it be developed for houses and the like, you know rebuilt barns, things like that?"

Phil pondered the question. "Shouldn't be, not really suitable. But round here, who is to say? The local council, as you know, are a law unto themselves. Why, have you heard of somebody with an interest?"

"No, not as such, I was just thinking aloud."

Phil stood up to leave. "OK, I'll keep an eye on it. Well same time next week?"

"Absolutely."

As he walked through the clubhouse, the steward bade him good evening. "Bye Mr. Knowles, see you soon."

Stanley watched his partner cross the car park and glide away in his new Mercedes. It had been parked next to Stanley's Vauxhall. The steward approached his table. "Yes Mr. Stanley?"

He handed the man his empty glass without looking at him, "Gin and tonic. Large one."

CHAPTER 18

This time, when Curran arrived at the car park in the woods, the BMW 4x4 was already parked up. The soft dash board glow outlined the immense girth of the driver, the lone occupant. It was heavy cloud dark night and a gentle wind pushed and shushed the tops of the trees. Curran turned the engine and lights of his car off. The dark of the night immediately filled the void where there had been light. He remained at the wheel of his car for a brief time, staring into the void. He looked up.

"Well, let's get man mountain sorted. How can Yorkshire's godfather, the head of the criminal family be some sodding thick neurotic doom brain?" He stared into the dark. "Because he maims or kills anybody who gets in his way I suppose."

He climbed into the passenger seat of the off roader, tonight the diesel odours were complimented by those of fish and chips. The windows, being firmly in their place despite the fact that the evening had not let go of all of the day's heat, ensured the miasma that greeted Curran, was full bodied. He brushed aside wrappings and some empty drinks cans on to the floor. "Jesus, Lenny, do you ever think of clearing the shit out of this car? It's like a mobile fire hazard. Are you trying to grow your own botulism or something?"

"What's the matter with you, who smacked your arse? I don't tell you what to do with your car."

"Yeah, yeah, alright, Lenny. So what's new, what's happening, got anything to tell me?"

"Well, not much, nothing, except..." He hesitated. "You're not, you know, you're not, I mean you haven't any?"

"Lenny, if you ask me one more time about bloody bugs and recording devices spy satellites or non-stick frying pans that whistle 'Dixie' so help me I'll send round my little green men in their space suits and beam you up to diet land, alright."

Both men were silent, Curran was already having second thoughts about his outbreak and made a note to remember what his evening companion was capable of doing to those who did not amuse him. Lenny was gripping the steering wheel tightly and twisting his hands around it. However, Curran noted that, although steering wheel abuse was one of Lenny's lesser, albeit regular misdemeanours, on this occasion there was a growing intensity to his actions that appeared to grow to match his increasing heavy breathing. Curran could almost sense the rumblings.

"Nobody ever talks to me like that, nobody." The last word was barked and was delivered with venom. "I don't give a toss who you are, you are no different to anybody else. You can't touch me. I can feed you to my dogs and nobody, I mean nobody, will ever even ask me about it. Just watch your mouth, copper. You bent copper, I've got a dozen of you."

Curran waited for the rumbling to subside. "Funny you should worry about me wearing a wire. I've got one tonight, I've recorded you threating to kill me and telling me you consort with corrupt police officers. Nice one. As we speak, it is being beamed by a satellite-guided, multi-linked, computer-controlled system to huge split 3D screens with surround sound in New Scotland Yard. Why don't you give a little wave for the cameras? Go on, show them your best side."

Lenny squirmed violently in his seat. "You what, you bloody what?"

Curran half turned to face Lenny and looked directly into his now contorted features. "You daft bastard, you daft thick bastard. Do you think I would come out to deal with you and not have some form of insurance? Lenny, for Christ's sake stop looking, there are no cameras or bugs. Let me tell you this though, Lenny, if anything happens to me, right, every meeting we have ever had, every deal we have ever done has all been noted. If I am found floating in the canal, or I go missing because your dogs ate me, or I am late for my line dancing class, it will all be published. Not in this country where the top brass would try and quash it, but somewhere. Somewhere, Lenny, a journalist has our history. He is dying to publish it, it would make a great story. It's not just you, it's all my little side lines and what I know about all my other colleagues. If I am dead, I don't give a toss, you will be well in the frame. So, let's cut the crap, you are not going to do anything to me. We will continue, if you want to, to develop our own little schemes. It's a matter for you. Frankly, I'm getting to the stage where I have had enough anyway. I make money from things like this, but I've got to hide it, I can't spend, not in the way I want to. So what is the point? But, Lenny, my friend, be under no doubt whatsoever, if anything happens to me, your number will be well and truly up. I always carry insurance. Now, where were we?"

For once Lenny was still. With his mouth agape, his gaze met Curran's unflinching visage.

"You bastard, you absolute bastard. You're not kidding are you?"

Curran's mouth showed the makings of a smile. He shook his head slowly but definitely. Lenny let loose with one more 'you bastard' then, with an expenditure of energy not employed for some time, he bumped and slid his way out of the vehicle and stood in the centre of the car park with his back to the vehicles. Curran returned to his car calling out to the night, "Lenny, you've got five minutes, then I'm off." Curran's vision had by now become more accustomed to the almost complete darkness. He could just about make out the frame that was Lenny, standing stock still, legs akimbo his head, moving with a gentle rhythm up and down. Curran lit a cigarette and told himself he would give Lenny five minutes to either stay out in the cold or come back in to continue the proposition at hand. He reflected on what he had said to Lenny about having enough of underhand and clearly illegal manipulation of information that came to him by virtue of his position. There were times when he had investigated fraud, only to perpetuate it. In the past he had reasoned with himself that these ventures usually did not progress to prosecution because of lack of evidence. As such he was merely making use of ideas or opportunities and, therefore, his actions merely brushed past what was considered to be unlawful.

If he was honest with himself, and the irony did not escape him, but he was reaching the point where he just did not have the stomach for this anymore. He had harvested not an untidy amount in cash. But spending it was difficult. Luxury items such as fast cars or exotic holidays, perhaps once in a blue moon, could be acceptable. They would still give murmurings as to how they could be afforded. Several years ago, a sergeant explained away his ability to take delivery of a brand new convertible each year and have several far eastern holidays and dine out most nights, on the fact he had won the pools. Not just once, but on two occasions. His continuing and unlikely luck brought the attention of the rubber heel squad. He received a prison sentence for fraud and his chief superintendent, who on occasions accepted a lift home in the hot wheels, received a reprimand for being so gullible. Apparently to win the pools once was unfortunate, to win twice was careless.

Curran had come a fair distance from a council flat in inner London, his parents scraping a living, mother a shop assistant, father rising from the ranks of labourer to junior management with the local council. Summer breaks used to be holiday camps reached by train. Later the family progressed to package holidays in Spain. On return, his mother would fly around to neighbours and friends, before her tan, frazzled on under lashings of olive oil, had time to fade. His father would seek refuge in the local pub, the Londesborough Arms, where, usually sitting alone, he would nurse a beer with his roll up, taunting gravity as it adhered to his bottom lip, burning like a slow fuse. What was he doing here? Why did he prostitute himself under the feet of people like Lenny? It used to be a buzz. In London, as he progressed through the Met, he was swirled into the dirty whirlpool of a core of colleagues. Many, who were aware of the culture, warned him against it. He was regarded as a more than capable officer who had potential. He was flattered to be given a tug on the sleeve and invited to partake of the carrion.

One old inspector told, "Be careful, son, you are stepping over a ten pound note to pick up a shiny shilling." Now he realised what that meant and how true it was. Just hang on to the Spanish accounts, an inspector's wage is not too bad and, all being well he would have his thirty years in within the next six or seven years. Kick all this into touch, at least he would sleep better at night. No worries about a late knock on his door or arriving at work to find the contents of his locker in exhibit bags, his 'phone records checked. That's a point, he had been getting a bit careless with the use of his official phone. Better watch it.

'Sod Lenny, I'm off, no more of this old horse feathers.' He flicked his cigarette butt out of the window, turned the engine on and flicked the headlight stalk. Standing right in front of the bonnet, in a halo of light, was Lenny peering into the windscreen. His face, lit from below gave him a look of a movie horror monster. His sudden appearance shocked Curran.

"Jesus. How the hell did he get there? What the hell. Look at him, he's like a bloody roundabout on legs." Lenny maintained his unmoving stare into the windscreen. A thought flicked through Curran's mind. Was Lenny about to do something stupid? He grabbed his mobile phone tightly in his fist. He thought that a severe blow with the 'phone to the side of Lenny's head might stun him enough to allow an escape.

Lenny waved his hands to indicate that he was prepared to talk. "Turn it off, turn it off." Lenny grabbed the passenger door and wrenched it open.

"Hey, easy on, Lenny, that's official property." The car bounced under his weight as he sank onto the front seat. The 'phone slid back into Curran's pocket.

"Alright, we can do it. But I don't want you telling your journalist about this, but we can do it."

"So you won't kill me and feed me to your dogs."

Lenny's reply was immediate and sincere. "No."

"OK." Sixty seconds earlier he would have been driving away from this. He thought for a few seconds, then, under his breath, with fatalistic undertones, he muttered, "One more time then, and that's it." He switched the engine and lights off.

"Right, Lenny, what's it to be? We are talking about this place that can be developed aren't we? I'm not going to bugger about, I will fill your inside straight and you will pay me, in cash. As I said last time, it's either a one off for the information. The owner has a load of money, and I mean a lot. He is completely half baked, not an ounce of sense. I give you the details, then I am out of it, gone. It is then up to you to do any negotiations with this punter. You will not have to lay out a penny, you do the building and all that, and charge him whatever you can. You will note that I am not guaranteeing anything. This bloke may take a dislike to you, though God knows why he would do that, if that happens you could be left with diddly. You understand that?" Curran wanted the security of an answer, which demonstrated Lenny's comprehension of the proposal and, if it went belly up, there could be no come back against him. "Well, do you understand?"

Lenny's mind was already whirring. Who was the punter? How much could he make out of it, what if, what if. "Yeah, yeah, sure, sure. I know what you are saying."

"It's an investment, Lenny, and, like all investments there are risks. If this information becomes public knowledge, I am telling you there will be a string of outfits like yours a mile long waiting to knock on his door." As Curran was chanting this out, he had a heavy feeling in his stomach, something that weighed him down. He continued. "Option number two." He sang the words out as though mocking a game show host. "I throw my hand in with you. We both take a chance on getting our foot through his door. If we don't, then I get the square root of bog all, but it doesn't cost you. However, if we go down this road, I want a cut of every piece of work you do, say twenty percent. All you have to do is to load your prices to give me my cut. This bloke can easily stand at least a million pounds of development costs. If we do this, there is a distinct possibility that I, in my official capacity, would be able to deal with some of the obstacles that may arise from time to time. That's it, my friend, it's up to you now; you pays your money and takes your choice."

Lenny scratched his stubble. "Who is this bloke anyway? I've had my snouts out, but they can't come up with nobody like you're talking about."

"Now, now, Lenny. It's make your mind up time. I need to know now or I'm off."

"Have you got someone else lined up for this, you haven't have you?"

"Lenny, I'm going in one minute, one minute from now. I really don't give a toss what you say or what you do. You tell me. The clock is ticking." He reached for the ignition keys. Deep inside, he hoped that he would be able to drive out of the car park with no deal done. The idea of letting go of scams like this was growing in strength.

"All right, hang on, hang on, we can do something."

"Well do it quickly, I need to be out of here."

"How much are we talking about for the first one, I pay you for the information."

"That, Lenny old luv, will cost you fifty grand, not a penny more."

"Fifty, fifty grand, you are joking, you are having me over. Fifty bloody grand, no way."

"Lenny, you could raise that in a morning's collection from the pubs and clubs that you, shall we say, look after. It's peanuts to you. It's not even one of your metal deals, you know the ones where you send goons round to collect payment for stock dumped in dealers' yards that nobody asked for or wanted."

"Oh, you know about that one?"

"Yes, I know about that one. You dump low grade steel then demand payment for high grade. I think it's called extortion. It just might be that that trade sector is working with the fraud squad on that one. They just might be coming up this way to have a word with you."

"Do you think they might?"

"Yes, I think they might, I think they might come up here within the next few weeks. You can have that one for free. What will you do? Drop it on a sales manager who was bent but now has had it on his toes, who not only embarrassed you, but ran off with all the purchase and sales records. I mean, you can't lose any more records in unexplained fires."

"I suppose not."

He took a deep breath. "Right, forty grand, I'm not going to talk about it, it is 'yes' or 'no' now." He reached down and turned on the ignition. "Close the door on the way out, Lenny."

"How about I give you..?"

"No 'how abouts', Lenny, let's do the forty grand one now, or I am off." Curran turned the ignition key and revved the engine. "Bye, Lenny, close the door, mate."

"All right, I can do the forty grand, I'll have it for you tomorrow. So who is this bloke?"

"Now, now, I will play when you pay, OK. Another thing, when you call me from now on, can you use the number ending 2103, the one you use is my official phone, so the numbers to and from it can be checked. I don't want my super to start making things awkward for me."

"Who, Stanley? I wouldn't worry about him. He uses his official 'phone all the time." Lenny's response was off hand and was made without giving any thought to the impact it might have and what it could convey.

It wasn't a complete surprise to Curran, but it answered a few questions. "Yeah, I know he does, but be careful, there could be somebody checking his phone. Maybe the fraud squad who are coming up in a week or two? I would box a bit clever if I were you. I've told you before, don't trust him. Call me tomorrow."

"Hang on a minute, just wait there." Lenny left Curran's Ford and went to his BMW. He used the interior light to search for and identify a key from a bunch he removed from the leather blouson jacket he was wearing. He then opened the rear passenger door and pulled back the floor carpet. His key opened the safe installed in the floor of the four by four. He held up some of the contents from the safe to the light in order to make an inspection. Eventually the key locked the metal box and the carpet was replaced. He walked back to Curran's car.

"There you go, forty grand. Check it if you like."

"Check it if I like, of course I'm going to check it. Not that I don't trust you, it's just that, well, I don't trust you. Got to say, nice touch, the floor safe in the. Nice and cosy."

"I'd appreciate it if you kept quiet about that, I'm getting rid of the car next week anyway. Right, you've got the money, now who is it. This better be good."

"Lenny, do you mind? I'm counting, hang on a minute. Do you always have so many fifties? They're not that easy to get rid of. For some reason they attract a lot more attention than twenties."

Lenny drummed the dash board and shifted in his seat. "Can't you be still for minute, I still trying to count this?"

Curran was satisfied that the full amount was all present and correct.

"Come on, who is it then, who's this bloke then?"

"Daniel Hamblin."

"Daniel Hamblin? Daniel Hamblin?" Lenny's face dipped and contorted with the effort of trying to bring to mind the owner of that name. His struggles came to an abrupt halt, he sat upright as though he had received a shock. "Hamblin, the old bloke that got done, he's the bloke that got done. He didn't have a penny to scratch his arse with. Are you pulling my chain? Here, give us that money back. Come on, give it back. Bloody Hamblin."

Curran remained still and smiled at Lenny. This confused him.

Eventually, finding no response from Curran, his wailings died down.

"Yes, Lenny, you are quite right. Old man Hamblin, who owned one of the crappiest farms around here, got blown away by somebody who was after his wallet, which they got. He leaves behind a son, Daniel, who is not very bright, to put it mildly. In fact he is rock-thick. Here's the good bit, the bit you have been waiting for. On the day that old Sam Hamblin got blown to hell, by the way, it wasn't you that did it?"

Lenny swatted out a 'no' without giving it any consideration. He was too engrossed in his future potential to make money.

"That's alright then. Where was I? So, the old boy gets blasted, but, and this is the good bit, he bought a lottery ticket earlier that day."

Lenny was beginning to find this tedious and was considering the most appropriate manner in which to re-appropriate his forty thousand pounds.

"The ticket is a winner," Curran paused to let it sink in. "It is a winner."

Lenny snapped out of pondering where in the woods would be a good place for a shallow grave.

"How much?" The question was urgent.

"Over two million quid."

Some people find beauty and contentment in a new born baby, a meadow of wild flowers or a rainbow. For Lenny it was money. If there was ever such a phenomenon as a 'g' spot, and if Lenny had one, it just erupted.

"Over two million?" He couldn't hide his incredulity. "Over?"

"That's it, Lenny, two million plus. We will have to wait for the money to come through from the lottery, but that shouldn't take too long. Now nobody outside the police knows about this, so, although I don't need to tell you this, keep it under wraps. If you want confirmation, go and put the squeeze on Hunters, he is the newsagents in town. That's where he bought it. Now, Lenny, go; go and make money."

Lenny seemed to shuffle in his seat in his haste to leave the car. His eyes widened and his face was acquiring a messianic aura.

As Curran wound down the driver's window, Lenny was heaving his bulk towards the BMW with surprisingly dainty steps for such a big man. He called out, "Remember, Lenny, he hasn't got the money yet. I have spoken to his lawyer and told her to put the claim in for him. Even she wants a cut, but I think there will be enough left for you. You could get things moving by using your contacts to get the planning permission in place." The rear red lights faded as he made his way along the rough track.

Curran flicked through the cash he had just prized from Lenny. He used one wad as a fan. "Forty grand, nice one. But let's leave it alone after this." In the dark, the light of his 'phone gave a faint eerie glow that just about reached the extremities of the interior of his car. While he waited he mumbled a wordless tuneless theme.

"Hi, Barry, how's it going? Up to much? Oh I see, good, that's good. Listen, you know we spoke about, shall we say, 'capitalising' on recent events, the lad and the farm and all that. Right, listen, I've just done a one-off deal. The information was worth quite a bit to one of my contacts, who wants to use it in the way we discussed. You know, development. What has happened, in exchange for the information, we have received a fee. So you will be getting your share, twenty-five percent, that's right. Well that comes to five grand. I did better than I expected to. Yeah, nice result. I'll come round to your place tomorrow, when we've signed off and sort it."

CHAPTER 19

Curran hovered at the open door of Stanley's office.

"Come in Malcolm, shut the door, grab a seat." At his desk he was in shirt sleeves, red braces traced the contours of his torso. He lowered his head to look over his half-moon glasses. Curran seated himself, legs splayed, his frame pushed back into the seat at a slight angle. Stanley dropped his glasses on the desk and rubbed his eyes. "We've got the brass coming over in two days' time. Obviously they will want to go through the usual inspection stuff, but we know they will concentrate on the Hamblin killing. They will be asking about progress. Where we've been, where we are and where we are going. So, how are we doing, I take it there is no word of the ticket?"

"No, we have searched the areas in and around the farm, put the squeeze on the lad just in case. What I did do was to tell the brief who is holding the lad's hand to put a claim in on his behalf. When I told her how much it was, she nearly wet herself. Of course, her firm will rip the backside out of it on fees. She couldn't wait to get off the phone. I've told her to keep me in the loop."

Stanley rubbed his chin. "She works at Baxter and Martin. Martin is not around much these days, but James Baxter is still going, bit of a sticky character. Still, if it means extra fees, he's not going to sniff at it. So, from the top, what have we got? What can I tell this inspection team?"

Curran rocked back in his seat and screwed his face up. "OK, from the start. Old boy seen in town on market day flashing a large wad of money to all and sundry. He goes home, after several pints in the Golden Fleece, where, apparently, he tries to chat the landlady up, good for him. Right, there is nothing on CCTV, or anything from any witnesses that we can find, that suggests he was followed home. It is possible that somebody who knew him went to the farm before he left town. There were quite a few cars and vans, and tractors come to that, which went from town in the direction of the farm. As usual, the CCTV resolution is crap and no number plates can be read or occupants identified. As I say, all we can say is that they went in the direction of the farm, there is no recording apparatus after the outskirts of town."

He paused and sighed. "We get the call, ambulance there before us, call came from a neighbouring farmer, Reece, and he had been notified by Hamblin's son who, according to Reece, was bricking it and in a complete state. The lad claims to have been working in some fields from where he couldn't see the farmhouse or the road leading to it. We have checked the location, you cannot see the farmhouse or the road and there were signs of fresh digging by a stream, which confirms that part of the lad's story.

"Hamblin is dead, just inside the door of the house. Single shotgun wound to the chest, twelve-gauge according to the doctor. There were twelve-gauge cartridges in the house, just lying around in drawers Death would have been instantaneous. The wallet he had been flashing around was missing, as was the shotgun. We are making the assumption that it was his shotgun that was used. Then what? Right, the doctor said Hamblin's heart was so knackered, that he probably would not have lasted more than a couple of months anyway."

Stanley was making notes. Without looking up he asked, "Did Hamlin know about his heart, it wasn't some form of clever suicide?"

"Apparently not, his medical records, such as they are, showed that he hadn't been near a doctor for many years."

"Were there any other relatives?"

"Doesn't look like it. It seems that he married a local girl about twenty-five years ago. But she died, very shortly after the birth of the lad. It was an accident on the farm according to reports. They had not been married very long. So the old boy had to bring the lad up himself, couldn't have been easy. They, the locals that is, reckon that's when the farm started to go downhill. In the old days, he wasn't the best farmer around, but he held his own. He always had a reputation for being really tight with his money, really tight. But no, no other relatives can be traced."

There was a pause whilst Stanley caught up with his notes. "What about this tyre track, we're not dismissing that are we?"

"No, absolutely not." Curran's brain raced to recall the details of the tyres. "On the day, it had been raining, quite heavily, but, on the drive up to the farm Scenes of Crime found tyre marks in the shelter of a barn that could have only been made that day, otherwise they would have been washed out. We checked them against the farm vehicles and the neighbouring farms, but no matches. One tyre had a distinctive split on it. From the dimensions, it looks like a some sort of four by four, maybe a short wheel-base Land Rover. What is interesting is that Scenes of Crime are now saying that they are pretty sure that the tread marks were made after old Sam drove home that day. It could be that somebody left town earlier and was waiting for him. Any footprints that might have been would have been washed away by the rain."

"So witnesses of any use. Suspects, who are the suspects?"

"Witnesses?" Curran was beginning to feel a sense of unease. Stanley's questions were being delivered in a staccato monotone. There had been no eye contact, no small talk. No jokey asides to old Sam's demise. He came to realise that his senior officer, was creating and maintaining an aloofness, a cool distance that had crept up behind him like a slow wave. Most telling was that there were no references to the lottery money and the money making opportunities it offered.

"Yes, witnesses." The abrupt tone of the reply further enforced Curran's assessment. He stiffened in his seat.

"As you well know, Superintendent Stanley, there are two main witnesses who, in the absence of anybody else, are also our suspects, namely the farmer Reece and the son Daniel Hamblin. Alright?"

Stanley did not change his demeanour and continued to make notes. Curran, feeling anger curdling up into his throat, was about to launch into an offensive when Fenwick entered the room and, unbidden, took a seat. Curran. He was surprised to see his constable in the room and his face showed it. "What are you doing here? I thought…"

Fenwick looked towards Stanley who took his cue. "I asked Barry to be present as he is part of the investigation team."

Fenwick lowered his head slightly to acknowledge and accept the explanation. Curran noted the apparent unease of his young constable, who shifted in his seat and gave an almost silent, but unnecessary cough. He tried to return his inspector's gaze, but the floor held more interest for him.

Stanley, in trying to push past a situation, which, although was expected, came earlier than he had anticipated. "Right, shall we get on then? I was just asking Malcolm here how you two ace investigators are getting on with the Hamblin shooting, and what progress you were making."

"Progress? About the same as last time." Curran's response was delivered in an offhand manner that lacked any semblance of deference. Having answered that question, he waited for the next. The silence that followed, although not more than a moment or two, nudged Fenwick into trying to answer. He had said just three or four words, when Curran, staring straight at Stanley, put his arm across Fenwick's body to signal him to stop. Curran sat impassively, his eyes not moving from those of his Superintendent. Stanley looked down and shuffled some papers.

"Look, if you have nothing to tell me, I suggest you best be off and find something on this case, the pair of you. It's been over two weeks now and you haven't got a lot to show for it. It's disappointing, very disappointing." Curran greeted this faltering display with indifferent nonchalance and remained silent. Fenwick's face was flicking from one man to the other. The silence ticked on. Curran, still maintaining his laid back attitude, sniffed loudly then took a degree of interest in his fingernails. He concluded that they passed muster. He looked up at Stanley who in trying to return the gaze, hoped his seniority would take preference over the unease he was feeling. He started to mouth some words, but was brought to a halt by Curran.

"Listen, you fat useless twat, you complete and utter useless armpit, you who only got your rank by kissing arses or stabbing people in the back. You are about as much use as a cuckoo with an egg timer. You great fat panjandrum." He turned to Fenwick, now a mere spectator, and casually remarked, "Good word that, 'panjandrum', it means a pretentious barrel of lard who is under the misapprehension that he is of importance or use. Just like Nigel here. 'Panjandrum' - try to remember that, a good word, one of my favourites."

"Inspector Curran, I would remind you that…"

"You would remind me of what? That you are a superintendent and I am an inspector. That you are my superior officer?" His voice was low and guttural; the words hissed out like steam from the fires of Hell. "What you are, what we all are, are con men, swindlers, cheats. We are lower than the pond life we arrest. You have no authority, you are not a senior police officer, you are a crook swimming in the same sewer as me and Fenwick. You are the accused. You have no 'authority'."

Stanley mounted a last challenge, he had nothing to lose.

"Now look here, Malcolm, I would remind you…"

"Blow it out your arse, Nigel. You've been pulling your strokes again. If you wanted 'progress' you would have done a press conference disclosing details of the ticket. Too much attention on your investments, eh, Nigel?" He turned his attention to Fenwick, who appeared to be shrivelling in his chair. "Well, constable Fenwick, what really brings you here today?" The constable did not move nor speak. "Come on, lad, you will have to speak louder than that. Although I think you have made it clear what is going on. Worried about your investment, Nigel? Concerned that there won't be enough left in the kitty for you and your mate to screw the lad for the odd hundred grand?" The room was very quiet, the oxygen of normality was being pushed out, displaced by something more noxious. "So, constable Fenwick, what does bring you to these parts?" Fenwick's interest was still the floor. He briefly looked up towards Stanley who was continuing to busy himself making notes. No solace, no rescue. Accepting that his options were very limited, he opted for an attempted explanation, starting in a low soft voice. "Well, Malcolm."

"It's Inspector Curran, or Sir, OK. Right, continue, constable."

Curran's verbal explosion came as a shock to Fenwick and pushed him back draining the few drops of confidence he started with. Stanley attempted to speak.

"I think that what is wanted here is…"

Curran's glare, loaded brim full with contempt and anger, stopped Stanley in his tracks.

"Sorry constable Fenwick, you were saying?" His tone was falsely conciliatory.

Fenwick cleared his throat, sat up and tried to control his voice. He pulled the sides of his jacket together and fastened the buttons. "Inspector Curran."

"Good start, constable, keep it up." The inspector was now feeling as if he were the senior figure running the meeting, Stanley having played his hand was left with nothing to back it up, and Fenwick had been reduced to a state of terror being played by two rods on opposite banks.

"Look, Sir, the Superintendent spoke to me about all this, Hamblin's ticket. He said there was enough to go round if we went along with his idea. He said that your way of thinking would only make things more awkward and difficult to manage. The more people involved, the more likely it would be blown. He said his way was much safer and more likely to get results than yours."

"So he is completely au fait with my proposals is he? And why is that?"

Stanley decided it was time for him to come back to the party. "For Christ's sake, Malcolm, what do you think I would do? How long have we worked together? I have seen half a dozen of your hare brained schemes, you always seem determined to get shopped. If you start sucking up to this lot round here, involving them in your stupid plans, and by God, I have seen some stupid ones, you are not only committing professional suicide, but you are likely to end up being banged up. As soon as a local gets the hump with you, bang, it's gone. Anonymous letters and 'phone calls to headquarters, they all add up. That lot, in their shiny blue suits and silver pips would love to get a scalp, especially an inspector. Grow up. Get real."

Stanley threw his pen onto the desk. Then, becoming aware that the raised voices in his office may have reached a wider audience, he looked through his window blinds, but oblivion still appeared to hold the upper hand outside. He continued in a lower key.

"Of course I knew you would have your own scheme. You can't blame Barry here, I did push him. He did try to stick up for you, but, you know, it's a young bobby up against an old super. Look, if we do this my way, we will all get a good deal. It will be split evenly between the three of us."

"You think I would trust you? You would sell me down the river without even thinking about it. Listen, and I say this in front of Constable Fenwick here, if you try anything, anything that you think may cause trouble for me, and we know what we are talking about, I will drop you in it, so deep and so fast, that you will spend the rest of your life behind bars. Do you understand that? Do you understand what I am saying?"

Stanley blinked slowly. Curran was on his feet his left hand on his hip, his right jabbing towards Stanley as though trying to flick off venom.

"So, my schemes don't work don't they, they're hare brained are they. Well mine is sorted. Done and dusted. If you get in my way, I will have no hesitation in dropping you in it." Without taking his eyes of Stanley he added, "By the way constable, that five grand, forget it. Go back to mummy and ask her for more pocket money."

Stanley addressed his focus to Fenwick, who shrank at the thought of the question that was about to come his way. "Five grand, what the bloody hell." Then he fell back into his chair and started to laugh, quietly at first and then louder, cupping his hand over his mouth to muffle the sound.

"What a sad group of bastards we are. Ripping punters off, then each other before the punters pay up, farcical." He sat forward, elbows on his desk arms raised with fingers interlocked and pressed onto his face under his nose. He maintained a silence that held the attention of the other two men. His gaze was firmly fixed on his inspector.

"Malcolm, I'm only going to say this once, then, my friend, you can do what you like. One of your sayings is, 'Never take a skunk on in a pissing competition.' I like that one. I'm asking you, no I'm telling you to take note of that. At my rank, and I don't mean just me but other senior ranks, there's a group of us, well, we're the skunks. We are like the musketeers, we stick together, but there are quite a lot of us. If you want to take us on, you will lose. You will lose very badly. If they get a sniff that their boats are being rocked and they think they can lose a lot, believe me the Mafia has got nothing on them. You, my old son, will be buried. You have got no idea how far their tentacles stretch. A long, long way. We are owed a lot of favours from a lot of people, some of them very powerful people."

Curran made for the door. "Mafia, bollocks. And you, constable, will stay in the office from now on writing reports. Perhaps you could start off with the musketeers and tentacles."

Curran left the station and made his way to the nearest bar where he ordered a pint of lager with a large whiskey. Then he ordered the same again. The first round of drinks was beginning to make its impression. It was starting to shave off the edge of his anger, and his fear.

In a whisper, only audible to himself, he muttered, "What are you doing, what the bloody hell are you doing? Stanley wouldn't stroke me, I've got too much on him. He would lose more than me. How could he, what could he do? He knows I would take him down if he crossed me. This is the last one, right, the last one." He left his drinks on the table and went outside so that a cigarette would be able to add its effect to the alcohol that was now sending tiny slivers of ice through his system. He looked up towards the end of the street. He wasn't more than sixty yards away from his station, he could easily make out figures moving about inside. He was just as readily visible from the station. However, he did not see the very slight movement of a window blind. He crushed the end of his cigarette with much more force than was necessary and returned to his drinks. He sat with his head on his chest, eyes closed.

"Well, Matey, if you are going to do it, let's do it now. Or give Lenny his money back, saying it was a mistake, or it wasn't a mistake, but have this one on me." He gave a short snort of a laugh and fatalistic smile. "Sod that, that forty grand is mine. Little mummy's boy Fenwick has blown it. Yeah, forty big ones will not do me any harm at all."

From the bar, using the public 'phone he made a call. Before he spoke, he checked the area around him. There were a couple of patrons not too far away, but they were engrossed in a robust discussion of the merits of some football team. "Safe enough." The drink was working.

"Hi, it's me. How are things?" His tone was almost cavalier. "That's good. Look, I need to see you as soon as. No, I'll come to you. I'll give you the details. And listen, this is absolutely between you and me, nobody else is to know, absolutely just you and me. OK. I'll be in touch."

Stanley was alone in his office. The thoughts of the meeting were still echoing around his head. Moments after Curran had hung up, the 'phone in Stanley's office rang. It was a call he wasn't surprised to receive. He listened without speaking, occasionally making a slight nod of his head to indicate that he understood the contents of the call.

"Thanks for that, I'm not surprised, I did speak to him about the consequences of going alone. You can sort it can't you? When you have more details, let me know." He clicked the cradle. "You are a silly boy, a very silly boy." He reached into his drawer and located his bottle of Famous Grouse. He blew the dust out of a glass and poured a generous measure and savoured his first sip.

Raising the glass, as in a toast, in a low voice he said, "Enjoy it, Malcom, enjoy it while you can." He gave a slight rumbling laugh, then took another sip. He punched some numbers and waited for an answer. "Hello, all well with you I trust. Good, that's good. Remember we spoke about you coming over here for shall we say, 'investment opportunities' yeah, that's right, not too much detail just now. I think it would be better if you put off coming over here for a while. Some things need to be sorted out." He paused to listen. "No, that's still OK, don't really see a problem there, it's just that it might take a little longer that we had planned for. OK, I'll be in touch."

CHAPTER 20

It had been over three weeks since his father was shot. His time at Mrs. Knowles's guest house had now past. So much comfort had caused him unease. Mrs. Jones had urged him to stay at the guest house, but the farm was what he knew, it was his proper place. That short passage of time, and the loss of his father, had changed him. Now he had the space and opportunity and the need to make decisions for himself. A lifetime of waiting to be told what to do then acting on those instructions had fixed an attitude so deep within him that now having to think and act for himself filled him with a dread. Usually this was because he might make the wrong call. Surely this would attract attention and anger from somebody; he was bound to be chastised and ridiculed. If this happened, which as yet it had not, there was nothing he could do about it except agree. Inside he knew that if he was being true to himself, he would rather not expose himself to always making himself subordinate to others. Having made this decision, the idea of being back at the farm, gave him a sense of security.

When he was at the guest house, rather than actually deciding on a course of action, he would lay an idea before Mrs. Knowles: "I was thinking of going into town," and "There is a shop that sells books about cars, I am of a mind to get one." Mrs. Knowles never took much notice of what he was saying, but there would be a comment, "Are you, Daniel, that's nice." He would wait for her to deliver an opinion as to whether or not such adventures met with her approval. He would watch her as she busied herself and wait for a pronouncement, but none ever came. She would look around, in a somewhat absent minded manner. "Are you still here, love? I thought you would be off into town." This neutral stance did not give him the direction he sought. She hadn't said not to go and waste his money, and to stay and occupy himself with some mindless chore. But neither did she say that his proposals had her express approval. He took to remaining in her presence, being occupied with some delaying tactic such as flicking through one of the magazines on the hall stand and waiting.

"Still here, Daniel, thought you would be gone by now. It's not a bad day, a walk would do you good, a bit of fresh air." Only when he was completely satisfied there was no objection would he move off. But even then, not without suggesting that he was actually about to leave the premises.

"Well, I'll be off then, Mrs. Knowles, I'm off into town, I'll be back later." He would then walk the path to the road, looking over his shoulder in case he had misunderstood and that he would be recalled. At the gate he would look back, just in case. His journeys started off with a hesitant stride that lengthened as he approached town.

Now he was back. The farm buildings had not changed, the feel and smell of the place was almost a comfort. He found there was a degree and orderliness to the house that hadn't been there before. Perhaps it was the way the police searched houses.

Although he found it difficult to deal with Mrs. Knowles's direct closeness and friendly ways, there were things about staying at the guest house that he enjoyed. What buzzed around him most of the time, was his change in is appearance. He now accepted regular showers and trips to the barber. The novelty that gave him the most pleasure was the array of clothing supplied by Mrs. Jones from social services. In the secrecy of his room, he would try different combinations of jeans and shirts. He decided to wear sweaters whilst he was in the guest house, but favoured a jacket if venturing further afield. He had taken to a beige corduroy, which was almost new. He postured and turned in front of the mirror, smoothing down imaginary creases and tugging collars and lapels into shape. It was this, this transformation, into anonymity that made his pleasure rise. Now he was able to pass along a pavement, cross a road, walk into a shop without being noticed or attracting comment. He still was on his guard in case the magic wore off, but nothing happened. He felt as though he was invisible; nobody saw him. He was just another soul who had a right to walk the length and breadth of the town.

When he returned to the farm, the first place he went to was his secret room above the old coach house. He made sure, or so he thought, that his actions were unobserved, looking down the lane and across the fields, then hesitating again at the threshold of the building. Looking at the entrance into his private space, he could see why the police had not noticed it. Even from a few feet away, it looked as it was originally intended to, the end wall of the building, where a clutter of implements and wooden items lay against it. Only if the very last small stout wooden door, which had previously served its time as a loft hatch, was pulled away would the opening to his space surrender his secret. If the general area had been searched, the lack of disturbance indicated that not much more than a perfunctory use of effort had been applied. The space in the coach house held more than a measure of interest for him. He remembered when the police were organising rummage teams, someone in charge said not to waste too much time with the more remote outbuildings, as the offender was likely be in a hurry to get away and there was little point in him hiding, either himself or the stolen items, which were easily portable, in an old barn.

Even though he was alone, he maintained his cautionary approach, moving slowly and quietly, making sure the small door was replaced once he was inside. Once in his room, he would remain still for a few minutes as though to allow the weight of the outside world to disperse into the ether. Although he still regarded the room as a retreat from the pressures from beyond, his attraction to his collection of secret artefacts was waning. His exposure to society, though abrupt and limited, had started to affect his values. Now, as a bourgeoning citizen of the world, other matters were beginning to fill his life. His treasure now was losing its lustre, well the old items were.

The approach of a vehicle dragged his attention away. Through that small portion of window he could see, towards the bottom of the lane, a car approaching, churning up a wake of dust as it bumped cautiously along the mud-rutted path. He replaced his secrets and made his way to the space in front of the house. As it neared he saw that it was a small red Renault. The driver was a man who was a stranger to him. The passenger was Tracey Williams, the lady lawyer. Whereas he had welcomed and clung to her protection of him during those times at the police station, now he wondered why she had to see him. He felt no small degree of assurance now that his appearance was acceptable, but his unease at this sudden event was growing. Why did she need to come out here? He scattered glances around and noted that what he called home fell a long way short of the pristine standards set by Mrs. Knowles. As she stepped from the Renault, he made a slight involuntary gasp and felt his stomach inside turning in on itself.

"Hello, Mr. Hamblin, how are you today?" Today she had forsaken her cargo trousers for a pair of blue jeans. She had the same jacket on, which he thought looked like a man's and a black T shirt.

"I'm alright thank you." He accepted her proffered hand.

She turned towards the car that had just brought her to the farm. "This is Mr. Carter from our office. He kindly offered to drive me out here. I don't know this area too well, so Mr. Carter agreed to drive me. Also, it is normal to have a second member of staff present at times like this." She felt she was labouring the explanation for Carter's presence somewhat and abandoned any further comment. Daniel saw that Mr. Carter was a small nervous looking man who, despite the warm conditions of the day, was wearing an overcoat. He remained by the car, leaning on it in a way that suggested he needed some form of support. He didn't speak.

"Just a few things I thought we should go through Mr. Hamblin. I am sorry to arrive unannounced, but you don't have a phone. The lady at the guest house said we might find you here. It's not inconvenient for you is it?"

Daniel looked away from Mr. Carter and back to the lawyer. "What, oh no, it's alright, but what do you want? Has something happened?"

"There have been one or two developments that I would like to go through with you, if that is alright? Is there anywhere we could sit down?"

"We could go in the house I suppose."

Tracey Williams grimaced slightly. "Er, Mr. Hamblin, you don't mind me asking, but is that where, your father, you know, is that the place where…?"

Daniel's questioning look gave way to comprehension. "Oh, where me dad was shot, oh yeah that's right, it were just there by the door." His response was matter-of-fact. Carter stiffened visibly.

"Is there anywhere else we could have a seat?"

Daniel took in each building in turn. "Well not really, them's just barns and sheds."

"Perhaps we could use that bench over there? It's a lovely day, it would be nice to sit outside. Is that alright for you, Mr. Hamblin?"

"Yeah, it's alright for me."

As they walked over to the bench with Daniel in front, Tracey Williams turned and nodded towards Carter, and with some vigour, cocked her head indicating that he should join her, and join her now. Carter clung on to the car. Her urgings now carried greater imperative, her eyes narrowed, her lips pursed. Carter, unable to resist such demands, hesitantly released his grip on the Renault and stumbled like an unwilling groom towards the bench. When he was about ten feet from the seat, his advance wavered and then halted. There he remained. Tracey Williams abandoned any further aspirations of reeling him in any closer.

"So, Mr. Hamblin." It dawned on him that he was now being referred to as 'Mr. Hamblin'. Although there may be a reason for this, perhaps because of legal needs, he felt disappointment at this erosion of intimacy and friendliness. Tracey Williams was one of the first women to address by his first name, and she was the one who had robustly defended him against his adversaries. He didn't realise until now, but he had developed a closeness towards her and now it was drifting away.

"Before I start, I must tell you that I am here with Mr. Whelan's knowledge and approval. What I have to discuss with you today are issues surrounding your father's death. Usually your family solicitor would look after these matters, who up until now, was Mr. Whelan. However, certain circumstances have arisen that put obstacles in the way."

Despite giving the impression of following the explanation with due solemnity, it was clear that Daniel's attempt to grasp it fell at the first hurdle. She rewound, and, staring at the ground, started again. She looked directly at him.

"Daniel." the use of his first name lifted him. "Your father had a solicitor, Mr. Whelan, yes?"

"I've heard him being mentioned, when dad was selling granddad's bit of land, he's got his office in town."

"That's right, Daniel, he was your dad's solicitor. Usually, when a parent dies, the family solicitor would continue to act for the family, sorting out the will and things like that. Do you understand what I saying?"

"Yes, of course I do." His reply was tending towards being prickly.

"I knew you would. In this case, there are problems in that you and your late father may have conflicting interests." She hesitated. "You and your father may need different things, different guidance. That makes it difficult for one solicitor to act for both people. It might be difficult, or against solicitors' rules for Mr. Whelan to be your solicitor and be the solicitor who is acting for your dad's estate, you know how to sort out what he has left behind, any money or property, like the farm."

"Oh, I see." She looked at him, clearly he didn't see at all.

She took a deep breath. She saw that Carter had been inching his way back towards the car. She nodded fiercely at him to make him recover the lost ground maintaining her demeanour until he retraced his steps in full. Another wide-eyed nod indicated that he must remain there until the conclusion of the meeting.

"How can I put this? Daniel, normally when a father dies, all the things he owns are given to his family, including his children. Normally he would write a will. That is a sort of letter to his lawyers telling them what he wanted to give to each member of his family. There are a couple of things. First, it seems your dad didn't write a will. That doesn't always mean it is a problem, because it can be sorted out. It takes longer, sometimes much longer, but is usually sorted out."

She ran her hands through her hair then placed them on her thighs. She puffed her cheeks out. "The other reason why Mr. Whelan cannot act for you is because of conflicting interests. That means that what your dad may or may not have wanted for you may not be able to happen, well at least for some time. What I am saying, or trying to say, is that normally you could have expected to inherit the farm and any other property or money."

Daniel interjected. "He didn't have no other property, just the farm."

Tracey Williams decided to let it go. "What I have got to tell you, Daniel, is that, because your father was unlawfully killed - he was murdered - and the police do not know who did this, it means that you are technically a suspect in your father's killing." She stopped and waited for a reaction. The gravel crunched under Carter's shoes. Any thought of progress to the car was thwarted.

"Do you understand what I am saying? The police believe there is a possibility that you may have killed your father."

"Oh, I see." His reply was bordering on indifference. "I thought that was why those policemen were angry with me." He looked as though he had solved a riddle.

"Well, Daniel, while that is the case, you cannot inherit any of your father's possessions, not the farm, not the money. Do you understand what I am saying? Because of that, Mr. Whelan must look after your father's affairs and, as you are seen, at least to the police, as a suspect, it would be a conflict of interest if Mr. Whelan represented you as well. You need a different lawyer."

Daniel was quiet for several minutes. "Does that mean I can't have that money he got with that lottery thing?"

"Until this is cleared up, which may take a long time, I'm afraid so. It is a very sad state of affairs, your father dying. Had he died of natural causes, there would not be this problem. I understand that he was a very sick man and was not likely to have lived much longer."

He was quiet again. "So, if he hadn't been shot and just pegged out, I would have got it all, that lottery ticket money?"

"Daniel." She paused, took a deep breath and patted her knees. "I would like to clear up the matter of the lottery ticket. I want to be sure. What can you tell me about it?"

"Well, what do you mean?"

"Did you know that your father bought lottery tickets?"

"No, I never knew. I was right surprised to find out that he did buy them."

"So you never knew? He never mentioned it to you?"

"No, I never knew he bought them."

"So you have never given your father money to go towards the lottery?"

"I hardly ever had any money. If I did, I don't think I would have spent it on those tickets."

Tracey Williams made notes in her book.

"To answer your question, Daniel, if your father had 'just pegged out' as you put it, then yes, you probably would have been given all his money. I say probably because he didn't leave a will. He didn't let us know how he wanted his money to be passed on. As you are, as far as we know, his only living relative, it is more than likely that you would have inherited everything." She paused to judge Daniel's reaction. There was none.

"Daniel, I would like to ask you about the meeting you had with Inspector Curran and Constable Fenwick at the guest house. Can we talk about that?"

"I'm sorry. You said I wasn't to speak to them unless you were there. But they just sort of pushed me into it. I am sorry."

"Daniel, that doesn't matter now. They should not have done it, but please do not worry about it. What did they say to you about the lottery ticket your father bought?"

"They said it won a lot of money. A real load of money and that I could buy a car. I said I didn't want a car, anyway I haven't got a licence."

"Did they say how you might get the money?"

"That's right, they told me to say that me and dad bought it between us. To say that I always gave him money to help buy the ticket. But I didn't. I never had no money. They both told me to say it. I am certain about that." A fleeting mask of concentration swept past him. "Yes, they said I would have more money than I ever dreamed of and that people do it all the time."

"Are you sure that's what they said? Are you absolutely certain?"

"I am. I thought they were going on about it a bit much. They were serious."

Without appearing to show too much interest in the subject, he seemed to reflect on what he had said. "Was it alright not to do what they said?"

"Absolutely."

"Can I still keep the money that Mrs. Jones gets for me?"

"As far as I know, yes."

"Well that's alright then. But nothing from dad?"

"Afraid so. Even the farm. We, that is, our firm of Baxter and Martin, will continue to act for you for the time being. But under the rules, we should not be your criminal lawyers and your lawyers for family matters. We will suggest law firms to you, and you can chose one of them to act for you. In the meantime, we have to see if there is anybody else who may be entitled to what your father has left. I understand that he was married, I presume to your mother, but that she died very shortly after you were born. We have traced her to be born Mary Desmond on the twenty-fourth August 1961, died twenty-fourth July 1995, when you would have been about two years old. So you didn't really know your mother. Do you know if she had any relatives? So far we have been unable to trace any."

Daniel did not hear the question. He had been told, in the last sixty seconds, more about his mother that he had learnt in all his years.

"My mother, she died? He never spoke about a mother." A silence allowed him to start to absorb this previously unknown chunk of his life. "Do you know what happened? How she died?"

"From the reports we were able to uncover, it looks like it was an accident, here on this farm. It seems she was driving a tractor on uneven ground and it toppled over on top of her."

Tracey Williams looked at Daniel. In the short time she had known him, apart from annoyance with the police, she had never seen him display any emotion. Now he was stunned, sitting absolutely still with eyes tight shut, rocking slightly to and fro.

"You didn't know this? Daniel, you didn't know? I am sorry, so sorry. I assumed that your father would have told you. I am so sorry."

Daniel had heard her words. That was two questions she had answered.

"What was me mum's name?"

"Mary, Mary Desmond before she married your dad."

"When did they get married?"

The lawyer flicked through the pages of the file she was balancing on her knee.

"Our records show it was the tenth May 1992. She was a quite a bit younger than your dad, by about fifteen or sixteen years. Before I left the office, I had a chat to Mr. Baxter, our senior partner, about your mum and dad. He didn't know your dad personally, but he knew of him. Apparently he kept pretty much to himself. People round about thought he was a good farmer, ran this place in a reasonable way. We have managed to trace a photo of the wedding from the local newspaper archives." Again she riffled through the file. "There you are, a handsome couple don't you think? Your mum looks very pretty." She handed Daniel the photo. His thick stubby fingers handled it as though it was made of the most delicate lace.

"He's smiling, look, he's smiling. I don't ever recall him smiling. Is that me mum? Is that her? She's a right pretty lass isn't she?" He sought confirmation of that from Tracey Williams by staring into her eyes, almost daring her to disagree.

"Yes, Daniel, she is very pretty, very pretty indeed. Daniel, haven't you seen a picture of your mum before?"

"He never kept pictures or even spoke about her. I didn't even know her name. Why didn't he tell me about her? It would have been nice to know." He went back to the photo. "She is right pretty though, isn't she, right pretty?"

The lawyer nodded and smiled. "Mr. Baxter said, that meeting your mother was the best thing to happen to your dad. The town was a lot smaller then, but most people said it changed him for the better. He was still very careful with his money, or so they say, but he was very happy."

"What happened to her, how did she, you know, how did she?"

"How did she die, Daniel? We've a report from the local paper. It says she was driving a tractor near the stream on the farm."

Daniel stood up and pointed. "That'll be Small Acre field down by the brook. She shouldn't be using the tractor down there, it's too steep - it's bound to topple."

She handed him the cutting. His face seemed to question the actions of the mother he never really knew. "She shouldn't have taken the tractor down there, she shouldn't. What was he doing letting her do that for? He should have stopped her."

The file was flicked through again. "There was a coroner's hearing. Apparently your father did blame himself. He said he had asked her to drop some feed off for sheep, but didn't make it clear that she was not to go near the stream. She had not long learned how to drive the tractor. The coroner was absolutely clear that it was just an unfortunate accident and that nobody was to blame."

Daniel started to walk across the drive. Carter flinched visibly and stumbled backwards, then turned and then with short but rapid steps and holding his coat closed with one hand, he returned to the sanctuary of the car. Tracey Williams knew that, irrespective of the consequences, for the time being, Carter and the car would remain as one.

"Well why didn't my dad take the tractor down there then?" His question was delivered with rising anger and demanded that a reply be given. "He should not have let her take it down by the stream, it's too steep. You've got to be right careful. It would easily topple."

"You were ill, Daniel. You weren't very well and your dad was looking after you. After the accident, according to what people were saying, your dad sort of, well, gave up I suppose. He took her death very badly. Gradually he let the farm slide."

It was a lot for Daniel to take in. He was trying to unravel the threads of his history. He stood with arms folded and head bowed. "He was looking after me?"

"Yes, Daniel, according to the coroner's report, your father was looking after you. You were about two years old at the time."

He walked away from the buildings towards the edge of the yard and, with arms still folded, gazed out over the farm.

Remaining on the seat, Tracey Williams called out, "Of course, Daniel, if you still want us to, Baxter and Martin will continue to represent you in respect of your father's death, but Mr. Whelan can no longer be your solicitor for other matters. You can either choose a firm of solicitors to act for you, or we can give you a list of what we consider to be suitable lawyers." She waited, but there was no response. She walked over to his position and, standing behind him, said, "Speaking as your lawyer in respect of your father's killing, Daniel, is there anything that you want to say to me that you haven't said before?" After a moment of silence she continued. "You know sometimes things happen that we didn't mean to happen, there are accidents. If a gun goes off without someone meaning it to, that can be an accident. When that happens, the person with the gun cannot be really blamed for a deliberate action. They may have acted in a way that caused a death, but there would be no intention if they did not mean it to happen. If there is anything at all that you want to talk to me about, then it will be between you and me. I cannot tell anybody else about what was said."

He half turned towards her and seemed surprised to see her there. Then he completed the turn. "He was looking after me."

Tracey Williams and a relieved Mr. Carter at the wheel bumbled their way back down the lane the car raising small clouds of dust.

Peering out of the windscreen she said, "Thank you very much for your protection today. You know how to impress a girl." They drove on.

"He could be a killer, that man, a murderer. What if he had gone for us? I've a bad back, you know. I am the office manager, not a bodyguard. I will thank you not to ask me to do that again. I don't mind filing when other staff are absent, but do not ask me to confront murderers."

"Alright, Mr. Carter, no more murderers."

Daniel watched as the car trundled out of view. He felt as though he was standing in the middle of silence. He remained motionless until the very last sounds of the car had merged with those of the fields. He realised that he was still holding onto the copies of the newspaper reports. He held the cutting of the wedding gently between both hands and was transfixed by the photo. There was a headline:

SON OF LOCAL FARMER WEDS DAUGHTER OF FORMER DAIRYMAN

Samuel Hamblin, son of Stuart and Martha Hamblin, today wed Mary Desmond daughter of Richard and Bella Desmond, both now deceased. After the civil ceremony a reception for invited guests was held at the Golden Fleece Inn. A friend and neighbour of the groom, Mr. Bill Reece, said, "I never thought that Sam would ever get married, but we all know that Mary is the best thing to happen to him. She is a lovely bright girl, just what he needs." Mr. Hamblin will continue to run his father's farm who, owing to health reasons, cannot take on those duties.

He let his arms drop. He could only pick out some of the lesser words, but there, staring out of the photo was Bill Reece. "He looked after me. He looked after me." He then ran to his room above the coach house and, almost frantically, he moved the boards so as to reach his private hoard. There was something he had to look at.

CHAPTER 21

Curran threw his shoulder bag into the back of his car. Earlier in the day he had phoned in to say he would be absent from duty for two or three days, a stomach bug. He told his wife that he had to go away for a few days as part of an investigation into corrupt police officers. He explained that he was to lead a team of officers to try to establish whether an officer, in another force area, was covertly meeting with known criminals. It was all very hush-hush. It may even involve officers from the local area. So if there were any enquiries about him, she was to say he was in bed and not feeling at all well. But it was very important that nobody from his office was told he was working, all this had been arranged at a very high level. She said she understood and wasn't it good that he had been chosen for such an important investigation. Not to worry, if anybody called she would, as instructed, say he was ill. She told him she was very proud of him, and perhaps this could help with his promotion.

"Bye, bye, love you." She watched the car disappear. "I wonder who she is this time."

Curran drove to the outskirts of Newcastle to a rundown area dominated by industrial units. Many of the premises showed signs of being closed for some considerable time. He stopped outside a premises, which, according to the faded sign above the door, had, at some stage, been used for the assembly of furniture. He took a key ring from his glove box. The first key fitted the large padlock, the second fitted the Yale lock. He rolled the large door along its runners. The interior of the building, save for a few stacks of flat packs of assorted laminated cupboards marked 'Made in China', was empty. Just the packages and the puddles. He drove his car inside and switched the engine off. He looked around at the dismal emptiness and smiled.

"Thank you Terrence Conroy, thank you very much." Curran had been called in to assist the local Regional Crime Squad, which was conducting covert surveillance on a team of known villains. As this team were mainly local to the area and, more than likely, had made it their business to identify all the law officers who may cause them inconvenience, it was decided to use officers, fresh faces, from outside.

Curran had arrested Conroy, as a result of these investigations, five years ago for murder, GBH, handling stolen property, fraud and theft and tax evasion. Even though the murder charge was reduced to manslaughter and the tax charges were abandoned as being too complicated, he still pulled twelve years, so he would be tucked up for a while yet. During the surveillance, Curran had followed Conroy to this unit. At the time of his arrest, Conroy said that he had just bought the place with a view to conducting a legitimate business. No evidence was uncovered to show that the unit had been used for anything untoward. During the post arrest searches, Curran, whilst going through Conroy's car found, amongst other things, the keys to the premises. As the lock up, at that time, did not figure in any illegal activity, he decided to hang onto them. Since that time, nobody has asked for them. So, two or three times a year, when he makes this trip, it is a useful place to hide his car. He took the shoulder bag from the boot, changed into jeans, short sleeved shirt and a linen jacket and then locked his car behind the security of the anonymous semi derelict building. It was a half mile walk to the bus stop, which would take him directly to the main train station. There he purchased a single to Manchester Airport, a journey of under three hours. He knew that leaving his car at the airport posed considerable risks as it could be easily traced. The various law enforcement agencies monitored the car parks on a regular basis. With the systems in use, a car with a known registration could be located within minutes, together with footage of any occupants. This way was much safer and, once on the train, he could have a drink. On the journey he considered the circumstances that brought him to this place. What kept coming back were Stanley's warnings not to go off on a frolic of his own.

What he really meant was, "Don't rip me off when I'm ripping somebody else off, don't challenge my authority." But what could Stanley do to him? He decided that he held as much weaponry as his boss. If one of them let loose, neither was likely to survive. He had accumulated as much damaging and dangerous material against him as Stanley had against him. A Mexican standoff. Neither was in a position to move. Nah! Stanley was full of it, he is shooting the breeze because he is yesterday's man and he recognises me as his successor. All talk.

He had booked his tickets the day before on line. He used a bank card, which was attached to a savings account. It just wasn't in his name. He had obtained it from an acquaintance who hovered in the shadows of his life. The card worked. As required he supplied details of the passport he would be travelling on, which was in the same name as the bank account. That too worked. He was confident it would be accepted. It was one that had been 'acquired' in Spain. A Mr. Edward Walsh had applied for a second passport and the Passport Office contact in Liverpool had proved a willing, and now slightly wealthier, assistant. Knowing that if there was any irregularity, the booking could not have been completed, he felt confident with his travel arrangements.

Manchester Airport was sufficiently removed from his area, that the chance of being recognised by any officers serving there, either patrolling or Special Branch who may have had a previous knowledge of him was extremely unlikely. Now there was the issue of getting a bag with forty thousand pounds through security. He understood that EU law was based on certain freedoms, one being the free movement of capital. In theory, and legally, he could move any amount of cash, without any formalities from one EU country to another. But, as always, there was an exception. If the authorities, police or Border Agency, found someone in possession of more than about ten thousand pounds, they could ask questions to satisfy themselves that the money did not come from the proceeds of crime and therefore be subject to money laundering regulations. If no satisfactory explanation could be given, the money could be detained. Then it would be up to the person carrying the money to convince a magistrate that it was legitimate. Apparently magistrates were not overburdened with claims that cash detained in this way was actually won at the dog track, and, as is usual, it was the government that obtained the benefit.

He strolled up to the security controls with a practiced nonchalance. Without being instructed to do so, he placed the bag, belt and watch placed on the tray and watched it slide into the scanner. As expected there was a nod from the guard monitoring the screen to one at the examination table. He worked hard at maintaining his relaxed approach.

"Could you open your bag please, sir?"

"Yes, no problem at all. It's the money isn't it? Glad to see to see that you guys are on your toes." The security guard, a short, dumpy woman of about fifty years, showed no signs of liking her job and, from her expression, much else in life. She exuded an air of apathy. He noticed that she wasn't wearing a wedding ring. Probably another casualty of divorce, and at a late stage in life when, instead of enjoying an existence of life without a mortgage and kids, she had had to find a job. No experience, no qualifications, long hours on her feet.

"Do you want me to show you the money, Miss? Here we go, it's about forty thousand."

She looked at her watch, it was nearly four o'clock. He posed the question silently to himself. "Shift change time?" He rummaged through his bag and produced the money.

"Been a long day for you has it?" He smiled down at her determined not to say anything further until she spoke. Eventually, under the awkwardness of silence, she relented.

"I've been here for nearly ten hours, six in the morning start, it has been a very long shift."

"I don't know how you do it. I mean, how do you keep your concentration for all that time? I imagine you have special training." She looked at her watch again. "I know you have to be careful with money, something to do with the law isn't it?" She gave a conspiratorial nod and for the first time looked at him.

"Yes, we have to work with the police a lot. We do training with them."

He smiled again. "I can well imagine. There's the loot. It's for a holiday apartment I am buying in Spain with my brother-in-law. He's a police officer, chief superintendent I think, he's in charge of this detective stuff. So the money is OK then?" As he spoke he started putting it back into his bag. "Sorry, I do go on a bit." The guard made a half-hearted gesture towards the bag. "There are some real bargains out there now, and they all want cash. I think it's one of those cash no VAT things, but it's the only way at the moment. Right, I'll be off." As he moved away, the guard looked at her watch again, nodded to her supervisor and left. Curran found a seat at the bar, and ordered a large whiskey. From his inside pocket he took an envelope and removed the contents.

"Plan B." On official headed notepaper from his station, he read, 'To whom it may concern. The bearer of this letter is a senior police officer engaged in important undercover duties. Please offer him any assistance you are able to. If you wish to verify any of the above please contact me by telephoning Superintendent Stanley.' He smiled to himself. The letter detailed two telephone numbers. One was his own mobile, the other was a number for members of the public to report any suspicious circumstances, the 'Thief Buster' line. It was never answered, but a recorded message asked the putative sleuths to leave all the information they had. He smiled and returned the letter to his pocket. The information signboard indicated that his flight was ready for boarding. He followed the signs for the gate, handed his boarding pass to a gum chewing bored looking young girl, who, with a complete absence of acknowledgement that she was dealing with a human being, returned his stub. He was on his way.

CHAPTER 22

Tracey Williams peered around the door. "Hi, James, is this a good time to go through my case load?"

"Come in, Tracey, come in. With you it is always a good time, grab a seat. So how are you settling in to the esteemed and venerable firm of Baxter and Martin? I imagine it's a bit dull for you."

James Baxter senior partner founded the firm, initially as a single handed entity almost fifty years ago. Now it was a practice that currently employed fifteen solicitors and ten support staff. He was a man of gentle curves that were flattered by immaculately tailored suits. Today he was wearing a grey pinstripe with a dark green tie ad matching silk handkerchief lolling in his top pocket. Although in his early seventies, his full head of black hair, which was swept back, had only recently acquired side wings of grey. His face had a natural tan that suggested he spent a considerable time in a warm climate. His blue eyes were gentle and matched his natural charm. His look was of one who found life to be a series of enjoyable episodes in which there were occasional interesting challenges. The measured timbre and rounded vowels of his voice confirmed that he had come from a privileged background and that he assumed, that when speaking, he would never be interrupted.

Tracey Williams, with her spiked hair and ear studs, was surprised when she was offered a position in what she considered to be an old-fashioned and conservative firm. She took the view that her individual appearance and her outgoing and confident personality would have been a barrier. Not only was she embraced, but considering her limited experience, she was given a considerable degree of freedom as to how she approached her duties.

"Tracey, I wish we had a dozen more like you, we need to keep moving with the times. You are welcome to stay with Baxter and Martin for as long as you wish, but I feel we are a bit too limited for you. Enjoy your time here, then move onto somewhere where you can gain the experience that suits you. Criminal law is a good head of law to cut your teeth on, it gives you exposure to the magistrates' and Crown court system. However it is in the lower end of the legal profession. There is nothing wrong in making a career out of it, but you are a talented lawyer, well qualified and you have the knack of cutting through the verbiage and homing in on the relevant issues. I wish all my lawyers could do that, not many can. What are your ambitions, what heads of law attract you? I could see you getting to grips with some juicy corporate stuff, mergers, takeovers. Very interesting, very lucrative."

"That's kind of you, James. I really like it here. I think you were brave to take me on. At the moment, I enjoy criminal, I know its small time stuff, but a lot of those caught up in it, well it isn't always their fault. No proper home life, no parental control. Most of their grandparents, never mind their own parents, have never had a job. I just feel a lot of them have no hope, no aspirations. For the majority of them, there is no stigma in breaking the law and getting caught."

James closed his eyes and sighed, his smile grew slightly. "Do you know, I used to feel like that, except I defended the grandparents of today's lot. You make me think that I have become a bit cynical, somewhat case hardened. Tracey, I don't think I need to tell you this, but keep thinking the way you think today. Always maintain your integrity, lose that, you have lost everything." He leaned forward, elbows on the desk. "Sorry, today's lecture is over, back to business. What have you got for me?"

Tracey Williams took a few moments to absorb the senior partner's words.

"Well, mostly guilty pleas to minor matters, assault, theft from vehicles, taking and driving without consent, drunk and disorderly, so it is a matter of mitigation. Trouble is, most have a lot of previous and it doesn't always help to churn out the same, 'He's a reformed man now, got a family to look after,' or 'He is deeply ashamed of stealing his fifteenth car.' I am aware, now, that the local magistrates see the same faces time after time, so they are not inclined to feel sorry for them."

She shuffled through her papers, placing some on James's desk. "One or two are, at the moment, going not guilty, but that will probably change come the day. Some further bail applications, which should not be a problem. Now, the tasty bit. The killing of Samuel Hamblin at his farm."

"Yes, how is that progressing, any decent suspects yet?"

She ran her fingers through her hair with the result of making it slightly less spiky. "Well, I think the answer is 'no', but, and this is the 'but' that concerns me, the son, Daniel Hamblin. I think, in the absence of any others, he could be considered to be a suspect. Father and son did not get on, they lived together in stressful conditions, the son was very unhappy with his lot. He didn't receive any pay, well hardly any and so on."

James took advantage of the slight pause. "This son, is he the one who is meant to be, shall I say, somewhat dysfunctional, has learning difficulties?"

Tracey Williams, found the relevant folder and flicked through it. "I'm no expert, I have been with him for some time. I would say he has problems, but how big those problems are, I'm not sure. The thing is, as I was saying, the police do not have any real suspects that they have identified. If it were me, I would say that, at the moment, the son is all they have and, in the absence of anybody else, they should concentrate on him. But they hardly seem interested."

"Do you think he could have done it?"

"Yes, he could have, he had the opportunity and, I suppose, a motive of sorts, but I can't see it. With his difficulties how he could shoot his father and not leave any evidence, well any evidence that the police could find. What I am saying is, he could have pulled the trigger, under what circumstances I don't know. But has he the intellectual capacity, even considering the police's lack of rigour in the investigation, to carry out such a crime and arrange it so that the police do not consider him to be a suspect?" She started to flick through the folder, then gave up.

"They seem to be hanging their hat on the fact that the father, on the day of his death, was in town with a lot of money in his wallet and wasn't being too discreet about it. They are convinced, or appear to be, that somebody, having seen the money, followed him from town and did the deed. The only evidence to support that is that there is an imprint of a vehicle tyre at the farm that doesn't come from any farm vehicles, or the neighbouring farm."

James rearranged some papers on his desk. Without looking up he asked, "How are you getting on with the local police? Who are the officers involved?"

Tracey Williams closed the file, put in on the floor then placed her hands in her lap. "I don't think I am getting on with them. They are arrogant, slipshod and unprofessional. They do not bother with any aspects of the law. I don't think they have ever seen the Police and Criminal Evidence Act let alone read it. The constable is called Fenwick and the inspector is Curran."

"Oh, him. I see what you mean. I have not heard of Fenwick, he must be new. Curran has been around for a long time. When he first came here he was a good policeman, seemed as though he wanted to do a good job. But that drifted quite quickly. He has a reputation, not a good one, whether he deserves it or not I couldn't say. It's a shame really, over the years I have dealt with many good policemen. It just takes one."

Tracey Williams patted her lap once with the flat of her hands. "There is an unusual aspect to this case." She waited.

"Go on."

"On the day Mr. Hamblin was killed, he bought a lottery ticket, it was a Friday. When the police conducted their search, his shot gun and the wallet, which apparently contained the lottery ticket, were not to be found. The assumption made that the killer made off with them, as I said the wallet was said to contain a large sum." James shifted in his seat. "It transpires that this ticket won over two million pounds when the draw was undertaken the next day."

James looked slightly shocked. "You are not serious? Yes you are. Well, in all my years, I have never heard of anything like that. Two million pounds you say, well I'm amazed. That's one for the next local solicitors' meeting. Poor Mr. Hamblin, still, I imagine his son will be able to claim it."

"I don't know. It was one of the police officers, Curran, who called me to tell me about the ticket. He claims they are keeping it under wraps as it is part of the investigation. They are of the opinion that whoever committed the offence stole the wallet, which, they seem to be sure, contained the lottery ticket. Find the ticket, find the offender."

James was still thinking of how the story would go down at the next monthly meeting of local solicitors. "So, Tracey, it is possible that a person responsible for a homicide, and the presumption is that it was undertaken in order to take possession of a wallet containing an amount of cash, now has the wallet and a lottery ticket with a value of more than two million pounds. Most offenders, as we know, will dispose of the wallet once they have removed the cash. Just imagine the situation if he becomes aware that he has hold of an item that has a potential value of millions. There must be a strong temptation to try to cash it in. However, as you say, the police will immediately link the ticket to the offender. Well I never." With pursed lips, his head moved slightly and slowly from side to side as he rolled the idea around his mind. "Well I never."

Tracey Williams waited until her senior partner's attention drifted back towards her. "As I was saying, about this 'phone call from Curran?"

"Oh yes, yes, the 'phone call."

"He suggested that we make a claim on behalf of Daniel Hamblin on the basis that he has an entitlement." She paused, James immediately picked up the point.

"Yes, I see."

"Yes, he went on to imply that not only would it be of benefit to the son, but would be advantageous to our firm as Daniel would move out of the legal aid bracket and we would be able to apply our usual 'extortionate' fees."

"Did he by Jove? You said spoke of the son's basis for entitlement to the father's winnings. I imagine you have something to tell me about that?"

"Yes I have. I think I have a pretty clear idea of what is acceptable and what isn't."

"Ah, I feel a legal theory is about to be aired. Go on, what have you got for me?"

"Well, if a ticket is lost, and I presume stolen is the same as lost, the owner of the ticket has up to thirty days to make a claim. If a claim is made after that time, the issuing body has a right to refuse to pay and the likelihood is they would refuse to pay. There is a case that is persuasive, but it seems there are firm grounds for not paying. A lottery ticket has a life of one hundred and eighty days from the date of the draw for which it was purchased. If it is found in the street before that time has elapsed, anybody can make a claim on it provided the original purchaser cannot be located."

"So, Tracey, what are the issues in this case? Can the son make a claim on the basis that the ticket is lost?"

"I don't think so, not directly although he may benefit indirectly."

"Go on."

"Well the father, who was the purchaser, died on the day he bought the ticket, a Friday. The draw took place the following day, Saturday. The father never made a claim. He couldn't, he was dead. At best, if a claim were to be made, it would be made in order to benefit his estate."

"But surely the boy would benefit, to some extent at least, from his father's estate. Although, knowing farmers from these parts, it is highly unlikely that he made a will. Intestacy rears its ugly head. Administration of Estates Act, do you know the year?"

"1925."

"Well done, I knew you would have it, not bad for a criminal lawyer. Now, I think you are going to tell me why it is that there is some sort of impediment in respect of the son claiming directly against the ticket."

"Yes, it was not a joint venture, the son had no idea that his father had even bought a ticket. Apparently, it was a regular practice that the son was completely unaware of. It is common knowledge that there was no real relationship between the two. Daniel stated expressly in the interview in the police station that not only did he have no idea what was in his father's wallet, he had rarely seen it. He made no mention of lottery tickets, he couldn't have done. He had no knowledge of the father's penchant for these things. There was a complete lack of knowledge of his father's lottery habit. And it was a habit, apparently he bought one every week."

James stood up to face the window, hands in his pockets with his back to Tracey. "So why does the son not just sit back and wait? Let the intestacy procedure rumble on and then, when it is finalised, assuming there is no will found that is in favour of a distant relative or charity, the son - Daniel is it? - becomes rich. I think you have an answer for that, haven't you?"

"Despite the police's general indifference towards Daniel and their general faffing about," James's eyebrows did a quick flick upwards, "he is still regarded a suspect. I mean he has got to be even though there is a lack of evidence. When I asked Curran if Daniel was a suspect, he confirmed he was, he said something to the effect that nothing was ruled out. Mind you, I think he thought he was doing me a favour in that by continuing to represent him, we could still submit fees."

James pressed down on one of the horizontal window blind slats in order to obtain a better view of the High Street. "And your point is?"

"You cannot benefit from your crimes." James nodded gently and smiled to himself.

"Quite."

"As long as he is a suspect, he will not be able to take hold of any of his father's estate, not the lottery, the farm or any other assets. Although the lottery people were tight lipped about it, very tight lipped, I feel that they would not be able to release funds until the case is completely finalised."

"And by 'finalised' you mean?"

"I think the view would be taken that as long as there is an appeal process open, the case is not closed, well I assume that is how the lottery people would see it."

James resumed his seat and smoothed his tie down with his right hand. "And so do I. Are you saying that if a Mr. Smith is, in the first instance, found guilty, the case is not finalised until he, Mr. Smith, has exhausted all his avenues of appeal?"

Tracey Williams took a deep breath, then exhaled slowly. "Yes. As long as there is a possibility that Daniel could be found guilty, there will be no pay out."

"I agree with you, I agree completely. Tell me, you say the son, Daniel, could have done it, do you think he did?"

"I don't know. There has been nothing of an evidential nature that points towards him, but there is hardly a shred of evidence that would point to anybody else. As we are all too aware of, in most cases of homicide a friend or relative is found to be responsible. He had the motive, the opportunity. The *mens rea* and the *actus reus* - the guilty mind and the guilty act. James sat back in his chair. Do you know, now that I think about it, criminal law can be quite interesting at times? Takes me back to the old days. What about this Daniel, he has difficulties, could he really pull the wool over everybody's eyes?"

"I'm no expert, but I feel the aspect of his, so called difficulties, may have been overplayed. I don't think he is overly bright, but he has been, well, brutalised by his father, he has not been allowed any form of social development. He has, more or less, lived his life in a vacuum. I think he could do it, but whether or not he did, I just can't say. There have been cases where people with limited intellect have committed similar crimes and almost got away with it. They may even have got away with it, we wouldn't know would we? If I'm honest, now that I think about it, most of the defendants in my files, are probably of similar intelligence or thereabouts. Perhaps they may have had a slightly better start to life."

"What about the son, what is his knowledge of this missing ticket?"

"He is aware that his father bought a ticket, well he is now. He knows what the value is, the police told him. Whether or not he can comprehend what it means, I have no idea. The officers did rather hammer the point that if they find someone in possession of it, they are likely to have found the guilty party. Daniel has told me, and the police, that not only did he not know his father bought a ticket, but he has never seen it or the wallet where it is assumed Hamblin senior put it. The police, including Curran and constable Fenwick, have devoted considerable resources to look for the wallet, and I suppose the gun, which is also missing. Apparently, as you say, it is usual for a culprit who steals items such as wallets to take what cash there is then throw it away as soon as they can. It is possible, if the offender went to the farm by vehicle, and there are the distinctive tyre marks, that he could have driven miles before throwing it away."

The room was silent for almost a minute. Tracey Williams waited for the verdict from James.

"Well done, Tracey, I think your analysis of the lottery situation and Daniel's ability to benefit from his father's estate is spot on. Of course he could have killed his father. The trouble with the police today is that they want to look for complications, too much television. Many of these matters are straightforward. I am concerned, strictly between the two of us, at the behaviour of the local police. Clearly the son must be regarded as a suspect and that must be pursued with rigour by our constabulary. But they chose not to. Why? What do we have? A susceptible young man who, on the face of it, is worth a lot, an awful lot, of money. Am I getting five from two and two? What do you think?"

Tracey Williams folded her hands in her lap and looked straight ahead. Her voice was softer than it had been throughout the meeting. "After Curran called me, I had, shall we say, concerns. I went out to the farm to see Daniel Hamblin, I took Carter with me."

"I know, he came to see me to complain bitterly about being employed as a bodyguard. Bodyguard indeed." James rounded his sentence off with a short sharp laugh that indicated the irony of the claim.

"I asked Daniel about the meeting with Curran and Fenwick. I asked him straightforward questions. He is absolutely sure that both Curran and Fenwick put considerable pressure on him to say that the purchase of the ticket was a joint venture between father and son. I must say, it makes me feel extremely concerned."

James let the silence fill the room. "I am not surprised, I too feel extremely concerned. Is there anything we can do about it?"

"I don't know, really I don't know. I realise that you and I are very suspicious about the behaviour of the police. I kept saying to myself I was being too fanciful, it was too unreal. Do you believe that Curran would deliberately put pressure on Daniel in order to manipulate him to gain access to the money, or come to that, blackmail him? Although I am convinced that Daniel is telling the truth in respect of the ticket, if he did go along with the joint enterprise idea and was put on a witness stand, or in front of any official meeting, he would be torn to shreds. Could the police really be that corrupt? Also, I now have direct knowledge, well Daniel's version, of the situation. If he agreed to throw his hand in with the police, I would not be able to continue to represent him."

James was quiet for a moment. "I am trying hard not to think it. We are in danger of losing objectivity here. Perhaps it is just very sloppy police work where they show no interest. But, in this back water, a potential murder, or even manslaughter, is a very rare occurrence. Would have assumed that the boys in blue would have made the most of it. There is always talk of closing the police station down here, the level of crime is not very high and tends to be general run-of-the-mill stuff of low calibre. A successfully investigated murder or two would do a lot to keep the station open. If it were to be closed, all the staff here would be sent back to the big city and become smaller fish in a bigger pool. They wouldn't want to lose the idyllic country life style they have become used to, lords of the manor sort of thing." He paused to collect his thoughts.

Tracey Williams took the opportunity in the moments of quietness to reflect. "Is there anything we can, or should do? All we have at the moment is criticism of lazy police and an awareness that there is a possibility, and only a possibility that the officers involved may try to manipulate Daniel to get him to lie with a view to, somehow, making him part with his money. They may try, but by their own efforts, they have made sure that he is not likely to be a rich man for quite a long time, if at all."

"Yes, it has the makings of a delicious irony. Look, leave it with me. I suggest that you carry on as normal. We will keep this strictly under wraps. Let me have a think about it."

"OK, James, just one point. If a lawyer was to make a claim on the father's behalf, shouldn't it be his family lawyer, not us? We are just looking after the potential criminal side."

"That point had not eluded me. I know the family solicitor, Whelan he's a one man band in the town."

"Should we inform him?"

"I think so, Tracey, but all we can say is, 'Your former client's son is probably not entitled to claim his father's prize. I know Mr. Whelan, probably not the most assiduous lawyer I have encountered. I think it is only right he is given as much information in respect of his client, well now former client, as possible. I am aware of the circles he moves in. Knowing that, I think that maybe, the local constabulary will weight their options as to whether or not they will involve him, which is a matter for them. I will speak to Mr. Whelan. I suggest that under no circumstance do we discuss any part of whether or not Daniel will benefit from his father's estate with anybody, especially the police. May I also suggest that if they make any enquiries with you as to the progress of our firm making an application to the lottery people on Daniel's behalf, we merely say something to the effect that we are taking the appropriate action, but obviously it is covered by confidentiality. It is not really a false trail, but why not let them dream."

CHAPTER 23

Daniel knocked rapidly on the already open door, waiting to be invited in. In his hand were the newspaper clippings that Tracey Williams had given him less than half an hour ago. He held them delicately between finger and thumb as they had been given to him. Not folded. He had carried them in that way for the twenty minutes or so it had taken him to walk the mile and a bit to the farm. Mrs. Reece answered what she took to be a rather urgent summons.

"Hello, Daniel, what brings you up here? Are you alright? How are you getting on? Back at the farm, I hear. That's nice for you, it's always nice to be in your own place. Come in I'll put the kettle on. You are looking very smart I must say, very smart indeed."

"Is Mr. Reece about? I need to talk to him. What I mean is I would like to talk to him please." A sense of urgency had overcome his natural hesitancy. This change in him did not go unnoticed by her. "Of course you can, come in, I'll sort you out with a cup of tea, then I'll fetch him for you. He's around here somewhere. Probably over by the milking, he said he had something to fix in there. You do look smart, Daniel. It is nice to see you like that, instead of, well, perhaps we won't go into that."

She settled the young man at the table with a steaming mug of tea. In the short time he had been there, she perceived a difference in the boy she had watched grow up. She became aware of his sense of haste and the unexplained papers he was purposefully holding onto. "Right, Daniel, I'll fetch him for you right now." She showed a slight unease, but a greater feeling of intrigue and surmised that something of interest was in the air.

Bill Reece threw his cap onto its peg as he came through the door. "Hello, Daniel lad, is there anything up?"

Daniel rose to his feet. Reece waved his hands indicating that he should resume his seat.

"That's alright, sit down. What is it, Daniel, has something happened?" He turned to his wife and with an affirmative nod of his head confirmed, that he would have a mug of tea.

Daniel pushed the papers towards the farmer. "Me mum, me dad?"

Reece spread the papers on the table. His quizzical look flowered into a smile. He read the words and inspected the photos. Acts that called for him to rely on his glasses, which he removed with care from a distressed case.

After a several minutes where all those present maintained a breathless silence, Reece looked up and, exercising the same care, replaced his glasses back into case. He smiled gently at Daniel.

"That's taking me back a bit. Look, Susan, that's you in the background, that wasn't long after we were married. You know that's your dad there, Daniel, don't you. And that's your mother, a lovely girl. Where did you get this from, this newspaper stuff?"

"It was the lawyer, that lady, Williams. It's to do with me dad's will or something." He filled his chest with air and held it. As the air rushed out, so did his questions. "Did you know my mum? What was she like? Dad never said anything about her, he never talked about when he was married. I didn't know until the lawyer showed me this stuff."

"Ah, so your dad didn't mention her. I must say, I'm not surprised. There have been times over the years when I have tried to mention it to him, let him get it off is chest so to speak, but never a word."

His wife gave way to her growing impatience. "Bill, the lad wants to know about his mother and about Sam. He wants to know what happened, he needs to know. Daniel, your mother was a lovely, sweet girl, made a world of difference to your dad."

Reece resumed his role as the authority on the subject. "Yes she was a lovely lass, a lot younger than your dad; was it eighteen or nineteen years."

"No, Bill, not that much, it was more like sixteen or seventeen. Don't you remember she was born in the same year as my sister's girl."

"Oh, right, sixteen or seventeen" Reece could feel Daniel's pressing need for information on his family history. "We never thought that your dad would ever get married. He was a bit, how shall I put it, a bit of a loner, not given to socialising. Never one to go to the farmers' dances that we had in those days. Kept very much to himself. If I am honest with you, he could be an awkward cuss at times. He guarded every penny he had."

Mrs. Reece's impatience again rose to the surface. In a voice that was clearly intended to reprimand her husband for not adhering to what information their visitor sought.

"Bill, the lad doesn't want to hear that, he wants to find out about his mother." Deciding that he was wandering off the subject and that she was in a position to supply the details required, she proceeded. "Mary, your mum, worked in bakers in town, in those days it was at the top of the High street, where the electrical shop is now. Your dad would go in there once or twice a week. Your mum took a real liking to your dad. As Bill said he could be a bit on the dour side and he was very careful with his money. Well, your mum, as patient as you like, would chat to Sam when he came into the shop. It just seemed to grow from there. He didn't stand a chance, she had the loveliest smile you ever saw. Just a little dot of a girl. We reckon that she asked your dad out first. When they started walking out - that's what you did in them days, not like now – well, everybody was talking about Sam. He must have been over forty then, never been out with a girl, not as far as we know, and if he did we would have known, I can tell you that for nothing." She sat back and let the history of the events and times wash over her, smiling to herself.

Taking advantage of a pause where his wife's pensive mind recalled the events, Reece added, "Then they got married." She regarded this merely as a further spur to her muse. Suddenly her mind reached the surface of the current time and she continued airing her memories.

"That's right, registry office then a very nice do at the Golden Fleece. Her parents both were dead, they were an older couple, very nice mind. She made a lovely bride, beautiful. Bill was best man on account that Sam didn't know that many people too well. She changed your dad, he would come into town with her, he was pleased as punch, very attentive. Holding hands; Sam Hamblin holding hands for goodness sake." Her left fist was lying on the round of her stomach, she gently slapped it with her open right hand to mark the memory. "Then you were born, a good year after the wedding mind. Now Sam was pushing a pram, we never thought we would see the day. If she let go of it, Sam would grab the handle and take charge of you. If she tried to take it back, he would pretend not to let her. He was a changed man. Then…" Her mood darkened. She looked towards her husband. She had said what she wanted to say, now Bill would recount the long buried details that she did not want to give light to.

Daniel's gaze switched from her to the husband in anticipation of the events that seemed to have marked his life. The silence that suddenly visited was broken by the rustle of the papers and the scrape of a chair. Reece tapped the papers with his forefinger.

"Daniel, did the lawyer say what happened? Did she tell you about the accident?" Daniel looked straight at him without speaking. The slightest of nods indicated his awareness of events.

Reece reflected on what he was going to say. "OK, I think you deserve to know everything that happened. As Susan said your mum and dad were as happy as anyone could be. Perhaps it was just the early signs of their relationship." His wife's scowl at such a typical male suggestion hit him like a gust of wind. "Well, yes, they were genuinely very happy."

"They were in love, Bill, you know that." He took the scolding and continued. "As I was saying, they were very, very happy together. At that time Sam ran a good farm, he knew what he was doing, he was a bit inclined to take the odd financial short cut, but all in all he kept a tidy farm. Your mum was determined to help out as much as she could. Wanted to learn all about farming. Hard worker, she was up all hours all weather, only small but tough and determined. She learnt to drive the tractor. You were just a nipper when it happened. You were going through some childhood illness, high temperature something like that. The sheep in that lower field needed some feedstuff. Your dad stuck some bags of feed on the tractor, then said to your mum that she should take it down. If she wanted to be a farmer's wife, she should have a go at all the jobs around. Well, she didn't want to be away from you as you were suffering. She asked your dad to take the bags down so she could look after you. Your dad put his foot down, she was to go he was to stay.

"We always thought it was because he wanted to look after you himself. He was right proud of you. He used to say to me, he had to keep the farm in good nick so that you could run it for him when you grew up. So off she went. He told me that as she drove off, he shouted at her not to go down by the stream. It was too steep for a tractor. But, with all the noise of the engine she didn't hear him. He made to run after her, but he was holding you. So he watched her go. Then it happened. It rolled over on to her. She... well she didn't suffer much."

Susan Reece stood and put an arm of comfort around Daniel. He didn't notice. Reece himself found going over the facts an emotional drain. He steadied himself. "The coroner and the police were satisfied it was an accident, mainly due to her inexperience. They made a point of saying that there was absolutely no blame attached to your dad. After that, he went downhill. Gradually he gave up on the farm. The worse it got, the harder it was to bring it back. He didn't care, he was grieving for your mum. He had found something that he thought he could never ever possibly have, a wife who thought the world of him, and a son. From when they first started going out until the accident was less than four years. He thought he had a lifetime in front of him, but it was only four years." Susan's arms held Daniel tighter. Now he was aware, and, what surprised him, he felt no discomfort or embarrassment. She stared at her husband with hard unblinking eyes. His response mirrored her look. Following her unspoken bidding he pushed on.

"He had the farm and you. I think he went a bit crazy." His wife moved forward as an act of admonishment. He brushed it aside. "No, I think he went a bit mad. He blamed himself for her death, and we think he put a lot of the blame on you as you stopped him going after her. It's not logical, or reasonable, but in situations like that logic and reason don't play any part. He had bouts of drinking. There were times when you were a nipper that you spent more time up here with us than you did with him. We were worried that the social would take you away. We even thought about adopting you. We wanted to, didn't we, Susan?" His wife's mind was back at the time of Daniel's infancy.

She dabbed her eyes. "We really wanted to, you were such a lovely child. We thought hard about it, but then we reckoned that if we explained why, they might take you off him and we might not see you again."

Susan nodded her confirmation of the facts of the story, dabbing a tear. Her husband continued. "I went down to see your dad and have a bloody good talk with him. I said he was being stupid and wasn't being like a man who had responsibilities. I was there with him for over an hour, we were shouting at each other, bawling and shouting. Suddenly he stopped and started sobbing his heart out. I told him that he must look after you. I think, inside, there was nothing left, he was empty. From being on top of the world to being in the bottom of Hell in minutes. It was as if he died as well as your mum. He said he would look after you properly, and he did, sort of. He stopped drinking, most of it anyway. He fed you and clothed you, but, in his mind, I don't think he could ever forgive you, even though you were only a child. He turned against the world, worse than he was before, much worse. He tried to make a go of the farm, but it wasn't in him to nurture a place that killed his wife. I honestly think he went mad. He just couldn't care about the farm and, as is painfully obvious, he couldn't care too much about you. Every day of his life since then, he would step out of his front door and look down to where his wife died. Every day he would see you and know that if you had never been born, his wife would still be alive today."

This wasn't what Daniel had expected or wanted to know. When he walked into the Reece's farmhouse, he had been told not thirty minutes earlier that his father, at some stage of his life, had cared for him. Now he had found out that his father had damned his very existence. Until recently, his life had been a continuum of daily routine, one day followed another with minimal variation. Now, in a fraction of a day, he had been raised higher than he ever thought possible then had his elation snatched away to be taken to a despair that consumed him. He took the papers from the table and without a sound and with slow steps, walked out of the door. In the house the husband and wife remained motionless.

Susan was the first to speak. "I don't know that we should have told him all that, perhaps we should have only said that his father was a bit strange."

"I don't know, Susan. I have thought about this, about telling him, for a long time. I think he has a right to be told everything. Wouldn't you want to find out the truth? With all this going on, the police and lawyers, it was bound to come out one way or another. It's better that he hears it from us rather than get some twisted story from those who don't care about him."

They both understood the silence that followed.

"He was nearly ours, Susan. I often wonder what would have happened if we had pushed harder for adoption, instead of leaving him with Sam. He's been treated like a slave and had his mind poisoned by his own father. Do you remember when he was only a toddler and we used to fetch him to stay with us when Sam was hitting the bottle. I have never seen a kiddie looking so lost, so vulnerable. It used to break my heart. I often wonder what would have happened if we did adopt him. Do you know, I think the best thing that ever happened to Daniel was Sam getting shot?"

"Bill." The name was exhaled loudly. "That's a terrible thing to say. You shouldn't.

"Is it, is it such a terrible thing to say? Sam was a nasty piece. How could he go through life blaming and punishing a helpless child? He was a coward, arespectt least now, Daniel might have some chance of a proper life. It won't be easy for him, I realise that, but he has a chance. We can help him now, help him with the farm."

"Perhaps you're right, Bill. It just seems wrong to wish a man dead. But he tormented that lad. Perhaps Daniel will make a go of it now."

CHAPTER 24

"Superintendent Stanley, I've come to a decision, I want out." Fenwick had walked into his boss's office, unannounced, uninvited. He slumped heavily into a chair. "I don't want to do this anymore." The wriggling discomfort he had displayed on the last occasion in that office that made his tongue feel like lead and his brain even heavier, had gone. Now there was a confidence that suggested substantial changes to the relationship.

Stanley, no matter what he felt, showed no reaction to the constable's sudden arrival. He placed the papers had been perusing on the desk, carefully removed his glasses then put the end of one of the arms in his mouth. He sat back and assessed what he had in front of him. The complete lack of respect from the young officer and, if anything, an air of being not really interested. There appeared to be a new balloon of courage that Fenwick had suddenly acquired. Stanley's stance did not alter. He placed his glasses on top of the papers. His actions gave no indication of any emotion, he continued to view Fenwick as though he was merely an object of some little significance. Fenwick sensed more puncture wounds and was now considering the appropriateness of such a head on approach.

The words of his instructor on interview techniques came back to him: "When you are the only one to whack it on the table, all you have done is expose your tactics and yourself." He could feel the lead returning to his tongue.

"What's all this about, lad? You don't want to take any notice of Curran, he's on a self-destruct mission. He's trying to take me on and become top dog around here. Well that is not going to happen, believe me it won't. Do not worry about him. He cannot do anything to you as long as I am looking out for you. He thinks, I am yesterday's man, I think that is the phrase he uses. If you stick with me, not only will you reap a nice little benefit, with absolutely no risk, if you are on my side, I will see to it that your career could get an early leg up. I know you're new to plainclothes, but you are a good copper, you show real promise. I mean that." He sat back to assess the impact of his words. Fenwick, who lacking the years of experience of his mentor, was now showing signs of one losing a battle. Stanley pressed his point home.

"Curran has probably done a deal with mad Lenny. If that goes belly up, Lenny will have some serious mischief brought down on Curran's head, very serious."

Fenwick tried not to trip over his words. "When I said I wanted out, I meant out of the job, all this is getting too much." He ditched his proposed speech about wanting to serve the public and enforce law and order, having decided, considering his past relationship with his current audience that perhaps it should be saved for the future. "I feel, well, I feel that it is not right for me. It's all too, sort of…" He was struggling to find the words. Stanley still did not reveal any emotions. "I just think that another career path would be more suitable."

"Oh, it would be more suitable would it? And what career path did you have in mind?"

"My mother is a director in a large multi-national, she's got a position there for me."

Stanley sat back, his mouth curved down. "A position, I see, a position no less."

"Yes, quite a junior one to start with, but the pay is not bad. But I have decided to do more studying, business studies. I wasn't bad at school, meant to be quite clever, but I buggered about a lot. If I get some qualifications, I could go up to senior management eventually."

Stanley's mouth remained turned down. He sniffed. "Senior management."

"Yes."

"Have you decided, is your mind made up on this?"

"Yes, pretty much, yes I have decided." He reached into his pocket and handed over an envelope. Stanley placed it on his desk without looking at it.

"What's to be done then? How much leave have you got left?"

"Three weeks."

"Right, I will say that you are suffering some form of stress, I will authorise a week's sick leave, don't worry it won't be shown on any leave entitlement. We work hard, harder than most; long irregular hours; can be very stressful as well. I think we are entitled to take full advantage of these allowances. I regard them as perks of the job. I think we are justified in making use of them. So in all, you will have four weeks paid leave. Not bad. And that will cover your month's notice."

"That's very generous of you. I could do with a good break."

"As long as we understand each other. I suggest, that as tomorrow is Friday, you come in clear your desk, sort out any handover stuff. Just give that to me. I wouldn't mention any of this to the rest of the troops. If you just slope off, I will do the explaining."

At his apartment, Fenwick disposed of any items that may have been inclined to decay in his absence. He would put the place on the market tomorrow. He would drop the keys into Knowles's estate agency and let them get on with it. He pressed his mother's number on his phone.

"Hi, Mum, where are you now?"

"Hi, darling, how are you, have you done it yet?"

"Absolutely, handed my notice in, didn't seem to be any problems."

"At last, I am so pleased. You see, it was worth all my nagging. You're not suited to be a policeman, you will be much better off working with me."

"I hope so. Where are you now?"

"Hong Kong, some sales convention. You will probably be here next year."

"That sounds very exciting, mother dear."

"Don't take the pee, I'm running it, it's my show. So what happens now?"

"Well, the way I worked it out with my boss, is that I get four weeks paid holiday starting from tomorrow evening. Mind you, with all what has been going on here, I think I need it. When did you want me to start at your place?"

"That's a matter for you, there is no rush. It will take a bit of time to sort out the contract and stuff like that. Why do you ask, I know that tone of voice, you're up to something."

"What I was thinking of doing, seeing as I have four weeks of freedom, is to do something I have always wanted to do, drive down through France, maybe into Spain. Take off and see what happens, maybe stay for a month or so."

"You won't get much luggage in that little two-seater, it hasn't got a very big boot.

"It's big enough; shorts and T-shirts, mum, that's all I need. I've really fancied this for some time now. Quiet roads with the hood down."

"That's fine with me, wish I could go with you. Perhaps not, wouldn't want to cramp your style. Don't go and get married to some French girl and live over there, I want you back and working for my company."

"Right, I will try not to get married."

"Mum, I've put the flat on the market. Is it OK if I give the estate agents your number. I don't know if and when my 'phone will work.

Anyway, you are much better at negotiating stuff. You don't mind do you?"

"Not a problem, I'll make sure you get a good price. I've got to rush, have a lovely time in France, darling, call me when you get back. I can't see you phoning your mum when you are being chased by all those girls."

CHAPTER 25

George was waiting in the arrivals hall at Marbella Airport. The doors from the baggage hall slid open, Curran strolled through with his bag slung over his shoulder.

"Jesus," George whispered to himself. "He looks as rough as old boots."

Curran's enthusiastic bear hug greeting confirmed to George that, indeed he had taken full advantage of the in-flight service. His face glowed, his lips unable to fully perform the function of retaining the oral fluids whilst he spoke. The smile a lopsided leer.

"George, good to see you, man. You're looking good as always. The climate must agree with you." There were more hugs, which were not reciprocated. George wondered when somebody would come up with a different greeting.

"Good flight?"

"Yeah fine, well as good as a cheapo can be I suppose. Car outside?"

"Yep, ready to go. I've put you in an empty apartment that I look after. Hardly ever see the owners, probably only come for three or four weeks a year. Must be loaded." They headed south for the thirty mile drive to Marbella. Curran was straining to come to his senses, realising that his lack of cohesion wasn't a big hit with George.

"Sorry, George, bit pissed, a few on the train from Newcastle, a few in the airport lounge, then a bit of a top up on the flight."

"That's alright, Malcolm, got pissed myself once."

"Oh yeah, once." The humorous remark eventually collided with Curran's brain.

"Listen, Malcolm, do you want to do the business tonight, or should you leave it to tomorrow? You look a bit wrecked at the moment. It's up to you. If you wanted, you could meet up with a couple of the boys tonight, have a few drinks, a few more drinks. I wouldn't worry about it, they will all probably be in the same state as you. There's not a lot to do out here, so some of them go on the lash most days."

"I'll be alright after a shower. Listen, George, it's quite a big one this time. I've got forty grand in English notes, can you shift that?"

"I imagine so, it will need a bit of running around to exchange it. If any of the bureaus ask, we tell them that it is rent from apartments and villas, where friends and relatives pay in cash. Mind you, most of the banks round here don't give a toss. They are all struggling, they are desperate for business. They will more or less take anything. Five percent for my fees, that OK?"

"No problem, that's fine. I'll give you the bag, just take it. How much have I got in my account now?"

"Let's see, you've just have the one haven't you? That's right, I had a look yesterday when you said you were coming. In total it's about three hundred and fifty thousand Euros. After my cut, this should bring it up to round the four hundred mark. Tell you what, you are slipping way behind most of the others, you are going to have to work harder to catch up."

"I'll see what I can do."

In Marbella, George showed Curran into an apartment. "You can crash down here. I look after it for the owners. What do you fancy? Have a shower and I'll give you a knock in about an hour, that alright? I'm only across the road, a short stroll to the bars. You will see the usual mob and some new faces. A couple have handed their warrant cards in, one or two found it convenient to take early retirement and remove themselves from any scrutiny that might be going on. Give you a bang on the door in an hour then?"

"Yeah, fine."

"Tell you what, Malcolm. Give us your bag and I'll make a start. Do you want some spends? How long are you here for anyway?"

"Going back tomorrow night."

"I'll get you about five hundred."

Curran entered a night of back slapping and bravado. One or two faces were known to him, others he had heard of. The stories that filled the evening were of how they had beaten the system and ended up in Marbella. There was as much bravado as there was drink. But sun and time and drink and boredom and self-serving heroics had pushed the facts of these tales so far down the line that they had lost their definition and became increasingly blurred. The tellers of stories often invited a former colleague to confirm facts that increasingly took on a Salvador Dali concept. Conferring a more important role on the putative witness was the price paid. The tales grew like soufflés and had the same substance.

The banging on the door to Curran's apartment roused him about ten the next morning. He stumbled to the door in boxer shorts and T shirt.

George conducted a visual inspection of the property as he walked in. No damage, but the place was steeped with the odours of last night. Curran had drunk so much that he almost sweated alcohol. The odours and that of stale tobacco smoke seemed to permeate the entire apartment. George opened all the windows.

"Bloody hell, Malcolm, you look like something the cat has stopped chewing on. Come on, we'll get some coffee, get you sorted. What time is your flight today?"

"Christ, George, one at a time. What is the time?"

"Just gone ten."

"Right, yeah coffee sounds good. The flight is twenty-five to six this evening. I trust you can do the honours?"

"Not a problem."

"How are we doing with the cash, all gone in?"

"Not quite, getting there."

The two men sat outside the café which was on a main street. By the time the first cup of coffee had gone down, Curran was on the edge of entering the human race again. George excused himself, he had to get some cigarettes. "George, while you're there, you couldn't get me a couple of cartons of my usual filter tips could you."

"Malcolm, I always get you a couple of cartons of your usual filter tips. Where do you think I am going?" Curran eventually managed another cup of coffee and flicked through an English language newspaper.

Taking advantage of the lull, he reached for his phone. "Hello, could I speak to Tracey Williams please? It's Inspector Curran here." He was asked to hang on. He sat facing the sun, luxuriating in the warmth so rarely encountered in North Yorkshire. He lay back in his seat, eyes closed, feeling at peace with the world.

"Hello." The word had a definite upward inflection towards the end. "Yes, I am Inspector Curran, from the local station. I was trying to get hold of Tracey Williams."

A clipped male voice replied, "I am sorry, she is in court at the moment. My name is Carter, I am the office manager; can I help you?"

"Yes, Ms, or Miss Williams was going to let me know how the claim on the lottery ticket in the Hamblin shooting was progressing, I am the investigating officer and I have been liaising with Ms Williams in respect of Mr. Hamblin's position. This information, the lottery ticket, could be of considerable assistance." He smiled at his subtle subterfuge. "It could be very useful to our enquiries if we were to know how the claim is progressing."

"Oh yes, the Hamblin case. I see your name on the file, Inspector. We discussed it last night. It has been concluded that the younger Hamblin, in all probability, does not have an immediate claim. As you realise, more than most, he is a suspect and it seems the ticket buying was not a joint venture. Our conclusions are that there is no way that the lottery people would entertain a claim under those conditions. He may have a claim through his father's estate once that is settled, but as there is no will, nobody can be sure when that will be. Of course the younger Mr. Hamblin may have no entitlement at all. The younger Mr. Hamblin will be looked after by another firm of solicitors who will look after family matters and the like. It was felt that because of the potential conflict of interests between the two Mr. Hamblins, they should have separate representation. Time will tell, Inspector. I hope that has been of assistance. Thank you so much, goodbye."

"What? What are you saying? I need to speak to Williams." He was on his feet roaring into the phone. People in the street initially showed signs of alarm, then decided it was only another Englishman who had started his drinking early. He continued shouting into the unconnected phone. "I need to speak to Williams." He slumped back down and slammed his 'phone onto the table. "Jesus, that can't be right, it can't. I am dead, big Lenny, I am dead." His face was ashen, eyes bulging.

With trembling fingers he tried to send a text to Tracie Williams. His panic and lack of coordination required several attempts. Finally he managed, "Call me as soon as possible, *urgent*."

A waiter from the café, on seeing and hearing Curran's reaction, asked him, "Sir, is everything alright? Can I get you something for you?" It took some seconds before Curran became aware of the offer of assistance.

"What? Yes, brandy, a large brandy. Big brandy. Anybody but big Lenny. Oh, Jesus, I am dead."

George arrived at the same time as the waiter was serving the drink. He saw a man terrified and in the depths of dread. "What the hell. What's going on, are you feeling OK? Still a bit rough from last night?"

Curran gulped at the brandy as though he had just climbed out of the desert. "Big shit, George, big, big shit. I am right in it, up to my bloody neck."

"What is it, what is going on?" Curran ignored the question, he had a flash of inspiration. A life jacket of hope.

"George, how quickly can you get that forty grand back? Can you do it now?"

"What you talking about, Malcolm, I've nearly finished putting it in."

"I need it, George, I need it now. I need it now." As he spoke, he was thrusting his index finger towards the pavement.

"Have you gone crazy? What is going on?"

"George, I need forty grand in cash now, I mean now, or I'm dead. Perhaps with good behaviour, I might just be severely maimed. But believe me, I need forty big ones, like, now." He was starting to recover.

George scratched his chin. "Right, first thing, calm down. Whatever it is, I am sure we can fix it. Tell me what do you want?"

"Forty grand, in sterling before I take off this evening." George appeared lost in thought.

"OK, Malcolm, I need to make some calls. I think it can be done, but it is going to cost you, sorry about that, but it will cost you. I reckon ten to fifteen percent. How much did we say you've got in your account here? About three hundred and fifty thousand in Euros. So you're covered, but I will need to take it from your account here, OK? Let me make these calls and I will get back to you. You hang around here, I'll see what I can do. I will call you in a couple of hours."

"George, what can I say? You're a star, but get it sorted."

"I'm sure it can be done, I'll have to call in a few favours though, Malcolm, so it is going to cost."

"Whatever it takes, George. Will there be any trouble getting it through security at the airport here?"

"Don't worry about that, I can put a call in, and that one is free."

Curran ordered another drink and started to settle. In appraising the situation, he realised that it was going to cost him maybe five thousand but considering the options it was a sound investment. The money in his account was not hard-earned by the sweat of his brow. There will be other times to make up for it. It is money well spent. Big Lenny had been suspected of being involved in several murders, but he always had cast iron alibis courtesy of those who worked for him, or he arranged for an outsider to act on his behalf whilst he was on holiday, ironically, he favoured Marbella. Curran played around with the idea of not paying Lenny at all. After all, he had all the tapes of their meetings. But they only showed that Curran was as much a criminal as Lenny was. Despite calling Tracey Williams about every ten minutes, she was not available. He spoke to Carter again asking him to confirm that facts that led him to say why the lottery winnings could not be paid. Carter obliged. The fear he felt continued to ferment inside him, growing bigger in large bursts.

It struck him, during the several hours he waited for George to return, that Stanley was very unlikely to be in possession of the information from the solicitors' office that Daniel, in all likelihood, was going to remain a poor young man, as poor as they come. So Stanley could expect to incur the wrath of some con man or other. "Oh yes, you bastard, I hope you get well and truly screwed over. I wonder if he is into big Lenny as well." As time dragged, he had a tightening feeling that was growing inside him. He ran the situations in a loop around his head.

"Suppose George can't make it, or he can't do it. If I have to, I could stay here another night. George wouldn't rip me off would he? Nah, he couldn't do that, as soon as he does it to one, he loses all credibility with the others. He's on a very nice earner, he's not going to screw it up." But it was getting close to take off time. As George appeared from around a corner by the café, his heart lifted. George was smiling.

"Here's your bag, mate, forty large ones. Check it if you like."

"No need for that, George. Are we OK for the flight? It's getting a bit close."

"Don't worry about that, you've got time if we go now. Car's in the apartment car park, let's get going. I've put your fags in as well."

"George mate, you are a star, an absolute solid gold star."

The car pulled into the traffic and headed north to the airport. Curran did not believe the sense of relief he felt.

CHAPTER 26

It was decided that a condition of Fenwick's leaving, would be it was low key. He would just leave the office Friday afternoon and not come back. Staff were told he left for pressing personal reasons. He was happy with this arrangement; he was no fan of backslapping bonhomie, when the consumption of alcohol went up, so did the declarations of affection. Stanley had been more that generous with the severance terms. It was obvious that the main reason for authorising what was in effect four weeks paid leave was to get him out of the office as quickly as possible and to buy his silence. He was happy with that. He certainly did not want to cross swords with Stanley. The man was not the greatest police officer to wield a truncheon, but he had reached his elevated status by being a bare knuckled street fighter. Call it a talent or an ability, it didn't matter, in that jungle he had the biggest teeth and sharpest claws and the proven strategies. Leave it alone. And Curran, what about Curran? He was OK to work with, but he kept a distance from his colleagues. There was something a bit too slick at times, it wouldn't do to trust him too much. He had shown him into some pretty iffy practices. Although, fair enough, he didn't need a great deal of pushing. Now he had turned on him because of Stanley, and had totally gone totally ape. He defied anybody of his experience and rank to try to stiff Stanley.

On the day he resigned, he put his apartment on the market. He arranged with the estate agents to hold the keys and notify his mother as to progress on the sale. He packed up his effects in large cardboard boxes. The estate agency agreed to let the removal people in to send the boxes of his effects to storage.

He packed for his journey, it was not much more than he told his mother, shorts and T-shirts. The boot, despite his mother's concerns, easily accommodated what he needed. Drive south, stop overnight short of Dover, early start and try and get as close to the south of France in one day, then go wherever his bonnet pointed. He sat with his boxes around him, the apartment seemed to have more of an echo. But, his thoughts, his ideas were still nagging at him. Let it go, leave it behind. But, if it worked, he would get more of a share than either Stanley or Curran could have imagined. It was worth a go, what was there to lose. Nobody would know, not now.

Daniel was sitting in his secret room. The closeness of the walls gave him a feeling of security. His wounds were still raw from being told his father held him as being the guilty party in his mother's death. A deep and burning anger showed no signs of subsiding. The narrow room helped to hold it in. Suddenly a scalding fear made him leap from his seat. At first he had no idea what it was. Then he saw the small door to his hideaway being pulled back. A voice called his name.

"Daniel, I'm coming in, Daniel." A face appeared, it was the policeman, Fenwick. He had intruded into his private space, now he might get to see his secrets. Daniel's mouth moved for some time before he was able to form any words. Now on his feet against the wall facing the tiny entrance, he felt this intrusion was fuelling his already volcanic anger.

"What do want, what you doing here? Go away, I don't want to see you. I don't like you or the other one. That lawyer said she must be here when you speak to me. She will tell me off and she'll tell you off. Go on, go back."

Fenwick unfolded himself into the room. It struck Daniel that he had never seen him dressed this way before, jeans and trainers. "It's alright, Daniel, I just want to talk to you, just a talk that's all."

"How did you get here? I didn't hear your car. Where's the other one? Why didn't I hear your car? Where is the other one? Is he down in the yard? I want you to go. I am going to tell Miss Williams, then you will be in trouble."

Fenwick held his hands up, palms outwards. "Daniel, I honestly just want to talk to you. Look I am on my own, the 'other one' isn't here. Nobody knows I am here. I'm not even a policeman any more, I've left. I left today. So you can talk to me. Believe me, Daniel, nobody, not a soul, knows I am here. They think I am on my holidays driving to France. Whatever we say will be between you and me, nobody, absolutely nobody knows I am here. So if we talk, it's just me and you."

"How did you get here? I didn't hear a car. You didn't walk that's for sure, it's too far for you to walk."

"I left my car down the drive, before the bend. Then I walked. I thought I would find you up here."

"How do you know about this place, about my room? Nobody knows about this. It's my place, my own. I don't want other people coming here, you best be on your way."

"Daniel, I've been watching you for some time now. Watching you come and go. I used to see you coming into this place, then stay for hours. When you were in town, I used to come here to look around, then I noticed the dust on the floor leading to the wall had been pushed away by footprints. I've got to say, it took me ages to find this. I only discovered it the other day, but you came back from town so I had to leg it. It's the first time I've been in here. You see, those other police officers just don't care, they don't think. I was meant to be a detective, so I did detective work. I must say it is very cosy in here."

Daniel considered punching him. He didn't look like he could hold his own. "I want you to be off, now. Go away." Fenwick moved into the room, treading on a loose floorboard. He was very still, he could hear Daniel's deep breathing.

"Daniel, you killed your father didn't you? I know you killed him. I don't know why, whether you meant to or not. And I'll tell you something; I don't care. I don't care that you killed him, but you did kill him."

"You, you're talking rubbish, it's rubbish. Go on get out, leave now. I am going to tell that lawyer."

The words bounced off Fenwick, he continued to smile at Daniel. "You know what, you are a lot brighter than most give you credit for. I am here to help you. I don't want to take you to a police station, I can't. I'm not a copper any more, I am taking a break, going on holiday. Going where nobody can contact me. I mean it, I have packed in being a copper, left the force. I am, Daniel, leaving this place for good. So, tell me about it, killing your dad."

"You're stupid you, you're talking rubbish. Stupid. Why are you saying I killed me dad? What you saying that for anyway?"

"Let me see, where shall we start? You had the motive. You didn't like your father. For years he used you as cheap labour, wouldn't let you mix with people of your own age. So that's a start. On the day of the shooting, you were working in a field, with a digger, I remember. You had been there for a couple of hours. That's right isn't it?"

"You know all that, I've told you that before."

"It was raining that day, raining quite heavily, lashing down, in fact. When we arrived at the farm, there were puddles everywhere."

"I don't know what you are talking about, I want you to leave. I am going to tell that lawyer about you." The anger within him was such that, for the first time in his life, he was arguing, trying to take command of a man who he previously would have automatically placed in a category as being 'better' than he was, a simple farm hand.

"Thing is, Daniel, you weren't wet. You were a bit wet, but you were not soaked through to the skin as you should have been, if you were working in the open for a couple of hours."

Daniel was silent, glaring at Fenwick, breathing heavily through his nose.

"You were working in one of those fields down by the stream. I know that. You weren't wet because you were wearing waterproofs. It only struck me a while ago that when we searched this place, there was only one set of waterproof clothing. They were bone dry, your dad's I presume. So where were yours? Where would be a good place to hide clothing like that if you had access to a mechanical digger? May I make a suggestion, in the ground perhaps?"

On top of his anger, Daniel was now feeling the chilling fingers of fear starting to pull taught the muscles on face. He started to speak, but abandoned the idea when Fenwick put his hand out to stop him.

"I reckon that you came up to the farm, shot your old man, realised that your outer clothing, your waterproofs, were splattered with blood. That's why there were no traces of blood on the clothes you were wearing, that is other than where you touched him afterwards. Some stains that would be normal from holding a person who had been shot, but not the blood spatters you get when you blow somebody to pieces with a shotgun. Then you went back to where you were working and buried them." He bent forward so that his face was within an inch of Daniel's. "I know that's what happened, because, Daniel, you didn't bury them very deep, did you? No you didn't, bit of a rush job I would imagine."

"You're a policeman and you are trying to make me say things, you're trying to trick me."

"Believe me, I am no longer in the police. I have left, I am going to work for my mother's company when I get back from touring France, which I hope will be in four or five weeks from now. If you look at my car, you will see that I have my case in the boot, and look, here's my passport. Daniel, it is important that you believe me. I don't care that you shot you father, I really don't. Look, nobody, and I mean nobody, knows I am here. This is just between you and me."

"I don't believe you."

"Well listen, matey, you have got to believe me. Where was I? Right, so we have found your blood-stained water proofs. Then there was the gun. Everybody made the assumption that an intruder came up here to steal your dad's wallet. Your dad had been to the market, had more than a few pints and was probably asleep when he was shot. He was obviously sitting in his chair. There were no scuffles, no marks to suggest he tried to defend himself. So why would a thief, looking for a wallet, blow a sodding great hole through a sleeping man's chest when that was probably where the wallet was, in his jacket pocket. He would have to wake him first, then take the wallet, then shoot him. But that would have given your dad the time to at least stand up and start to defend himself. But no, everything points to him copping it when he was either asleep or half asleep. I've not been in the police all that long, but people who steal wallets are not in the habit of shooting their victims once they have what they want. They just leg it." Daniel now had his back pressed against the wall. His little sanctuary was starting to close in on him. Fenwick persisted with his story. "And how did an intruder get his hands on a loaded gun? Did he walk in, pick up a gun, look for cartridges, load it and bang? No person who keeps guns leaves them lying around loaded. You told us, when we interviewed you that it was an old gun, a bit patched up from what I remember. I would imagine that the trigger assembly would be a bit worn. Dangerous combination, knackered gun and ammunition. No, Daniel, you came up here, your father was asleep. Even if he was half awake, he would not have taken any notice of you, even if he saw you with the gun. Then you got rid of the gun. Buried that as well did you? Must have gone a bit deeper with that."

Having made the point, he straightened up. His gaze was fixed on Daniel's eyes. He waited. His breathing was becoming heavier. "Where was the wallet, Daniel? In his pocket, in the drawer? Where was it? I am here to help you, not to arrest you, I don't want to do that. Where was the wallet?"

He stared at the young man, his lips pressed small with growing frustration and anger. He exploded and roared out, "Where was the wallet, where was it?" The shock waves of his voice ricocheted around the walls of the room as if searching for an escape route. Daniel rocked back in shock. He found the silence that followed oppressive.

Then he heard himself say, "In his jacket pocket. It was lying open, I could see it. I lifted it out. He never woke up." Inwardly he gasped. "Why did I say that?" He knew then there was no way back.

"See, Daniel, that wasn't so bad. Before we go on, where did the split tyre come from? That has been bugging me."

He gave the impression of relaxing somewhat. "It wasn't on a car, it was on the trailer hitched to the tractor. I was using it to carry stuff down to the field. When you lot came, you never looked at it, you kept on saying it was a car that somebody drove up to the house in. It was a trailer, I made it myself. I used the wheels and axle off an old Land Rover that was clapped out. It wasn't a car. It was the trailer."

"On a trailer, not a car. Of course we would miss that. Trained investigators. And I suppose you buried those tyres once we left?"

Daniel nodded and in a low soft voice said, "Yes."

"After you did it, pulled the trigger, you went to Reece's farm. He said you were in a real state, crying and panicking. What was all that about? You weren't acting were you?"

Still in the soft voice. "No, I was frightened, I was really scared. I sort of did it in a rush. I was scared when I thought he was dead and I might get done for it, then I thought that maybe he was wounded and they could fix him in hospital and I still would get caught. I was pretty sure he was dead like, but well you never know. But I was really scared, I thought I could go to prison for ever. I felt sick. It's not like shooting an old heifer, I don't mind that."

Fenwick's 'phone bleeped indicating he had a text message. He ignored it and pressed on.

"Why did you do it, what made you shoot your old man?"

"I was getting fed up with him, he was always going on at me, telling me I was too daft to run the farm. He kept saying I was simple. I'm not, I didn't go to school very much, but I can read a bit, I did it myself from books, nobody showed me. He never gave me any money. He owed me money for all the jobs I did. He kept saying he would give me some, but he never did. When I came up that day, when he got back from the market, I went up to the house for a cup of tea. He was sitting in his chair, drunk like he always is when he comes back. He started saying how I was daft and how I shouldn't go into town because people know I'm not right."

Daniel's confession was becoming a cathartic outpouring, as he relived the episode, he did not want to omit any detail.

"He had his wallet in his hand, I could see all that money. That was my money; that was mine. He put it in his pocket, but I saw it. Then, after a bit, he went to sleep. I thought, I'd have that, all of it. It was mine anyway. As I lifted it out of his pocket, he sort of woke up, not properly. The first thing he did was to feel for his wallet. He looked right confused. I thought, 'You are the stupid one now.' Then he saw me holding it. He didn't move, he just went all red in the face, like when he gets real angry. The gun was there, I grabbed it, and then, well it went off."

Fenwick gave a benign grunt of approval. He knew his guile and cunning had paid off. The hours he spent, most of it off duty, watching the farm, had borne fruit. Now he was going to reap the harvest.

"The thing that puzzled me, Daniel, was how you managed to tell all those lies so convincingly. I mean with you being the way you are. You had me convinced for a while. But the lies, how did you do it?"

"After I did it, I was frightened, I don't know if I really meant to do it. I was really scared. With me dad, I learned to say things that wouldn't make him mad. I said things to stop me getting in trouble. He'd ask me if I had done all the jobs, the jobs he set for me. I would tell that I'd done them all even if I didn't. He never knew. He couldn't even remember what he said half the time. I just told him what he wanted to hear. I would make sure he couldn't catch me out. I didn't want to get into trouble, you see. If I was to fix things, I made sure that the parts I was meant to fit were hidden, but I left the tools lying about to make him think I'd done the job. Sometimes I said I was fixing something and there wouldn't be anything wrong with it. I did it all the time. He never found out. I knew the police would be asking me questions, so I made a story up. All I had to say was that I found him and no more. You never asked me if I did it, nobody ever asked me if I shot him."

"Well, Daniel, I am impressed. I said you were a lot smarter than some people said. And you are."

Fenwick slowly rubbed his open palms together, looked up to the ceiling then slowly lowered his gaze. "Now Daniel, this is very important. This is where I can help you and, at the same time, you can help me."

"What do you mean, I can help you?"

"Daniel." Fenwick paused and steadied himself. "Where is the lottery ticket? You haven't buried that as well have you?"

"What do you want with that ticket? What can you do with it?"

"If you give me the ticket, this is what I will do for you. It's worth over two million pounds. Now, Daniel that is a lot of money, an awful lot of money. If you give it to me, I will make sure that you get half, that's over a million pounds for you. You will be rich, you could buy what you want."

Daniel pondered this proposition. "What do you get?"

"The other half."

"Why should I let you have all that money for? It's dad's ticket."

Fenwick's sigh was exaggerated. He looked down at Daniel with arched eyebrows. He spoke as though he was giving kindly advice. "As we have only very recently established, you, my friend, are a murderer. I've got your confession and the evidence, your waterproof clothing, and we can dig the split tyre and the gun up. Don't worry, your waterproofs are where nobody will find them. But I've got them." He paused to let his words sink in. He held his hands out imitating scales, one rising as the other fell.

"It is make your mind up time, I'm afraid. Now what is it to be, a million pounds in the bank, or a lifetime behind bars? Because, without my good will, that is where you are going to end up. I get my share and you will never see or hear from me ever again."

"You said you weren't a policeman, now you're saying you are going to lock me up. I don't like this."

Daniel's returning anger had no effect on Fenwick; his hands were still playing at being scales. His voice was now higher and his words were almost sung out.

"Where's the ticket, Daniel, where is it? We don't want to go to prison do we?"

Daniel had the look of defeat. He removed the floorboard and reached into the space. After feeling around, he lifted up the wallet. Fenwick was seized with a momentary paralysis, then he snatched the wallet. He saw the edge of the item protruding. Gently, with finger and thumb he removed it as though it was as delicate as a butterfly's wing. There was a long, almost inaudible sigh. His mouth was rounded and his eyes bulged and gleamed. He studied every corner of it. Without looking away from his prize he asked.

"Daniel, when were you born?"

He closed his eyes to concentrate. "Sixteenth June 1994."

"Is there somebody with a date of birth that is something like, let's see, the seventh July?"

Daniel's hand scrabbled through the darkness under the floorboards and withdrew the newspaper cuttings recently handed to him. His stubby finger traced the script line by line. "Seventh July 1961."

"Yes, that's it, was that somebody's birthday?"

"It is, it's me mum's." He looked at Fenwick in awe. "It's me mum's birthday and mine."

"Hang on, I am trying to make out the third line, two, seven, could be twenty-four."

Daniel had traced the date, interrupting, almost shouting. "Twenty-fourth July 1996."

"Yes, that's it."

"That's the day me mum died." He let the moment of excitement subside slightly whilst he considered the implications of the dates. He looked towards the policeman to share the awe filled realisation. "He had my birthday and me mum's together and when she died. He must have liked me a bit. He must have done, he's put me and me mum together." Then quietly, for his own benefit, "He must have liked me a bit, he must have done."

Fenwick's gaze could not leave the fortune he held in his hands. He was almost oblivious to Daniel's arm ferreting under the boards for yet another trinket. Then he became aware that all movement in the room had ceased. He lowered the ticket from in front of his face. Daniel was facing him holding a shotgun. "Ah, there's the gun that did all the damage, that's the gun, Oh Christ."

The blast blew him off his feet and spread-eagled him up against the wall. As he slid down it, he revealed a broad, rainbow-shaped swipe of blood on the brickwork. The body arrived at a sitting position, then slowly keeled over to the right and stopped in a drunken slump. Daniel calmly replaced the gun under the floorboards and casually moved towards the body. His expression was of one slightly distracted as though trying to recall items on a shopping list.

"You think I don't know that you are trying to send me to prison?" Daniel bent down towards the corpse and whispered in its ear. "Well I'm not going." He took the now heavily blood spattered ticket that was still in Fenwick's right hand. He sat on his improvised chair, mopped some of the blood away from the ticket with his sleeve and peered at it. Now he could see what he hadn't noticed before, the numbers that represented his date of birth, his mother's date of birth and when she died.

"He's put me next to mum. He must have thought about that. He loved her, so maybe he liked me, he might have. All this time." He picked up the wallet from the floor and removed the tattered and frayed photograph that had until very recently perplexed him. It was of a young pretty girl holding a baby of about a year in age.

He sat with the ticket, now stiffening with dried blood, and the photograph for more than an hour. Outside the evening gloom was deepening. He replaced the shotgun and the wallet and its contents back into the dark where they resided. He left the room and returned with a tarpaulin. He dragged the body onto it. As he did so, a mobile 'phone slipped from Fenwick's jacket pocket and clattered onto the floor. In picking it up, he pressed a button. A message appeared on the screen.

"Solicitors have confirmed that the lad cannot, repeat cannot, have any part of his father's estate, including any winnings. Still think you are a prat. Do not, under any circumstances, tell Stanley. I will see at in office Monday." Daniel shrugged at the hieroglyphics, then smiled. This will be his new piece of treasure for underneath the floor. He saw the car keys sticking out of Fenwick's pocket. "That's two new pieces." Wrapping the tarpaulin around the remains, he dragged them to the ground floor. It was becoming darker. He drove the digger from the barn and, down the lane. He tied a rope to the front axle of the open top sports car, and fixed the other end to the digger. He dragged the car, without releasing the handbrake, to the yard. There, without any apparent effort, he lifted the tarpaulin and its contents and slumped it across the seats of the car. The vehicle and its contents were then pulled down to the corner of Small Acre field. At this point, he decided that the tarpaulin and the contents would be more secure in the boot. He bent and folded the remain so that they fitted snugly. "You'll be alright here, it's where my mum died." Within half an hour the hole was big enough. The car rolled in and settled at the bottom. Ten minutes later the digger and driver left for the house. He looked back. "Grass and weeds will soon grow over that." He was deep in thought. "He put me and mum on the same ticket, close together. I think he must have liked me really."

Being concerned as to why machinery should be operating in his neighbour's farm at this late hour, Reece walked across his fields to the hedge that marked the border between the two. Looking down into the field below, he saw what was causing the noise.

CHAPTER 27

Curran did not linger in making his goodbyes to George. His flight was due to leave in forty minutes. Although he had checked in on line and had no hold luggage, he still had to clear security and immigration control. He felt assured that by George arranging for local assistance, there wouldn't be any issues with the cash he was carrying. With a bit of luck he might be able to squeeze a drink in. It was all a bit of a rush and a lot had gone on. What was the story about the Hamblin lad and his winnings? Bloody lawyers, always find a way to cock things up. Inwardly he shuddered at the idea that Lenny might have thought he was ripping him off. He tended to act first then think later, much later. Probably he did overact at what he imagined Lenny's response to be, but there again.

He put his bag onto the screening tray and walked through. He thought the security staff seemed a bit ill at ease, maybe he was imagining things. Probably some local police chief had tipped them off to let him through. The old boy's network is in play even over here. He collected his bag and approached immigration. He was waved through by a disinterested officer. There was a slight delay, which gave him plenty of time for that drink. He cleared the formalities then after passing through the duty free shop area found a table for himself in the circular bar a few yards away. He ordered a large whiskey, took a sip and sat back. How much will George charge him for his services today? He looked up and saw two Guardia Civil and a man in plainclothes approached him with at a purposeful pace.

"Oh, the locals, come to collect for letting me through. Why didn't George tell me? I don't know if they want a drink or a bit of a bung." He felt his pockets. He had just over two hundred of the five hundred Euros left from last night. He took out two fifty-Euro notes. "There you are, a hundred Euros. That will have to do you, boys."

The plainclothes guy stood to the front with the two uniforms flanking him and slightly behind him. "You come with me."

He didn't move. "That doesn't sound too friendly. I take it you are George's mates. Look, I haven't got much time, but I am very grateful for your help. Would it be in order to make a small contribution to your Christmas fund? Or can I buy you a drink?"

"You come with me, now."

"What are you talking about, squire? Look I am a friend of George, I did some business with him. He let you know I was coming, yes?" Perhaps the touch of sarcasm at the end was not particularly necessary. The plainclothes officer nodded to the Guardia Civil. One stepped forward, grabbed the hand that was cradling the whiskey and snapped a handcuff on it.

"What the - what the bloody hell is going on. Do you know who I am?"

"Stand."

The order was somewhat redundant, as the two uniforms had moved behind him and using the handcuff as a lever, hoicked him to his feet and completed the handcuff set by fettering his other arm so that both limbs were behind him. One grabbed his bag, the other pulled the linking bar on the restraints sharply upwards, forcing Curran to bow from the waist.

"I am an English police officer, I don't know what is going on, but you bastards have made one hell of a mistake." When he received a sharp blow from one of his minder's knees to his upper thigh, the fear set in before the pain. By now he had been propelled across the concourse. He was shouting to other passengers in the hope that some form of message may get through.

"I am an English police officer, these men are kidnapping me, 'phone the embassy, somebody please 'phone the embassy." He didn't see a rush for phones. He was pushed headlong through a plainly painted door with his head was used as an instrument to gain entry. The blow he encountered stunned him and made his legs buckle. He was dragged by his arms, which by now, were screaming with pain, to a small room and thrown at a chair. Although he made initial contact with the seat, the velocity he was moving at, caused him to overshoot and end up in a heap in the corner. He felt one eye starting to close up. One of the Guardia Civil unzipped Curran's bag and upended it over the table. He tried to sit up to make himself more comfortable.

"Stay still, do not move."

The two cartons of cigarettes were waved at him. "Where did you get these?"

Peering through what vision was still available to him, he saw the cartons being exhibited.

"They're cigarettes. George, a friend got them for me." A horrible fear started to wrap itself around him like a constricting snake. "Oh, no, oh Jesus no, no, no, no." He was sobbing. "I've been set up, those bastards, absolute shitty, bastards have set me up. Let me get my plane, please, please let me get my plane. Let me go home. Please, please." The rest of his words drowned under his sobbing.

A knife inserted into one of the cigarette packets taken from a carton caused a trickle of white powder to flow from it. "Cocaine. I think it is a kilo of cocaine." The words were a greater blow to him than any he had received today. He made a noise that was between a howl and a scream. The lead officer watched Curran a casual nonchalance.

"My friend, if you will cry, I think you must wait until you hear the judge gives you your sentence. I think maybe you will be an old man when you see England again."

The bundles of money were removed from the envelopes. A 'phone call was made. He was grabbed by the arms, but now he was beyond feeling physical pain, and dumped on a seat. His pockets were rifled. The plainclothes officer flicked through the passport and his ticket stubs.

"So, you are Edward Walsh. Where do you live, Edward Walsh? In Spain or in England?"

His sobs were diminishing, he was fighting to control himself. "No, no, not Walsh." He muttered the words to his chest. He looked up. "I am not Edward Walsh, do you understand? not Walsh." Then very deliberately he recited. "I am an English police officer, my name is Curran, I am an English police officer, my name is Curran."

"Really?" the plainclothes officer sat up in mock surprise. "Well, Mr. Walsh or Mr. Curran, whoever you are, I am arresting you for trafficking cocaine."

Curran was close to fainting. The letter, explaining that the bearer was an undercover police officer, was flourished.

"What is this? I see I must offer you every assistance. Who is this Mr. Stanley?"

"What, Stanley? He is Superintendent Stanley, my boss. He's the bastard that has done all this. Haven't you spoken to him today yet? He's the biggest crook of the lot. He said he would sort me out, didn't he just."

"Shall we, Mr. Walsh or Mr. Curran, 'phone this Stanley?"

Despite knowing that Stanley had orchestrated this charade out of sheer malice and spite, it was hope, the merest glimmer of hope.

"Yes, yes, by all means give him call, give him my best wishes. The station number is on my phone." His survival instinct kicked in. "Yes call him, let me speak to him, could you please let me speak to him." His words were those of a very desperate, angry and frightened man.

As the officer left the room, a woman in uniform came in and took the packages of money with her. The two uniformed men stood chatting animatedly about something that they found mildly amusing. Minutes ticked away. Although he had never, in his life, felt so terrified and sick, he tried to focus his mind on damage limitation. He must be allowed a call to the British Embassy at some time. He would come clean about the money, he would probably get time, hopefully in England, but it would be better and a lot shorter than doing it over here. The plain clothes one returned smiling. Curran's heart leapt.

"Can I talk to him?"

"Stanley tells me there is a Curran at his station. But he is at home, not well. This Stanley tells me he spoke to the wife of Curran. She says he is at the house now. So you are not Curran."

He slumped back and closed his eyes tightly.

"And, Mr. whoever you are, I also charge you with trafficking with counterfeit money. All the English money in your bag is counterfeit. In this area, there is a big problem with this fake money." He turned and left the room. What Curran had instinctively reacted to, the violent and public arrest, being found in possession of prohibited items, the realisation he faced a humiliating and public trial, it was dawning on him, no matter how hard he tried to suppress the thoughts, he realised that he could face a very long incarceration in prison, a Spanish prison.

"Oh my God, if I could just be given a chance, just a chance, I would never ever get myself into this situation again. If I only had a chance. I want to be home, I want my wife." As he started to sob again, he could hear the airport's public address system.

"Would Mr. Walsh, travelling to Manchester on flight JMC 235, please make his way to pier C, gate 56 where the flight is about to close." It crushed him.

He had been placed in a cell overnight. Proper sleep was impossible. Occasionally, he would doze then wake with a start. For a second or two, he thought his present situation was a bad dream. Very quickly the reality would move in, pushing aside what he wanted. Two uniformed guards came and unlocked his cell.

"Come." He was shuffled along to an interview room, where the plainclothes officer from yesterday was present, together with another non uniformed man. The man from yesterday spoke.

"My name is Salazar, Juan Felipe Salazar. I am the senior police officer for the Marbella Airport." He spoke impassively and with restrained gestures. He was the victor, the absolute victor and his foe in front of him was utterly defeated, no longer posing any threat. He did not need any language or body signs that would have been used in a contest. That was over; history. Now processes had to be adhered to.

"I have sent a photograph to the policeman, Stanley. He says you are Inspector Curran from his police office. So, Inspector Curran, you are in Spain with a false passport, you carried in your bag a kilo of cocaine and, in English money, fake bills of forty thousand pounds sterling." When he was addressed as 'Inspector Curran', a nascent seed of hope moved in the pit of his stomach. The recital of the reasons for his arrest, snuffed it out.

"Also we have traced a bank account, in the name of Edward Walsh. We know this is your bank account."

"Of course you do, you knew that before you lifted me. You knew that because Stanley told my very good friend George to tell you, before I even got here." Towards the end of his interruption he was shouting. Salazar did not react.

"This bank account, which we found today, shows that a lot of money was taken from it in the past twenty four hours. Enough money to buy a kilo of cocaine and counterfeit money."

Curran blinked at the information. He rocked back and started to laugh. At first it was restrained, then it flowed into an almost hysterical torrent. As it slowed, he said, between sputters, "You have got to hand it to them, you really have, not only do they stitch me up, they make me pay for it as well. Clever, oh, very clever indeed. Well done, boys. What a team of players. Tell me, Jose."

"It is Senor Salazar."

"Right, Pedro, so you are going to go through a trial procedure with all this old bollocks. You don't believe the courts here might think it has all been a bit convenient, you don't think that the British press - and believe me they will be interested in an English copper being banged up - you don't think that they will wonder how this all fell into place, in what, a couple of hours?" He was trying to hide the desperation in his voice. His whole body was shaking.

"The greatest bit of detective work since Sherlock Holmes. You must be mad, you're the one being stitched up. What do think will happen to you if the trial goes belly up? What do you think will happen when you are asked, 'So, Pedro old luv, how come you picked on this man within minutes of arriving at the airport. How did you find out and get access to his bank accounts so quickly and easily? Wasn't it a bit convenient that he had coke and counterfeit money on him? It's a pity you couldn't get your hands on a couple of machine guns, then you could have done me for that as well."

"My name is Senor Salazar, Juan Felipe Salazar. We have a different system in Spain."

"Listen, Pedro, the English press will be all over this, the English Police

Federation is a very powerful body. It will get the politicians involved. It will all be down to you. Do you think that a bunch of corrupt former English police officers who have no hesitation in dropping one of their own in it, that they would think twice about you? You wouldn't have a hope."

Salazar's demeanour was sliding into a semblance of concern. His fingers drummed on the arm of his chair. "But you were travelling on a false passport."

"You got me there, Pedro. Listen, this is what I want you to do, I want you to let me speak to Stanley. I am going to communicate with him sometime, so you might as well make it now. You can have me for the fake passport and the money, the legitimate money I brought in. I will stand trial for that in England. What you will have is the arrest of a bent English police officer who was stashing illegal money in a foreign bank account. If you go along with Stanley, you will be making a lot of trouble for yourself. Why risk a being involved with bent English coppers. You know that some of them cannot go back to England, you do know that don't you? Why take that risk when you can be a hero, you will have caught a bad English policeman. But I want to speak to Stanley now. Please let me speak to him, Senor Salazar." His attempts to establish an air of authority collapsed.

He sat back and tried to assess the effect of his attack. Salazar's victim had tried to rise from the grave. He thought he saw something flick across his inquisitor's face, perhaps for a fraction of a second. Salazar affected a look of insouciance.

"You may have a cigarette." He turned to leave.

Curran was left alone for over two hours. He was supplied cigarettes, coffee and some sandwiches. Salazar pushed the door to the room open.

"Come with me." They went to an office empty except for a table and a couple of chairs. There were two telephones, one on the table, the other, on a window ledge. Salazar indicated that Curran should sit at the desk.

"OK, speak to your Stanley." Curran looked at the life outside. He was about three stories up and the window gave a view to the entrance area of the airport. He thought that what held him there was the thickness of glass. "It is reinforced, the glass, you cannot break it." Curran continued to look.

"You will speak to Stanley now."

"Yeah, right." As he punched in the numbers, Salazar picked up the other telephone and put his fingers to his lips, suggesting that he didn't want Stanley to know he was listening.

"I wouldn't bother, he will know that somebody will be on the end of an extension. He may be a bastard, but he is not stupid." As he waited for a connection, his heart was beating as though it was trying to break out of his chest. He felt his throat tighten to a narrow tube. He hoped he would be able to speak.

"Put me through to Stanley." There was a slight pause. "Who the hell do you think it is? Get Stanley and get him now. Tell him if he buggers about, I will drop him right in it." As he waited, he turned to look towards Salazar. He heard some heavy breaths at the other end of the line. *That's good, so he is nervous.*

"Yes, what do you want?" Curran involuntarily gave a thumbs-up.

"I want to come home, what do you think I want."

"I think you have blown that. Drugs and fake money, I hear." Curran did not want to enter a debate, he wanted to show that somehow, he had some cards to play.

"I think the Spanish police are a bit concerned, I think they feel you have used too big a sledgehammer. I have been talking to Senor Salazar, he is the chief of police here." Salazar gave a nod of confirmation. "But then you probably already know that." Salazar shook his head to suggest that wasn't the case. "He is concerned that if this goes to court, it will look ridiculous and reflect badly on him and his force." There was no reaction from his captor. "You know that, under the proper scrutiny, it will show up as being so full of holes that it could only be a stitch up, a very stupid stitch up."

"Now listen, Curran, don't think…"

"Shut it, I'm not here to listen to you, I'm here to tell you. You thought that because I was out of England, you could have me. Well, I'm out of England and I can have you." There was silence. "What I want you to do, is to call a friend of mine in Holland, he's a journalist. He's dying to print a good story, and because he is abroad, you can't touch him. But, believe me, he has got everything, and it goes back for years. It starts with your escort agency scam. There are a few names, as you well know, who would be delighted to back me up. This is what I am going to do if you don't get me out of here within the next few hours. What I will ask my contact to do, is to either email some of the best of your performances to the Chief Constable, or ask for an interview with him. Then he will entertain him with some of the best of your business ideas. You have no idea who my contact is, the Chief Constable runs a very tight ship and is as straight as they come. You will go down, Stanley, and you know it. Your mates, your band of bent coppers, do not have any clout there. You will go down for a long time. I will bury you. So get me out of this place and do it now."

You are bullshitting, Curran." Stanley's voice sounded confident. "I have my office swept for bugs and all that stuff regularly. Nothing has ever been found, nothing. You're bullshitting as usual."

"Swept regularly was it? Did the sweeps pick up mobile phones? They make very good recording devices, put it on 'recording'. Stick it in your top pocket and away you go. And it's so easy to put it all on email." Curran waited for the reply he knew would come.

He could hear Stanley take a breath. "That would never stand up as evidence in court. Some murky 'phone recordings supplied by a bent drug smuggling copper. It's a bit thin, isn't it? What court will take that as evidence? Any half decent brief would have that slung out at a pre-trial review, and you are well aware of that. If I were you, I would start to learn Spanish, I think you will have plenty of time to practice."

"I've got recordings of every bent meeting I've had with you, every meeting where a copper has told me about your scams, every meeting I've ever had with a villain. Your name is always there, always. You will go down. All that information, all of it, is in an email account. There is this mate of mine, a reporter, not in England, in another country. You can't touch him, you can't get to him. He will release this a bit at a time. It going to be a cracking story for him, he'll make a fortune out of it. You think because you stitched me up in a foreign country I would not be able to retaliate. But I can. Just watch me, unless…"

Stanley's interjection was forceful. "Listen, listen to me, there is a big hole in your so called 'defence', a bloody great hole. We know your foreign friend is from Rotterdam, yes, that's right isn't it? Who signs your expense claims? Me, I do. So I have seen the number you call, we know where he is. I have sent a text to him saying that everything is fine, but for the several months, for operational reasons, I will not be contacting you. You know what?, he will get more texts just to put him on hold."

This was a blow to Curran, but his retaliation was instant. "You must be joking. In the not too distant future, I will be able to contact him, then it will all be released. Maybe not to evidential standard, but the Chief Constable will be asking questions. He will have information and intelligence. Your cage will be well and truly rattled."

Salazar was giving Curran signs suggesting that the call should be finalised. Curran had to think on his feet.

"Listen, listen, of course I know that it might, just might, not be admitted as evidence, but what the Chief Constable will have is a lot of information, intelligence, about you, and what he is required to do, is to start an enquiry to get to the bottom of it. He will investigate you, he will get the rubber heel squad, they will get hold of all the villains involved and offer them immunity, it's probably agent provocateur anyway, so they will get a free ride. But they will have you. It doesn't have to be like this; get this sorted, there is no need for us both to go down." Now Salazar was standing over Curran and trying to grab the phone. Curran twisted away from him.

He heard Stanley say, "Don't you worry, you are the only one going down. You don't threaten me with doing time. The Chief Constable is a…" Salazar hand had snatched the instrument and terminated the call. Curran looked up, his face was a mask of terror and despair. The Spanish officer opened the door and shouted out along the corridor. Within moments two uniformed officers appeared and half carried Curran's almost lifeless body back to his cell. Within a few hours, he was taken in a police van to Marbella's prison, the Alhaurin de la Torre. The vehicle drove through a large red entrance, above which, in faded lettering, were the words, 'Centro Penitenciario'. As the large doors slammed to a close behind him, Curran felt as though the breath of life was being squeezed out of his body and his soul.

After two days, he was taken from a cell, as dark as his tormented mind, up to an office to meet with a representative from the British Embassy, who introduced himself as Ian Davies. He started by saying that the meeting was in private and asked Curran to run through the facts of the case. Curran's responded in a flat monotone.

"I was stitched up. Give me your phone."

"I'm sorry, Mr. Curran; that would be frowned upon, it's not within the rules."

For the first time Curran looked his visitor in the face, his eyes were glazed and watery and virtually lifeless.

"The rules, the rules, what bloody rules? Have you ever been in here? There are no rules. Jesus Christ man, what planet are you from? Now give me your 'phone or piss off back to your civil service desk. Give me your phone." Davies was shocked by how much menace Curran was able to insert into the last four words. He knew that the meeting would be over unless Curran's demands were met. Reaching into his inside jacket pocket Davies produced a mobile phone.

"Mr. Curran, I should say, at this point…" Curran reached over and snatched the device from the man's hand. He punched in his home number.

"Christine, it's me. Listen, whatever they tell you, I was framed. Listen, I haven't got much time, I want you to do something for me, it's very important, have you got a pen? Write this down. I want you to call a Theo Mulders, a Dutch newspaper reporter in Rotterdam, Holland, he's a freelance and he owes me. Make sure you speak Mulders himself. I want you to give him details of an email account, the account name is 'Malccurrtheomuld358', and the password is 'stan999badboy'. Tell Mulders to contact the Chief Constable and to start releasing the information onto the internet. Do that for me, will you, Christine? Christine, from now on, you must think of me as being dead. Get on with your life, find a new man. God knows you won't do any worse than me. I will try to stay on remand for as long as possible, probably that will be about two years. Speak to the Police Federation, they will make sure that, until I am found guilty, my salary will still be paid. I don't know if we will ever see each other again, Christine, no bad thing for you. I am so very sorry. Make sure you contact Mulders." He ended the call and threw the 'phone at Davies. "Now you can piss off."

Mulders, as was requested of him, started to drip feed the information to the British public, using the internet and contacts with English papers. Corrupt senior police officer was not exactly hot news, but when it was connected to another officer arrested for allegedly smuggling drugs, it added a certain frisson that would make good reading. However, the objective of grabbing the attention of Stanley's senior management worked. Mulders was approached by UK government officials with requests to desist from releasing further information in order that a measured investigation could be carried out. The headline the next day in local and national British papers read, 'English police try to gag corrupt police scandal.'

A week after the initial release of the information by the Dutchman, Stanley, on returning to his station, was met with a concert of muted stares as he trod the corridors to his office. What greeted him when he arrived was no surprise. Two uniformed officers, one a chief superintendent, the other who had taken Stanley's chair, was an assistant chief constable.

"Hello, boys, what can I do for you today?"

"I am assistant chief constable Barker, this is chief superintendent Wilson."

"Of course you are. Now then what do you two buggers want?"

"Superintendent, surely you are aware of the information that has been released concerning your actions, or should I say your alleged actions."

"Oh, that load of old horse feathers. Am I being arrested?"

"Not at this stage, however I must warn you that, depending on the findings of the enquiry…"

"Oh, it's an enquiry is it, that's interesting. Load of bloody nonsense if you ask me."

"I would advise you that it is in your interest to seek either legal advice or representation from ACPO."

"You would advise me, would you? So, I am not under arrest. Tell you what Assistant Chief Constable whoever you are, move your arse, I want to get into my drawer."

"I should inform you that I expect my rank to be recognised and respected no matter what the circumstances. I would also inform you that we have searched your office and removed various documents."

"You should inform me, should you? Now move your arse, I want to get in to my drawer." He pulled his drawer open and removed his car keys. Without speaking, he glanced around his office, removed his overcoat from its stand, put his hat on and walked out.

A month after the visit to Stanley's office, the Chief Constable received a letter with a Spanish stamp. The headed paper showed it to be from Doctor Christopher Lyons-Wynne, from a clinic in Marbella.

"I have been treating Mr. Stanley for the past two months. I can confirm that he has suffered a complete nervous breakdown. In my opinion he has been affected by this condition from some considerable time before he became my patient. I believe that undue stress at work to be the main operating cause of his condition. It is my professional opinion that it would be deleterious in the extreme to Mr. Stanley's health to return to work. I understand from Mr. Stanley that he will be seeking early retirement due to ill health and that he will be contacting the appropriate department with a view to finalising the arrangements. Obviously, Mr. Stanley's request will receive my full professional support. Owing to his condition, I have advised that any travel should not be undertaken until he shows sufficient signs of improvement."

The two men parked their golf carts and found a seat that offered shade. *"Dos cervezas por favour."*

"Your Spanish is coming along nicely."

"Thanks, Adrian, or should I say *gracias*, Adrian."

"So you are all settled in. Your pad looks very tasty, very upmarket."

"Well, I worked bloody hard for it, it will do for the time being."

"So, is it all settled, pension sorted and all that."

"Yes, all done and dusted, I have it transferred into my account here. And thank you, Adrian for looking after me when I first arrived."

"No problem, you paid for the service."

"What about all that corruption stuff? Bit messy wasn't it. How did that pan out?"

"Withered on the vine, as was to be expected. You know what they are like, when push comes to shove and all that. You know they can walk the walk, but they can't talk the talk. I know them, there would be too much policy getting in the way. Good name of the force, all that old bollocks."

"Whatever happened to your constable, Fenwick wasn't it?"

"Oh, him. He took off to France for a long holiday. I reckon he got wind of what was going on and decided to stay there, don't blame him."

As the men sipped their beers, another golfer joined them. "Hello, Mike, how's it going?"

"Not at all bad, Adrian."

"Come on, join us for a beer. I don't think you two have met, Mike Parsons meet Nigel Stanley. Go on Nigel, show us your expertise in Spanish. Order another beer."

Printed in Great Britain
by Amazon